The Soil Is Dead
A Novel

Mitchell J Rycus

The Soil is Dead
A Novel

A Cataloging-in-Publication record by the Library of Congress has been established for this edition of,

Rycus, Mitchell J.

The Soil Is Dead

Library of Congress Control No: 2012907532
CreateSpace, North Charleston, SC

ISBN: 1-4752-2491-5
ISBN-13: 9781475224917

Over more than fifty centuries of recorded history, some ordinary people have found themselves unexpectedly overwhelmed by incomprehensible political actions. Some of them took on the challenge and tried to prevent the inevitable devastation from occurring. Their attempts, which frequently required great personal sacrifice, met with mixed success. More often than not, the even fewer valiant people who did succeed were rarely credited with saving untold millions from annihilation.

This book is about five such people and is dedicated to them and to the other ordinary individuals who have been confronted by potentially catastrophic events and persevered. It tells the world that—fortunately for the rest of us ordinary folks—their spirit has, in fact, always been among us.

acknowledgements: I would like to acknowledge the support of my family for their encouragement and belief in my ability as a writer of novels. I would also like to acknowledge my editors, Caroline Upcher and Lorna Lynch, and the editorial staff at CreateSpace for their professional work in making this novel not just readable but enjoyable.

PART I
ETIOLOGY
Fall 2010

chapter 1

It ALL STARTED in the fall of 2010 after I first uncovered them—the *Frankenslugs,* that is—and I showed my discovery to my thesis advisor, Margaretta Hawthorne.

"You say you found these slugs at our research site off Bemis Road?" Professor Hawthorne asked.

Margaretta Hawthorne was a world famous expert on gastropods and the most renowned malacologist in the Biology Department at the University of Michigan. Her joint appointment with the School of Natural Resources and Environment (SNRE) kept her very busy with more doctoral students than she would like, but she couldn't say no to any of us.

"That's right, Margie," I said. Even though her name was Margaretta, everybody—even her students—called her Margie.

My name is George Brachmann and, at that time, I was a doctoral student in the SNRE, majoring in environmental biology. I did my undergrad work at Oakland University in Rochester, Michigan, and was accepted into the doctoral program here at the University of Michigan in 2008. I picked up my MS degree along the way at the end of 2009. I was doing fieldwork on a piece of land that had once been a farm, and then later it became a commercial site where a variety of temporary structures were built and later torn down. The fifty-two acre site had remained unused for a long time now, but various attempts at farming and other ventures over the past forty years either failed or never got past the proposal stage. Many of us grad students used the field (with permission from the current owner) to dig up various life forms and take soil samples for research and analysis.

Margie carefully examined some of my find—about a half-dozen slugs—with her gloved hand. She picked up a small one and said, "I'm sure you know, George, that slugs have a very special life cycle, and this particular one looks like it's an infant, but this is much too late in the year to find new-born slugs around here. And it's been awfully dry this fall." Margie paused and, noticing the slug's orientation, she continued, "Also, it's a left-handed slug. Although not totally surprising, that too is a bit rare. But the mucous secretion you mention in your notes is the strangest I've ever seen. What did you say your analyses showed?"

"The pH of their mucous was much too low, less than four...so low that the acidity actually etched metal. I keep them in a porcelain container like this one and try to handle them carefully—I don't want to contaminate my equipment. But on the other hand, living with their high acidity doesn't seem to bother them," I answered.

"That is strange. Mucous should be slightly alkaline, if anything. That kind of acidity should cause severe internal and external stress on the animal's organs. It's like citric acid, and we can literally cook seafood in lime juice. What's keeping these guys from cooking themselves?" she asked, not really expecting me to answer. "These slugs were an invasive species, and once they were introduced into a nonnative environment, anything could happen. Looks like you have an interesting and probably unique research project here, George. I like that," she said with enthusiasm.

"I checked it out with other nonnative species of slugs and, as you know, simple garden slugs, like the ones here, should all have the same types of mucous," I explained. "But the ones I found at the site with this heavy mucous coat have this weird acidic characteristic unlike the common garden variety slug. I also noticed, just as you did, that most of them have a left-handed rotation, but I didn't think that was a problem...that is, until I noticed something else."

"What was that?" Margie asked, looking inquisitively into the bowl.

"Their sex organs are on opposite sides so they can't self-fertilize. They have to mate. Which, by the way, they seem to be doing quite regularly," I said with a smile in my voice. "In fact, these little fellows here are the next generation from the original sample I found."

"Oh, so that explains why he was born so late in the year. Are you putting them in an environment that's conducive to reproduction?" Margie asked.

I continued going over my findings until I noticed that Margie was not interested in all the minutiae I had noted. I'm not sure why I went into such detail, but I'd been in the habit of blinding people with science at that point in my life. Maybe it's because my family was so science oriented or that most of my friends were either in science or engineering fields, but it was a habit. Here I was talking to Margie—a preeminent scientist in her field—and I'm blinding her with science. *Not too smart*, I thought, but I continued doing it anyway; it was a hard habit to break, but eventually I did break it.

———

Shortly after the fall semester began, Margie had agreed to be my thesis advisor when she heard that I was interested in mollusks, especially the kind without shells. I wasn't expecting to find any slugs in November, but there was this whole batch of them under some of the debris on the site. I was actually scouting out places to put in traps for harvesting slugs later in the spring when I came upon my find.

I was originally interested in doing research on slugs to see if I could come up with new environmental markers—like a slug's health—that might predict the viability of farmland for supporting grain crops. I also just liked watching the critters.

I used to collect snails, slugs, and pollywogs as a kid growing up in the Detroit suburbs back in the early nineties. Snails and slugs were the easiest to care for, but I had to cover my terrarium carefully or else our house would be swarming with baby mollusks. The pollywogs would soon need to be out in the world and didn't stay with me long, but the slugs stayed a long time—some even lasted two years on a diet of rotting food from the fridge and some moist dirt to burrow in during the day. Being nocturnal creatures, they moved about a lot at night. I could actually tell one from the other; they really had distinct features and unique personalities—at least that's what I believed.

"Georgie," my mother would say, "why do you keep such dirty things around? Why don't you play outside instead of looking at such ugly things?"

Mom never understood my passion for animal biology. But she was a sweetheart and never really chastised me when my pets got loose. Mom talked in a heavy Dutch accent because she came to America when my maternal grandparents emigrated from Holland in the seventies. My grandfather, an automotive engineer, was hired by General Motors, so my mother's family lived in Warren, Michigan, near the GM Tech Center. My parents stayed in Warren after my mother married my father, also an automotive engineer who worked for GM.

You might say we were a GM family, but because of the economic slump over the last couple of years in the auto industry, my parents were concerned that they might have to move so my dad could keep working. However, after the federal bail-out of GM, the auto industry slump turned around and the family was doing all right—financially—once again. I was able to attend Oakland University on a scholarship, and when I was offered a teaching assistant position at the University of Michigan after graduating cum laude, I grabbed the chance. No automotive engineering for me. My little sister, on the other hand, was at Lawrence Tech, and she wanted to get her MS in automotive engineering, so the family tradition would carry on with her.

My conversation with Margie about my slug discovery convinced me to redirect my research towards finding out how these slugs might have come about. Maybe they were a new species, I hypothesized, and maybe their unique biology could be useful in land use planning, especially as it related to farming. I hadn't fully firmed up my final dissertation topic yet and here was my chance, so I was psyched. Little did I realize that my working life over the next dozen years would deal with my newfound *Frankenslugs*.

———

"So what do you think, Mackie?" I asked my little sister.

Her name was Marike, but I always called her Mackie, even though no one else did. She was either Marike or Mary depending on who was talking. Family members liked to call her Mary, but she preferred that her friends call her Marike.

Mackie had always been a good scientist, but her focus was primarily on the practical: what can I do with it? She planned to start working on her

MS next year and was well ahead on her studies. She even took organic chemistry, which was not required, but she loved the science involved. She believed that living organisms are like machines in that they consist of many complex sub-systems that must work together so that the whole organism worked as it was designed. "Even if just one sub-system is down, the organism doesn't function properly, just like a car," she would say.

She was looking at my notes while we were home together over the holidays in December. I couldn't get over how much she looked like our dad—light brown hair, ruddy complexion, Nordic features—but I thought she was kind of pretty. She was tall, nicely shaped, and had had a lot of boyfriends, but they were all too dumb for her.

"I think your data is corrupted. No living thing, even something as primitive as a slug, can have all these characteristics and still be alive, let alone functioning. The highly acidic coating with no apparent change in body composition is theoretically impossible. And the sex thing—that's much too weird for a hermaphroditic animal. Sorry, bro, but you got to redo your analysis," she said with some authority.

"Hello! I've done it and redone it on not just *one* of these guys—or girls—but on at least six and some of their offspring. I'm certain of these finding. I'm looking into their DNA and comparing it with other slugs, but I haven't got those results back from the outside lab yet."

Mackie looked over some of my technical notes again and said, "Do you wanna get some of these critters downstairs in our lab and take a closer look? Do you have any other slugs that we can use for comparison?"

"Yeah, I get garden slugs from this biological supply company down south that sells them by the gross. They raise them for scientific studies, not fish bait, so they're supposed to be a pure strain...a single species of the common garden slug, *Arion distinctus*." I looked at Mackie's expression to see if she was really interested before telling her, "I tried to mate the common garden slugs with these guys, but the garden variety all died. They got cooked in my slugs' mucous. After they were dead, my guys ate them. Not only are they weird sexually, they're also cannibals, which is a bit unusual for land slugs."

"Aren't there thousands of slug species? Maybe this is just a new species. If it is you can name it after you, *Arion brachmannus*. That's a mouthful for a slug-cooking slug," she grinned.

She loved teasing me even though, as the younger sister, I should have been teasing her. Then she got serious. "Okay. Look, I'll be around for almost two more weeks, so why don't you get those weirdo critters and some of the other slugs you got and we'll go downstairs to do some testing later in the week. What's today? Wednesday, right? Saturday morning looks good; Mom will want to do some last minute shopping so that'll be a good time. Say, after an early breakfast—I don't want to play with ceviche-eating slugs before breakfast."

———————

Our house was a two-story brick model that was built in the sixties, and it had a full Michigan basement. Many homes in our neighborhood had remodeled basements, adding dens or rec rooms, but when Dad bought our home in the mid-eighties, nothing had been done with the basement, and I think that was one of the reasons why he bought it.

When I turned thirteen and Mackie was just eleven, Dad built us a great chemistry lab in our basement. It was a complete wet lab with an acid resistant ceramic sink, a small exhaust hood with two Bunsen burners, and enough chemicals, reagents, and paraphernalia to do almost any kind of organic or inorganic chemical analyses we wanted to do. He built a photo lab down there for his own hobby first, but later, when he saw how interested Mackie was in chemistry, he simply added on to his photo lab. He also knew I was interested in small animal biology, so the microscopes were a must along with enough equipment to build a reasonable sized terrarium for my hobby.

But he really built it for Mackie, who would spend hours down there testing all sorts of things—as well as making some spectacular fireworks that Dad never found out about. He gave us a set of strict lab safety rules around using dangerous chemicals, but kids will be kids, and Mackie didn't always follow the rules.

I, of course, liked the microscope area the most. I looked at all kinds of pond scum, and on low power I could watch some of my specimens doing their various single-celled-creature activities. The lab was still there, and it would be fun working with Mackie again.

On Saturday morning—Christmas Eve day—an Alberta Clipper came down from Canada, dumping around a foot and a half of snow on Warren. Nobody went anywhere: Mom gave up her last-minute shopping trip, but it was easy for Mackie and me to go down into the basement and analyze my slugs.

"I hope you put your slugs in a separate place so that they don't contaminate all the other stuff we have down here," Mackie said to me as we went downstairs.

"Don't worry; they're in a well-controlled environment. They can't get out because they won't even come near the copper screen that covers their tank." I had made the small terrarium up at school using a copper mesh to contain the slugs. For some reason that no one can explain, slugs won't go near copper.

Mackie carefully picked up one of the slugs with her gloved hand and put it on her dissecting board. She immediately started slicing it open and began mumbling, "Respiration system, digestive system, circulation system, reproductive system..." as she took the critter apart and put its various organs into different glass containers. First she took pictures of everything on her board, placing the specimens close to the millimeter scale etched on the board's side. Then she tested the pH of each sample. I was quite impressed with her methodical approach to the whole operation.

"Wow, you're right about the slimy mucous being acidic. I get three point seven, like vinegar. But the other stuff, including internal organs and tissues, have a normal pH, near seven or so..."

She stopped working and looked pensive. "You know, Freddy,"—she called me Freddy because my middle name is Fredrik, but nobody else called me that—"there are some microorganisms called *acidophiles* that can live in a highly acidic environment, like even sulfuric acid, and do very well. It seems they have evolved some very complex acid stabilizing mechanisms that somehow keep their exposed tissue at normal pH levels. The big difference between these slugs and *acidophiles,* besides their size, is that *acidophiles* don't produce the acid they live in. But I wonder if these guys are doing the same thing: somehow controlling their proteins so that the acid doesn't eat them up..."

"So what are you two mad scientists working on?" Dad asked as he came down the stairs. We had been working for almost three hours when Dad came down. We filled him in—rather, Mackie did—on my slugs and their strange physiology and behavior. He listened for a while and then said, "If it's really true that they can produce an external acid coating without being cooked themselves, then you might have found yourself some very important animal specimens. Have you thought about other uses besides your land analysis problem?"

"Not really," I said. "It was all part of my dissertation proposal using normal mollusks like garden snails and slugs. I found these guys by accident, but my advisor suggested I concentrate on them for my research. Why, do you have something else in mind?"

"Dad's thinking electricity. Since GM is heavily into electric cars now, then new sources of electricity will be needed to power up the fleet. Am I right, Pops?" Mackie asked.

"That's my engineer for you, always a step ahead. And, yes, that's what I was thinking. If you have a biological source for acid that is sustainable and easily maintained, then it's not a great leap forward to think of an ionizing process that can pass electrons to either storage or transfer devices in the way the old-fashioned standard lead-acid storage batteries work. If you don't mind, George, let me pass this idea along to our research staff that is working on future electric vehicle design and production. They might be very interested in your slugs. Have you thought about patenting them yet?" Dad seemed quite excited over my slugs and the possibility that they could be a new source for generating electricity.

"I haven't got that far on my research yet to know exactly what I'm supposed to be doing." Then I asked him, "Why, do you think I should apply for a patent? I didn't make these guys, I just found them. Do you think I'd still be able to patent them?"

"That's for a patent attorney to decide. Look, let me take copies of the photos and notes Mary took and check it out with my lab. We have lawyers and other nonautomotive types working there so I'll just ask around, if that's okay with you, George?" Dad said.

"Of course it's okay with me. Why would you even ask?" I said.

My father headed up one of the many specialized research labs at the Tech Center, doing work on all kinds of advanced projects, and his staff consisted of people with various nonautomotive skills, including patent law. He couldn't wait for Mackie to get her MS so she could come in and work with him. I also liked to believe that he would enjoy working with me too, and maybe now would be our chance.

I couldn't get over how much my father and sister looked alike. I, on the other hand, looked like my mother: the fair-haired classic Dutch boy look. You'd almost expect me to have bangs. My complexion was like my mother's too, much fairer than Dad's. People told me I was nice looking; I think they meant in that soft way, not the angular good looks like my dad and sister had, similar to many other people with Teutonic ancestry. But I think I might have inherited something from my dad: blinding people with science!

As we finished our talk, Dad smiled and said, "Let's go upstairs and see if the snow has stopped. George, you'll help me shovel out, okay? And, Mary, will you help your mother in the kitchen? It's nice having the whole family home for meals for a change. I'm almost glad we got snowed in so we can be home together for dinner and you guys won't be running around. We can have one of our robust conversations again."

Mackie and I looked at each other with smiles on our faces. We knew what Dad meant by "robust conversations." It meant that he would be holding court. He would start out by asking us questions like, "Who's going to be Michigan's next football coach?" When we tried to answer, he would wait for about two sentences and then tell us why we were wrong. At times these conversations got quite heated, and my mom would get into it by yelling at Dad for starting arguments at the dinner table. We were supposed to relax at meals and have polite, noncontroversial discussions, but my dad liked "robust conversations." Mealtime at the Brachmanns' was always interesting for Mackie and me and brought back many fond memories as I grew older.

On Monday when Dad got home from work, I couldn't wait to ask him about my slugs.

"Well, first of all you're not going to be able to patent something you simply found in nature. But if you come up with a process, say generating electricity, that uses these specific slugs, then you may be able to patent that method. Applying for the patent could be expensive, but our group's lawyer tells me that if you work out a deal with GM, they'll help to jointly patent the process."

"Yeah, but that's not what I'm working on. Did you tell him that?"

"No, I didn't because right now patenting is pretty remote. What I did find out is that there is some interest in electrical-generating biological processes in our computer research area. In particular, they have a whole team working on something called protein design with DARPA, that's the federal defense research agency. I think they're mostly interested in computer—"

"I'm not sure I want to work with them, Dad. I think defense research is a far cry from my field of environmental biology. I don't think those guys are interested in what I'm doing, and I don't think working with them will help me get my PhD, do you?" I asked.

"No, no, I'm not suggesting you try for funding through DARPA or even GM. I'm just trying to show you where the current research in your field for new biological organisms is going today. That's all. I thought that you have to do a thorough literature review in your field before you proceed on your own research so you don't duplicate what's already out there. If there are people who are currently doing research on new, exotic biological sources— maybe even your slugs—then you should know about them."

"You're right, I should know more about what's going on in the field. But, you know, I'm really not interested in working with DARPA. The university doesn't support classified research on defense systems, and I want to make certain that my work is broadly seen." I must have sounded like a real anti-military snob, so I added, "I'm not against weapons research; it's just that I don't want to do it. Are you all right with that, Dad?" I knew that my father had been involved with Department of Defense work at GM, developing vehicles for the military, and I didn't want to sound like I was putting him down.

"George, I can fully understand your position. All I want to do is help you if I can. Look, I'm going to DC in a week, and I'll be near the DARPA facility that's doing the bioresearch. Would you be upset if I went in there and just asked some of my contacts about the nonclassified stuff they're doing in this field of protein design and find out if it's remotely related to what you want to do? I'll also try to get some papers on their work that's in the open literature for your background work. Will that be a problem for you?"

"No, of course not, and I really appreciate you helping me out here. I haven't fleshed out my research agenda with the slugs, so whatever they're doing that might tie into my work or give me some ideas as to how to use my data, yes, that would be great."

———————

I spent New Year's with friends in Warren and came back to Ann Arbor on Tuesday, January 4. Campus, as was typical the first week of the new year, was abuzz with registration, parties with friends and colleagues, and meetings. I saw Margie at the dean's party for faculty and doctoral students and filled her in on my progress and that my dad was going to contact his friends at DARPA on my behalf.

"So your dad has DARPA contacts—not bad if you're looking for dissertation funding. They fund a lot of dissertations in many areas; one would be hard pressed to relate many of those dissertations to national defense. But in your case with these *Frankenslugs*, as you're calling them, they just might want them, if for nothing else then to scare the enemy," Margie told me, I think in jest. She was holding a paper plate with hors d'oeuvres and a glass of white wine all in one hand.

"I have no interest in using my slugs for the military even if I knew how. My dad is just going to check on the current state of bioresearch in their protein design group, that's all. And I'm not looking for funding. I have my TA position and that's all the extra funding I need." I probably sounded a little cynical and regretted the way I just shot back at Margie.

Margie put her free hand on my arm and said, "I'm just teasing you, George. Don't get so defensive. I know you're not interested in weapons research, especially biological weapons." Margie paused and then said in a more serious tone, "But, you know, it wouldn't surprise me if those guys at DARPA are still into that stuff. They haven't been involved in chemical or biological weapon development for some time—in fact, I think Congress outlawed it—but they have to know what other countries are currently doing or might be doing. So your slugs might just interest them." Margie was apparently scanning the room for someone when she continued, saying, "Anyway, that would be taking a leap into something totally unknown. Stick to your own research goal. Have you come up with any models you'd like to test?"

"I'm looking into some highly acidic soil models that could be self-sustaining under various food crop growth cycles. But I've just started and I'm still doing my literature search. That's where Dad is helping me with DARPA," I said.

"Sounds good to me. Keep me up to speed and let's plan on meeting again early this semester. Maybe we should have a meeting with your whole committee around mid-term just to make them all aware of what you found. Does that sound like a reasonable short-term goal?"

"Yeah, I should be able to have something to tell them by then. Also, it will be nice to get some of their input on the slugs and if they feel it's of any value to keep the critters on as part of my project." I began to feel like I was taking up too much of Margie's fun-time and this party wasn't the place to have an in-depth discussion about my work.

"Then we'll leave it at that. I'm really looking forward to working with you on this one. I think it has great potential for two fields: environmental biology and malacology—my two loves. See you later, George."

And with that, Margie went off to schmooze with some of the other faculty.

All of a sudden, I felt anxious about my dad meeting with the DARPA guys tomorrow. I had this feeling that maybe the slugs could somehow develop a life of their own without my interests at heart. Margie would probably be interested in anything that came out of their existence, whether it was land use analysis or weapons. And if it was weapons that would certainly trump my work. I almost wished that Dad wasn't going to DARPA, but I knew it would hurt him if I asked him not to go now.

I wandered over to talk with some of my fellow TAs and get involved in some lighter discussions that would take me out of this funk I was feeling.

chapter 2

BORIS BETHELHEIM WAS a crotchety, wheelchair-bound DARPA deputy director in the Defense Sciences Office (DSO). He was in his early sixties and had been at DARPA since 1978, after getting his PhD in bioengineering from Penn. He was overweight and looked like a little Buddha, sitting there in his chair with his hair all a mess, dandruff flaking on his face and shoulders adding a little texture to his splotchy red complexion. His clothes were...well, let's just say eclectic. His jacket didn't match his pants, nor did his tie match anything else he had on. His shirt was stained with coffee and it looked like he'd been wearing it for over a month. To top it all off, he wore a white lab coat at all times, but he hadn't done any lab work in years. After describing Boris, my dad told me that he wore the coat to remind people that he was a doctor and that he wanted people who didn't know him to address him as Dr. Bethelheim, just as it was embroidered on his lab coat's pocket.

"Hello, Boris, and how have you been doing?" my dad asked as he walked into his office.

"Hey, Pete, how's GM treating you? You guys ready to do some work for us?" he asked. My dad's name is Pieter, the Dutch spelling for Peter, but most people called him Pete.

"Any time, Boris. You know we're already working with adaptive execution to develop the CROSSHAIRS vehicle." My dad was referring to a tactical detect and response system mounted on the latest GM version of a Humvee. The project was initiated to counter-attack an enemy's field-launched rockets. "But, I'm here on another topic that might interest your people in DSO."

"Oh yeah, what's that?" Boris asked.

My dad told him all about the slugs I found and asked him what was going on in bio-related systems that could be divulged publicly.

"You say your son's at Michigan. You know, we have a bio program going on over there called HI-MEMS—Hybrid Insect Micro-Electro-Mechanical Systems. That's some mouthful, like most of our projects. I know that's different from what your son is working on—slugs aren't insects—but they might have some common interests. One of their goals is to demonstrate technologies that can extract power from insects. I think your kid's work might tie into that."

Dad agreed and asked how I might get in contact with the group.

Boris thought for a second as he fiddled with his chair's controls before replying. Dad could see that something was going on in his head. "They're an interdisciplinary team out of the engineering school, and I think they'd appreciate someone from SNRE involved in their program. I've been telling them to get other schools involved in their work. Look, I'll call their project director and arrange to have your son—it's George, right?—meet with them. That way he can get his literature search done along with some helpful guidance on how it might tie into his topic. How's that work for you?"

Dad said that would be just fine and thanked Boris for going to all the trouble of getting me involved in such timely research. They exchanged pleasantries, shook hands, and agreed to talk again when Dad was back in DC.

What my dad didn't know then was that Boris was more than interested in my slugs.

———

Around a week or two later, my dad filled me in a bit more on Boris' background. Boris' father was a former WWII Marine reservist who was killed in action in Korea after being called back to active duty when the Korean War broke out in 1950. Boris was barely two at the time and remembered very little, if anything, about his father. But he was always bitter about his father's death and became a fervent anti-communist. He considered all communists, especially Russians, our enemies and wanted to destroy them for killing his father.

As he grew up, he turned out to be a wild, sometimes out-of-control kid. He was in a car accident in high school—they say alcohol was involved—that left him paralyzed from the waist down. Even though he hadn't shown any proclivity for a career in science, his attitude changed after more than a year of intensive rehab. Dealing with his own infirmity, he was determined to be a scientist in the hopes of discovering how to make people with central nervous system injuries walk again. Dad said that Boris felt if he could do that then maybe he could somehow avenge his father's death. That may sound strange, but Dad said that's how he felt. I was a bit surprised at how much Dad knew about Boris, but that too became clearer a few years later.

Dad continued telling me about Boris and how he got a scholarship to the University of Pennsylvania—a great Ivy League school—even though he and his mother lived in Ohio. He wanted to go to an out-of-state school and be on his own. His mother wasn't thrilled but thought it best to let him have his way. At Penn he learned to be less dependent on her and even became a little arrogant about being an independent paraplegic. As the sole surviving son of a Marine killed in combat, he was able to get a position as a research scientist at DARPA after getting his PhD, working in the DSO on biological warfare defense.

His mother had always been the one to settle him down. Raising a son who first lost his father in the war and then the use of his legs in an accident was extremely trying for her. His anger and moodiness were hard to bear, but she was always there to hold him and protect him from further harm.

"Boris, honey, you don't have to make up for your father's death. Korea is long over, and Vietnam is over too. With Carter in office now I think we can forget about the communist threat. And that's a good thing. Hate can eat you up. Work for the government and be thankful you got a job in these bad economic times, and just make sure we don't have to fight anyone anymore," his mother told him in her usual soft voice.

Boris listened politely to his mother but knew that once he got to work he'd be fighting those commie bastards with every ounce of knowledge he had gathered working on his degrees. He was not naïve and knew that atomic weapons were out of the question in today's world. He also knew that other weapons of mass destruction, like chemical warfare, would more often than not kill our own troops just as easily as they killed the enemy's. He knew that defoliants, like Agent Orange, were also ineffective as a tactical weapon and could have further reaching consequences than anticipated.

No, he was interested in developing the perfect biological weapon: something that destroyed a country's ability to maintain order, but when the assault was over the organisms could be brought under control again. They would need Boris' resources to return their country to an uncontaminated state, and they would be ready and willing to stop all hostile actions against our allies and us. Sort of a reverse neutron bomb but without all the political baggage that any nuclear weapon carried. That was his goal and he was determined to develop it, taking it out of the realm of science fiction and into the world of reality.

He knew that the government's biological defense effort was designed to protect the United States and its allies against other countries' use of biological weapons. But, as he so eloquently argued with his bosses, "How are we to know what weapons they're developing unless we can develop them ourselves?" That argument allowed him a lot of freedom in his lab. It also taught him that rules can be broken by people who have the courage and fortitude to persevere—and persevere was something Boris did very well indeed.

A day after meeting with my father, Boris followed through on his promise to connect me to Michigan's bioresearch program.

"Hello, Sy, it's me, Boris. How's it going?" Boris was calling Seymour Arvin, a professor of electrical engineering at the University of Michigan. "Sy, I have a favor to ask…actually, I might be doing you a favor. Are you still in need of more grad students to work on the HI-MEMS project?"

Boris filled Sy in on my work and what my dad told him about the slugs I found, and Sy was definitely interested. He was interested for two reasons: he did want grad students and faculty from other units to be involved in his lab; but more importantly, Boris was the DARPA program's manager overseeing Sy's projects—and if Boris was interested in my work then so was Sy.

Coincidentally, Sy was married to Margie and he was always looking for opportunities to work with her and her students. Sy knew that if I was working with slugs, then I was in all likelihood working with Margie Hawthorne, so it was through Margie that I had briefly met Sy a week or so earlier at the dean's party.

It was obvious that he didn't remember me when I went to his office on North Campus in the Electrical Engineering and Computer Science Building. "Come in, come in, George. Margie's been telling me all about your work and it sounds fascinating." The EECS Building was a relatively newer building like the others on that part of the campus. The ambiance seemed different to me: less traditional, I guess, than the older buildings on Central Campus that I was used to working in. His office seemed large for a faculty member, considering the small offices that my professors had in our building. Maybe his was larger because he brought in so much money from his DARPA research projects.

"Nice to meet you, Professor Arvin," I said. I didn't remind him that we had met just a few days ago. "Margie...uh, Professor Hawthorne suggested I come over here to tell you about my work. She seemed to feel that what we're working on at SNRE might be of interest to you. Also, you may be able to help me by filling me in on the latest literature out there on bioengineering that might be narrowed to my interest."

Professor Arvin told me to take a chair at the side of his desk so we could talk under less formal circumstances. "Yes, yes, it certainly is nice to meet you. I understand your father is a friend of Dr. Bethelheim over at DARPA. It seems he met with him recently to talk about your work. Boris contacted me and asked me to look into the possibility of having you do some work with us in our HI-MEMS program. Are you familiar with HI-MEMS?"

"Not really, but Professor Hawthorne seems to think that the potential for a bioengineered battery operating off of our slugs might be of interest to you," I said, making sure that he understood I was here as much to help him as for him to help me.

"Yes, of course, no doubt about it. We call it 'energy scavenging,' using the natural functions of insects to convert some of their mechanical actions into electricity. We can then use that electricity to drive the devices that are important to our sponsor—that's DARPA, of course. Currently we can actually control the flight of our beetles by using that scavenged energy, and then use the insects for reconnaissance and monitoring devices almost undetectable to an enemy."

When Professor Arvin used the term "enemy" the hair on the back of my neck stood up. I in no way wanted to work with anyone doing military research. I think he noticed my discomfort and immediately said, "Of course, the civilian applications for our products are even more important. As you know, we can't do classified military research—all our work has to be in the open literature. In which, by the way, I can help you find what might be of interest to you. But it would be disingenuous of me not to tell you that whatever DARPA does with our products is for defense; after all that's what the D in DARPA stands for. We look at the civilian applications for our research, but if DARPA sees other uses, well, that's pretty much out of our control."

He went on to tell me that his personal interest was in the micro-electrical systems because of the extremely large civilian applications. With nano research on the increase, smaller and smaller electrical generating systems would be needed, and there was no doubt in his mind that bioengineered electrical systems were the answer for driving future electronic systems. He further explained that developing those products tied into his environmental programs—like land use and sustainability—which were his ultimate goals, and it surprised me that his interests were so similar to mine. He also acknowledged that Margie felt the same way, and that was why they *both* (his emphasis) were excited about my work.

"Have you thought about doing a joint or dual interdisciplinary PhD?" he asked me.

"Not really. I guess I was always intent on just being an environmental biologist. I'm not sure my background has prepared me for working at the doctoral level in another discipline," I answered.

"Nonsense, of course it has. I've taken the liberty of checking your academic career—with your advisor's permission, of course," he said as he shuffled through some of the papers on his desk, "and I see that you've taken a lot of advanced math, computer, and other science courses. You'd have no problem getting your PhD jointly with EECS. Naturally, you'll want to sit in on our four hundred level MEMS class in the fall and maybe our bioengineering class this semester, but that should be no problem for you." He sounded very reassuring, and I couldn't help but smile thinking how happy Dad would be that I would be getting a PhD degree from an engineering program. "Look, let me be very honest with you. I want to make our MEMS effort much more interdisciplinary than it currently is and having a doctoral student with your credentials involved would be just what the doctor ordered."

I was certain that he was thinking of Dr. Bethelheim as the ordering doctor, but for some reason there was sincerity in his plea that I found genuine. After all, Margie wouldn't have sent me if she thought he was just using me. Professor Arvin went on to tell me that he'd already talked it over with Margie and that both of them agreed to jointly chair my dissertation if I joined his lab. I would have more than enough funding for my work and I would be working with a group of fellow grad students that had a common interest but a different perspective. He felt that I would flourish in such an environment.

"Professor Arvin..."

"Call me Sy. After all, if you do accept our offer we'll be working more as colleagues, in the same way you work with Margie," he said with a pleasant smile.

He was a nice looking guy and I could see why Margie married him. I knew that they had no children, so their careers—and each other—were all they had. Both were highly respected faculty members, having published many articles and even a few books, some of them jointly, so they worked well together. His offer was very tempting—and a little intimidating. I was afraid that if I refused then Margie may not want to work with me anymore, and if I accepted I might be co-opted by Dr. Strangelove—that's how I pictured Bethelheim after Dad described him. But that was probably unfair. After all, I'd never even met the man.

I continued, "Sy...I'm truly flattered that you would think I'm good enough to be part of your lab and you'd work with me on my dissertation. Let me talk with Margie first, if you don't mind, and then I'll get back to you. Will that be all right?"

"Yes, of course, talk with Margie and whoever else you respect. I know this would be a major redirection for you, so I don't expect you to say yes right now. Let me know what you decide, and either way I wish you much success in your work—and I definitely want to know how your research pans out." He waited for second and finished our conversation, saying, "I'll get you a list of current publications and websites that might be of interest to you and have them sent over to Margie. Will that work for you?"

Two days later I was meeting with Margie in her office. "So what do you think, Margie?" I asked. "Will I have to start all over—you know, get a new committee, write up a new proposal, and get admitted to the EECS program? I'm just wondering if it's worth all the trouble."

"You'll probably want to modify your proposal somewhat to address the issue of electrical energy generation using the slugs and, just as important, how did the slugs come into being? And if Sy agrees to serve as cochair, I think your current committee from the school will be just fine—that is, if they want to stay on. Sy will take care of you getting into their program with a minimum of paperwork, although you will have to formally apply, but that shouldn't be a problem," Margie said matter of factly.

I think she and Sy had already gone through the whole process before I even talked with her. I couldn't help but get excited about the new direction—or, I should say, *additional* direction my research was taking. This way if my original hypothesis about acidic slugs and land use didn't work out, I would still have the renewable energy generation model as another researchable topic that probably had a higher probability of success. Nobody ever got a PhD based on negative results—at least nobody at Michigan.

"Then let's do it," I said. I had a good feeling about the whole thing. "What do I have to do first?"

"Let's see, it's nine o'clock. I would suggest that you go to that electrical biophysics class at nine thirty over in the Biomedical Engineering Building. You've already missed the first class so you'll have some catching up to do. I think Sy already spoke to the instructor about letting you sit in, and I think he has an EECS doctoral student that he would like you to work with. Charlie Chen's her name. I've met her and I know you two will get along. I'll take care of all the administrative stuff from this end, but after the biophysics class you should go to the department office and take care of all the paperwork you need to do there."

I could tell Margie was excited about my agreeing to do the double degree when, wearing a broad smile, she shook my hand with both her hands. Not many doctoral programs had joint, or dual, degrees with other schools, and I'd heard that after people get those degrees they sometimes found it difficult to get academic positions. But that was something I'd worry about down the road. Right now I was off to the Biomedical Engineering Building on North Campus to sit in on the bioengineering class Sy told me about.

I found the class really interesting, and I had no difficulty understanding the scientific or engineering elements of the lecture. After class I walked up Beal to the EECS building and went to the department offices as Margie suggested. It was going on noon and the program secretaries were anxious to close the office for lunch. I was directed over to their registrar, who had been waiting for me. *Wow,* I thought, *things really move fast around here.* The registrar loaded me down with a ton of forms, program pamphlets, course books, and employment papers to either read or fill out. I found out I was to be an assistant research scientist in Professor Arvin's lab—one step up from a TA, and the pay was better too. She quickly explained everything to me and told me to fill out the forms and get them back to her after lunch. She said there was a grad student lounge I could go to and grab a sandwich as I filled out the forms.

I picked up all the materials and put them into my backpack and headed off to the lounge. It was crowded with students, and as I looked around I saw that they looked pretty much like the SNRE grad students, but maybe just a little neater. I smiled to myself thinking about that. Many were friendly; even though they didn't know me, they said hi and smiled. I got a sandwich and some milk from the machines and sat down at a table with a couple of other students who just looked up and smiled. At the table next to me was a small group of excited students discussing something that seemed of great importance. I couldn't help but overhear some of their conversation.

"You cannot put little bombs on beetles and have them attack someone. Don't be such an asshole," a beautiful Asian-looking woman was saying in a noticeably British accent.

"Charlie, you're so fucking naïve. You think that lab of yours is simply doing that HI-MEMS shit for the good of mankind? Grow up, kid. DARPA wants bombs," some older, bearded, geeky-looking guy was saying.

My ears pricked up; could that be the Charlie Chen I was supposed to be working with? The conversation got very heated, but all I could hear was that beautiful girl's accent and the occasional f-bomb coming from the geek. I couldn't concentrate on filling out my forms or reading all the booklets and papers anymore. Every now and again I'd hear the name Charlie and was more and more convinced it was her—or, I should say, more and more *hopeful* it was her.

A little before one in the afternoon the lounge began to empty out as the students went off to class or wherever they went in the afternoon. I heard Charlie say, "Got to go to work now. Catch up with you all later," as she left her table and headed out the door. I hurriedly finished filling out the forms and went back to the program office and turned them all in to the registrar. She directed me to go to the Systems Lab on the fourth floor and told me that someone would show me where my lab was located.

I found the HI-MEMS lab coordinator and she had me sign even more forms about my appointments. She then told me that Professor Arvin was not at the lab today, but Doctor Lasky was in and he'd like to meet with me at three if I was available. "In the meantime," she said, "let me show you your office and introduce you to your officemate."

My heart started beating faster. I knew it would be Charlie and I could hardly wait to actually meet her. But was I surprised when it turned out that my officemate was the geek!

"Gerry, meet your new officemate, George. George Brachmann, this is Gerald Kolaczki. I think you two will have lots in common. Gerry, would you show George around? I have tons of stuff to do or I would..."

"No problem, be glad to show him what's going on around here," the geek said.

It turns out that Gerry was a doctoral candidate in the Computer Science division and had been working on developing proteins for biological computer applications and was funded by DARPA's DSO office, as were most of the people in the lab. The lab itself was a hotbed of interdisciplinary research with students and faculty from many programs (mostly other engineering departments) in the university. However, to the best of anyone's knowledge, I was their first SNRE student to come on board. I also met some of the other students whom I saw eating lunch at the noisy table in the student lounge earlier. But I didn't meet Charlie and was curious about that.

"I couldn't help but notice you and your friends eating lunch today in the lounge. There was a young Asian woman there too, but I don't see her anywhere around here. Does she also work here?" I asked Gerry.

"You mean Charlie Chen; and yes, she does work here, but she's probably locked in her chem lab on the other side of the open lab," he said, pointing to some closed office spaces along the north wall. "She spends most of her time in there working on exotic chemical mixtures, trying to come up with more efficient green batteries since that's where all the interest seems to be today. Why are you interested in Charlie?" he said with a knowing gleam in his eye. "She's quite the looker," he continued, "but she's much too smart for the geeks that work in this lab."

I thought it interesting that he also referred to his fellow lab rats as geeks when I thought that if anyone was a geek it was him. But he was very nice to me and introduced me to most of our fellow grad students in the lab, telling me what each one of them was working on.

When we went back to our office he made certain I was comfortable with the desk, bookcase, and file cabinets I had assigned to me and that they had been emptied out and were clean. He showed me where to get office supplies and then got me officially logged onto the lab's computer network. We talked a lot about the work there and why, knowing that DARPA's main thrust was defense, it was hard for a peace activist like him to be involved with the agency.

"I'll take their money and do my work knowing that the civilian applications I'm developing are worth all the aggravation I get working for the feds. But as soon as I see a defense application for my research I'm out of here," he said with great conviction.

"But how will you know when that happens? I mean, how would you know when what you do has defense applications?" I asked, worried about the same issue.

"Yeah, that's the tough part. Working here you know that sooner or later some government lab rat will see what you're doing and turn it into some kind of WMD. But I'd like to think I'm smart enough to see that coming and be able to leave before it could happen."

I thought that was a bit naïve of him and recalled how he said that Charlie was naïve about her efforts.

It was getting onto three and I reminded him that I had a meeting with Professor Lasky. Gerry offered to take me there and introduce me to him. "He's a nice guy—an assistant prof with a PhD in electrical engineering out of Cal Tech. Just keep in mind that he's at that point in his career where you'll probably be in around five years, so don't be too impressed by him," he told me as we left our office.

It wasn't until the following week that Gerry filled me in on Mike's history. It seems that Mikhail Sergei Lasky was a Russian immigrant who came over as a small child with his family from the old USSR in 1985. His parents got permission to emigrate from Moldova to Israel, but instead of going to Israel, like many other Russians leaving as Jewish émigrés, they went directly to the United States after arriving in Europe. His parents were both trained as engineers in the Soviet Union and had no problem finding work in the United States. Mike, as he came to be called, got his PhD in California, but his undergrad work was done at Michigan. His family lived in Southfield, Michigan, a suburb of Detroit, and that's where his younger brother was born. According to Gerry, Mike liked to tell people that his brother can be elected president but he can't.

When a tenure track position in the Electrical and Computer Engineering division opened here at Michigan, Mike got the job. That was last year, but he's done well here and now, as the assistant director, he's sure to have an easy go at getting tenure.

When Gerry and I left our office we went to a group of larger offices along one wall with windows. The senior research staff and administrators had those offices. Gerry stopped at the second one in the row and said, "Mike, I brought the new grad student from nat resources over to meet you. George, this is Mike; he's our lab's assistant director, and he'll keep you honest by overseeing all your work and making certain you're giving the government their money's worth," Gerry said in his good-natured, folksy way.

"Come in, George. We've been expecting you and are delighted you're here. Thanks, Gerry. Would you like to stay while I talk with George?" Professor Lasky asked.

"No thanks, I gotta get back to my work. See you later, George, and welcome to the pit."

"It seems that some of the students—notably Gerry—refer to the HI-MEMS lab as the 'pit,' but I have no idea why," Mike said with a smile. "So you're the man who'll be developing our biological battery using...slugs, is it?"

After a brief welcoming speech and some other small talk, Mike said, "Let's see, it's almost four, so we should go over and meet your coresearcher on your project. Her name is Charleen Chen, but all her friends call her Charlie. I'm sure you two will get along famously," he said as we walked over to her chem lab on the other side of the large open area. Butterflies were in my stomach as I anticipated finally meeting that enchanting Asian woman with a captivating British accent.

chapter 3

CHARLEEN CHEN WAS a British citizen born to Chinese-British parents in Birmingham, England; her father was a professor of architecture and city planning at Birmingham City University. Charleen attended the University of Birmingham, a more prestigious school than where her father taught, and she received a *first*—that's the highest honor given—on her dual BSc/MSci degrees in chemistry and bio-organic chemistry. *Did I say that she was gorgeous?* Lucy Liu went to Michigan around twenty years earlier, but I remember thinking that Charleen had her good looks beat by a wide margin. She was wearing jeans and a warm sweater, but that didn't hide the perfect figure she had underneath. She was small, maybe five-foot-three, and probably tipped the scale at just over a hundred pounds. Her face could only be described as *China Doll.* As soon as I met her, I was totally smitten.

"Charlie, meet George, your new collaborator on that biologically-based battery you're working on. George has some very special pets that might make your work a lot easier. You two should get to know each other because I suspect your two dissertations will have a lot of overlap."

And with that introduction, Mike Lasky left the two of us alone.

"Hey, George. Sy already filled me in on your slugs, and I'm anxious to get started. When shall we begin?"

Her British accent was a delight but different from other Brits I knew. I asked her about it, and she explained that it was a Midlands accent, but she thought her *dialect* was becoming Americanized since being in Ann Arbor.

As we walked around the lab, Charlie showed me where everything was stored and how I could get more supplies and equipment if I needed it. Trying to make more small talk, I asked her when she got here, and she told me that she arrived here two years ago to get her PhD in electrical engineering.

"My focus is on green and sustainable electrical energy storage and production. I'm working on a biologically-based source—looking at microorganisms and some of the hybrid beetles used in the HI-MEMS project, but none of those sources have enough energy density to supply a meaningful amount of electricity," she told me.

By meaningful she meant a battery with enough stored or continuously produced energy to run a moderate-sized household. But the battery also had to be manageable and not larger than the house it was running. That was a tall order and probably not realizable during her PhD work. However, if she could come up with a smaller working model and enough research to convince people that the larger concept would work, then that would be enough for her dissertation.

We continued walking around the lab, occasionally sitting on the stools, and I told her about my slugs, how they were so physiologically strange, and how I hoped to use them for my research, which revolved around a greener approach to land use. We talked a lot about our interests and just general get-to-know-each-other stuff. Eventually, Charlie looked at her watch and said, "My gawd, it's almost six thirty. I can't believe we've been talking for that long." She stood up and asked, "You want to have some supper at my place?" in a voice that made my stomach tingle. Did I ever!

Charlie lived alone in a small student rental apartment near Central Campus, so we took the commuter bus from North Campus and walked over to her place. Over a dinner of leftover Chinese carryout, we continued talking about our work. Her father taught an environmental planning class in his city planning curriculum, so she was more than impressed that I would be interested in using natural systems for sustainable farming. She also completely understood my goals.

Sitting on the one small couch in her apartment, I felt so relaxed with her and I got the impression she felt the same about me. Occasionally as we talked, our arms or hands touched, and that tingling sensation was delightful…and I could almost sense the same was true for her. She was the first girl I ever really wanted to date—and not just because she was so beautiful. I became disenchanted with most of the other women I dated because they often didn't understand what it was that I wanted to do with my life, or they were only interested in telling me all about themselves. Charlie knew and understood what I was all about. More importantly, I completely understood where Charlie was coming from professionally. I also liked to believe that on a personal level she wanted to know me better, as I did her. We seemed to connect on so many levels that fate could never be so cruel as to have it any other way. I knew then and there that I had to be with this woman for the rest of my life.

"Mackie, you've got to meet her. If she wasn't Chinese, you'd think she was you, only much better looking," I teased my sister over the phone.

Mackie said, "Well, thanks for that, bro. Yeah, from what you're telling me, I would like to meet her." Mackie told me that she was coming up to Ann Arbor on Sunday to visit with some friends and suggested that I take her and Charlie out for dinner. We agreed to meet around six. She ended our conversation with, "How about if we meet at Gratzi's, or is that too rich for you? Let me know if it works. Love ya, Freddy."

I was excited about Mackie meeting Charlie but even more excited that I had an excuse to ask her out. "Hi, Charlie," I said as I walked into the lab on Friday afternoon. "I see you've been playing with my slugs. Any ideas yet?"

We talked a little business before I got up the courage to say, "Hey, I was thinking…my sister's coming up on Sunday to visit some friends. We usually get together for dinner when she comes up. Would you like to join us? We're going to Gratzi's."

I think I might have sounded a bit over anxious, but Charlie just smiled and said, "That would be lovely for a change; delighted to, George."

And so it was set, my first date with her—and my little sister as the chaperone! Not very romantic, but it would be a start. I always appreciated Mackie's advice and counsel. Even in high school, she told me what to wear on dates, how to act, and how to treat my date so she felt special. I was certain that if it wasn't for Mackie, I would have been a total social misfit with women by then.

On a mild Sunday in January, Charlie and I were seated in Gratzi's at a nice warm booth near the front window when Mackie walked in, came right up to us, and sat down next to me. "Hi, Charlie, nice to meet you. George has done nothing but talk about you since meeting you on Wednesday."

Great, I thought. *If that doesn't set me up for failure nothing will. Why would Mackie do that?*

She persisted. "Yeah, ever since he was a kid all that ever excited him was slugs and snails, so when he met you and found out that you liked his slugs he was in heaven..."

"Okay, Mackie, that's enough. I think Charlie gets the idea." I wasn't sure why she said all that crap, but I think Mackie was teasing me because she was finally realizing that I would soon be gone from her life. Her big brother would no longer be around to stick up for her and share secrets like only siblings could do. In any case, the teasing quickly stopped and Charlie was not at all put off by it.

"George told me what a good scientist you are," Charlie said to Mackie, "and you're going into automotive engineering. That's interesting. I should think not many young women choose that field, am I right?"

"To some extent you are. Automotive engineering used to be dominated by men, but now there are a number of us women in the field. I think that more women are concerned about the environmental impact the auto has on the world and they want to do something about that. In any case, that's why I'm doing it. Besides, my dad promised me a job at GM once I graduate," Mackie said with a big grin.

During dinner Mackie and Charlie got along extremely well. I thought it would be all science and engineering, but it wasn't. It was about music and the theater and almost anything other than science and engineering. You could see that they really liked each other and had a lot in common. I hardly ever got into the conversation, but I didn't mind at all. I liked the fact that Mackie liked Charlie and that Charlie was so comfortable with my little sister.

Later that night, around eleven thirty, Mackie called me from her apartment in Southfield. "You asleep?" she asked.

"Not yet, but if I was I wouldn't be now. What's up?"

"Just wanted to thank you for dinner and to tell you to hold on tight to that woman—don't let that one get away, okay?"

I had to smile to myself as Mackie told me that because I was thinking pretty much the same thing. "Okay, sis, I'll do my best. Love ya and good night. Oh, by the way, if I do loose her, it will be because of what you said to her about me liking slugs when you came in the restaurant. Good night!" I liked doing that to Mackie, knowing that she'd try to get even for it the next time we talked.

———

Early the following week, Charlie and I met with Sy for about a half-hour to bring him up to date on our project. Sy informed me that I was now enrolled in their doctoral program and that I should concentrate on getting candidacy by the end of the semester. We laid out a plan for achieving that and set some dates to possibly schedule a meeting with my committee to give them a status report. Charlie sat patiently waiting while Sy and I discussed my academic career. Then Sy asked her about our work together. "So, Charlie, I guess you know all about George's strange mollusks by now."

"I think he's done a yeoman's job of bringing me on board with his creatures. I can't get over the acid levels that their mucous holds. Should be perfect as a vehicle for transferring electrons. We're now sharing a lab and working together on the project."

"Good, good," Sy said and told us to keep him informed on our progress. Also, he wanted to make certain that we kept thorough notes and that we started to write up our research in anticipation of generating some journal articles. "You can't start publishing too soon. George, your slugs alone are worth putting in an article; and Charlie, if you have a model for a battery using those slugs, it's also worth publishing, so go for it," he said enthusiastically.

Charlie and I didn't know it then but Sy had recently talked with Boris to update him on my coming on board, and it was Boris who asked Sy about the status of my slugs. I found this out later when Dad called me about doing the dual degree with funding from DARPA. Dad said that he found out about it—he had been in touch with Boris—and about my speedy admission into the EECS doctoral program. Dad was quite surprised when he called me. He was thrilled that I was doing an engineering PhD—as I knew he would be—along with my SNRE work, and I was glad that Dad was so supportive of my plan.

In the meantime, my relationship with Charlie was really taking off. We were spending so much time together—working in the lab and being together like we were on dates or simply watching TV at her place or mine—that it was bound to get more intense.

"My turn to pick tonight's shows," Charlie said on Valentine's Day.

We had finished a pizza that was shaped like a heart and were sitting very close together on my couch. I think we both knew that it was just a matter of time before our hormones would kick in and take over the whole relationship, and it happened very quickly on that Valentine's Day. As fate would have it, the weather turned very cold that night. We frequently worked on our laptops, doing our research and writing up our notes, at my place because it was closer to our lab on North Campus; also, I had a printer.

It was too cold, at least that's what I told Charlie, for me to walk her over to catch the Central Campus bus, so I talked Charlie into staying at my place. I offered her my bed (luckily I had just changed the sheets that morning) and offered to sleep on the couch.

Sitting together and watching Charlie's comedy show, everything just happened naturally. We had sat close like that before and even made out a little without getting too involved. I had put my arm around her as was usual by then and could feel the warmth of her body coming through her blouse. I was getting very aroused, and I'm certain Charlie noticed it. As we started kissing, it was apparent that both of us were very turned on, and when I touched her breasts, even outside her blouse, it was ecstasy. I knew then that I was not going to be sleeping on the couch.

We had just gone farther tonight than we ever had before, and by news time we were both in my bed making love. Our hands and faces were all over each others' naked bodies. I couldn't get over how delicious Charlie tasted and how her body's fragrance was like perfume to me. The sheer joy of it all was awesome.

"George, I don't want you to think I'm this easy. It's just that you're so...so..."

"Shh," I said and kissed her. Almost immediately after that we merged, and I kept the rhythm of our movements as slow as I could until neither one of us could wait any longer and we felt the ultimate pleasure that love making brings. The thrill, the excitement, the pure pleasure we felt in each other was beyond description. After that we both knew we would be together for a long time, if not forever.

It was only a week or so later when I proposed to Charlie. "Charleen Chen, will you marry me?" I said very seriously one night after we made love. Charlie looked at me strangely at first, and then with tears in her eyes she said while sobbing, "Yes, George Brachmann, I will marry you and be your wife and life partner." With that we both hugged and cried and kissed and warmed our bodies with each other's and made love again...and again.

We soon got into a routine of work, dinner, sex at either her place or mine. It was amazing how much we accomplished. My analysis on the slugs and their habits was getting so detailed that I filled my lab book with notes and sketches in just two months. Charlie had been working on developing her battery and came up with a simple copper mesh anode and a carbon rod cathode. The copper mesh was based on the fact that the slugs, like other varieties of garden slugs, would not cross or even touch copper because it supposedly gave them an electric shock. She buried the mesh under the soil so that the slugs would not have to come in contact with it and then planted the cathodes at fixed intervals separated by a wall of copper mesh. The system she designed would then be a multi-cell battery, each with a fixed voltage of around two volts.

Not everything was always sweet and rosy with us, as I learned when I first asked her if she had ever heard of Charlie Chan. She gave me that look as if to say, *If I hear from one more American about Charlie Chan the detective I'll cut his liver out.* What she actually said was, "It's bad enough that I'm probably the millionth person of Chinese descent with the name Charleen Chen, do you have to further fuck up my identity with a fake Chinese detective?"

That was enough for me to know that I shouldn't mess with Charlie Chen's name.

———

We got the slugs' DNA results back in January, and their DNA was, not surprisingly, about 99.999 percent similar to the common garden slug, *Arion distinctus*, but there was a very slight variation—probably a mutation that affected their genes for reproduction. It probably also affected their mucous producing glands that gave them their special chemistry. The lab wasn't sure if it was enough of a mutation to consider them a new species, but since we had no way of knowing if they could reproduce with the common garden slug (because they kept eating them), it would be some time before anyone could make a case for speciation.

It's rare when a mutation like this occurred in nature, and if their progeny cannot mate with the parent species so that their offspring can be analyzed, then it becomes almost impossible to tell if a new species was born. In addition, historically when such mutants are found, they are frequently short-lived and die off before they can find an ecological niche to survive in. For now they were simply known as *Arion d. distinctus,* a subspecies of the garden slug they originated from.

We were staying at my place that night, and I had explained all this to Charlie. It was getting late and we were in bed when I asked, "I wonder how they became a mutant variety? I know that recombinant DNA can occur literally out of the blue, but it's a far more complex process and unlikely in today's world where most ecological niches are filled. I know that more often than not there is some mutating agent involved—a chemical, radiation, or some other physical operator at fault. But even then it's usually on just a couple of organisms, not a whole group of them."

Charlie responded, "We can go back and study their habitat more thoroughly later, but for now let's just assume that there was some environmental intervention at work there. Even if we can find out, or at a minimum come up with some plausible alternatives, I'm not sure what that buys us. Let's just go to sleep; I'm tired."

———————

Over the next month, Charlie and I became inseparable and planned on moving in together in the fall. Charlie was a little concerned about us moving in together; she was worried what her parents would say since she knew that they were conservative regarding premarital living arrangements. We were spending our nights either at her place or mine, and since my place was bigger and a bit more private, it was mostly over at my apartment. At that time I was living in the Huron Towers on Fuller Court right behind the VA Hospital. It was on the edge of North Campus, literally walking distance to our lab, so it was more convenient for us than her place on Central Campus.

Our work was going well and I had a couple of nice-sized terrariums in the lab to house my slugs and study their habits and physical characteristics.

A couple of months ago, I had sent some down to the biological supply house in South Carolina to farm them for me since I didn't have fields of my own to dedicate to them. The warmer climate would be more conducive for reproduction and the large, moist fields down there would be good for establishing larger colonies. Charlie was doing well in her research, establishing a battery model that might yield a promising amount of energy, so both of us were progressing when we got the letter.

In March a letter from the biological supply house had arrived at our lab. Charlie opened it. "The soil's dead," Charlie said to me as I walked into the lab. "All of it is void of nutrients, microorganisms, and any potential for growing anything but your slugs. And they'll only grow as long as there's dead organic matter for them to eat, even if it's each other's dead bodies," she said with some disgust. "It would seem that the soil acidity is so high from the slugs nothing else can live or grow in it."

"But the slugs live in it, and it's that high acidity you need to support your battery, so what's the issue?" I asked. Then I realized, of course, that my goal of some kind of farming going on in conjunction with these slugs was probably out of the question. That didn't bother me too much since my research was now focusing more on their origins and I was heavily into the mathematics of that process.

"Here, read this," she said, handing me the letter.

In essence, it said that they had to destroy all my samples because they were taking over their soil beds and killing off everything else. If they hadn't destroyed them then their fields would have been overrun with the slugs. I wasn't sure how to respond since my feelings were very mixed. On the one hand I felt that the news might jeopardize Charlie's battery, and on the other hand it had no major impact on my work. I said to Charlie, "What do you suppose that means for us? Is there any way we can control them? More important, how do you feel about it regarding your work?"

"You remember a while back when I tried feeding them to some of our HI-MEMS beetles in the hopes of finding a biological control," Charlie asked me, "but the beetles just died trying to eat them, and soon the beetles were all gone—killed and eaten by the slugs. With the weather getting warmer here, we might try feeding them to other larger predators...but I'm not sure how that will go either." As for her battery, Charlie wasn't greatly concerned because she planned on keeping them in a closed and controlled environment that she referred to as her battery farm.

It was then that I realized that our work was heading in directions entirely unanticipated. I felt a little nauseated knowing that maybe I would have to rethink my whole approach. But what was really making me feel sick was that the slugs were indeed becoming *Frankenslugs,* and I was losing control over their existence in the same way that Dr. Frankenstein lost control over his creation. I was torn between wanting to nurture them to see what their full potential was and destroying them before they got away from me... but I seriously doubted that I could destroy all of them now.

"You say that the slugs are killing the soil," Boris said to Sy over the phone. "No, no, keep the kids on the project. Charlie has a good, viable topic that will probably pan out, but you may have to redirect George to something else. Talk it over with his advisor in SNRE. She's your wife, isn't she? I'm sure the two of you can come up with something."

Boris was very excited about the way the slug research was progressing since it became more apparent to him that his hope for the perfect biological weapon was now a real possibility. "Sy, find out the name of that bio supply place down south for me. I'm curious how they got rid of the slugs and what other events happened down there...No, don't tell the kids. I can have my own people do it. Thanks for the update."

Boris sat there thinking for a while before calling in his chief chemist. "Beth, put together a team with you and two other people. I have a very important mission for you that I'll fill you in on once you pick your team."

And with that Dr. Elizabeth Munsing left his office, intent on carrying out Boris' orders.

chapter 4

ON A MILD St. Patrick's Day, I met with my committee and Margie introduced Sy as a new member and cochair for my dissertation. My dissertation
would focus on slug habitat and the environmental causes, or sources, of mutation that could modify their protein characteristics. One of the members
decided he would not be good for me, so he asked to be excused from my
committee. But with Sy coming on, I still had enough faculty members to
satisfy the graduate school's requirements. The other two members, besides
Margie, were delighted that I would be pursuing a dual degree with EECS.

Pursuing a dual degree meant that I would have to satisfy the requirements of both units, but it also allowed for a lot of overlap, which greatly
reduced the amount of time and money I would need to complete my studies,
and, best of all, only one dissertation would be needed.

Later that day, when I was in my office in the HI-MEMS lab doing some
research, Gerry walked in. I spent so much time in our chem lab—Charlie's
and mine—that I was rarely in my office when Gerry was there. Today was
different and our schedules overlapped. The few times we were in the office
together, we got very little work done while having some great philosophical
and political discussions. I liked Gerry and we were in agreement on so many
social issues—like being antiwar and embracing environmentalism—that it
was fun being with him. Also, he was a great help in giving me some solid
direction in understanding the engineering principles I needed to know for
my work. His help got me through my original anxiety about getting into
a graduate engineering program without having an undergrad engineering
degree.

"So what's this I hear that you and Charlie are off to DC next week to visit with the chief guru himself, Herr Dr. Boris Bethelheim? How did you guys swing that one?" Gerry asked.

"Sy arranged it. It seems that Dr. Strangelove wants to meet us, talk about our work, and, who knows, maybe even give us summer internships in DC."

"Wow! I bet he wants to put miniature torpedoes on your slugs and send them off to sink subs in the Arabian Gulf," Gerry kidded. "*Slug Sinks Sub!* What a headline that'd make."

I just smiled and let him have his fun. He would be defending his dissertation next year and was in the last stages of his work. All he had to do was put together his data and a solid technical report since his dissertation would mostly be a demonstration of the protein engineered micro-processor he helped develop at the lab with some other professors. The computer itself was still in the very early stages, and all they had to show for it now was a small demonstration model. The full-sized prototype would require a few more years of engineering and design before it became a technically viable product.

"So, you're sure that IBM is going to hire you to work with them on their bio-computers?" I asked.

"Yeah, DARPA promised to continue funding the project in a joint operation with IBM, and IBM wants me to come with it. I could do worse— teaching freshman computer classes at Podunk—so I'm taking their offer. You gonna miss me when I'm gone?" he asked with a smile, and then continued, "Well, I'm gonna miss you guys at our get-togethers, but I'll miss Charlie more. She's more fun to look at than you, and she's a hell of a lot smarter," he teased.

He was referring to our occasional lunches and Friday night Happy Hours that many of the grad students from the lab attended at a local pub downtown. We were all in different years in our programs, and the students who were farther along on their PhDs were a great source of information. Gerry was like the dean of the older class, having been at the lab the longest and, I think, looking the nerdiest. He always held court and would chastise us if he thought that any of us were doing weapons related work, but most of the other students were apolitical and didn't think about it either way. They did their work, hopefully for the betterment of all mankind; but they too knew that if DARPA, or the DOD, wanted to do other things with their discoveries then that was essentially their business. I felt more like Gerry and would make a serious issue of it if somebody wanted to use my research for something I couldn't accept morally, like weapons development.

I continued our conversation. "Yeah, Gerry, you ancient sixties-style *peaceniker,* we'll miss your sarcastic ass. But stay in touch, maybe you'll be able to come to our wedding in a year or two. Do you have a suit you can wear?"

"A year or two, why is it taking that long?"

"Because her folks are old-fashioned and I'm not Chinese. We may do a civil thing before, but don't tell anybody, okay?"

Gerry smiled like a big brother, shook his head, and went back to his writing.

"Welcome back, Sy, and welcome to you two as well. You must be George and this lovely woman is Charlie," Boris said to us as we entered his office at DARPA. "Here, sit down, get comfortable. We have a long day scheduled, so we should get started as soon as possible." Boris picked up a sheet of paper that looked like a one-page spreadsheet and read, "Let's see, it's nine now and at nine thirty you have your presentations scheduled. Then lunch, followed by the lab tour and discussions on the future of your project, and you're taking the six thirty back, so you have to be out of here by four thirty, DC traffic and all..."

Boris was completely organized, like any old Washington bureaucrat was expected to be. His office was kind of Spartan, I thought, for a deputy director: standard government desks, chairs, tables, and other furnishings all looking like they were purchased at a K-Mart sale. I couldn't get over how much he looked like I had imagined him to be: like Dr. Strangelove, only a little messier.

After our initial meeting with Boris, we left his office and went to a nice looking conference room. Sy, who had been to DARPA on numerous occasions, introduced us to the DARPA scientists and technicians that Boris invited to the presentation. My PowerPoint presentation went well, I thought, and the various lab reports, visual images, and movie clips seemed to keep them interested in the slugs. Charlie's presentation was shorter but more powerful. She took out a small black box, about six inches cubed, with two contacts on one of the sides. She connected the wires from her LED flashlight to the box and wowed them by pointing out that the power was generated by the slugs' acidity.

She fielded tons of questions.

"What's the energy density?"

"What kind of maintenance is needed to keep the cells viable?"

And so the Q&A went. I had very few questions other than how my work might tie into keeping the slugs alive in different environments.

Charlie answered all her questions calmly, professionally, and in good spirits. She was truly the hit of the morning session. I really felt proud to be her fiancé and colleague—in that order.

During lunch most of the DARPA staff wanted to be near Charlie to ask more questions, but I suspect it was her outstanding good looks that really attracted most of them. She was dressed in a fashionable pinstriped business suit and had on a pair of sensible but stylish black shoes. Her makeup was impeccable, and she certainly was the poster-child for Michigan's HI-MEMS lab. There was only one woman in the DARPA group—a chemist—and she was also taken in by Charlie. It was a slam-dunk for Sy. He had a mile-wide smile on his face after our presentations, and I could only guess that he knew that getting additional financing out of DARPA was all but guaranteed and that his future as a researcher and academic were established forever.

But the real highlight for both of us was the lab tour. If we thought our MEMS lab was world-class, it was only because we hadn't seen DARPA's. First of all it was gigantic: over two hundred thousand square feet, with numerous clean-rooms lining the interior walls. Compared to the cheapness of Boris' office furniture, the stuff in there was obviously the best money could buy—and it appeared money was of no concern. All the equipment was new and the mass spectrometers (instruments used to compute the abundance of elements in a test sample) were beyond state-of-the-art, not to mention the IBM mainframe that serviced them.

Our laboratory back in Ann Arbor looked like a high school chemistry lab compared to this. When Boris offered both of us summer internships to continue our research, we jumped at the chance. All we could talk about on the plane back to Michigan was what we would be doing and seeing in DC that summer. It was such a great feeling to be considered respected and credible scientists by people working in the scientific community. We were on a real high on that flight back and could hardly wait to get home to tell our friends and family what we had accomplished.

At that time we didn't know that, earlier in the week, three of the people we met at Boris' research center had gone down to South Carolina to visit the bio supply company I used to purchase my garden slugs. They introduced themselves as DARPA scientists and said that my slugs were part of a larger research project they and I were working on. They asked to see the bed where the slugs were first taken and asked if they could take soil samples back with them.

The company tech who was showing them around told them, "The soil is probably still heavily contaminated with the stuff we had to use to kill them. We first tried caffeine, but that simply kept them awake longer. We think that the acidity of their mucous neutralized the caffeine's ability to destroy them. We then used iron sulfate, but that had no lethal effect on them for probably the same reason. Finally we used an old-fashioned organic cyanide compound that did the trick. But it's most likely still in the soil and we still have to neutralize it so that we can use the bed again for other products."

"Why did you have to kill them?" the DARPA chemist asked. She was the one that we met when we made our presentation and seemed to be the person in charge of the expedition to South Carolina.

"Because they were taking over everything in their bed and it looked like they might be contaminating the other beds. They reproduced like crazy here in our warm climate. Not cold enough for them to hibernate, so they just continued laying eggs and growing bigger. I don't know how well they did up north, but down here they were really prolific. They killed everything living, ate it, and ate the slug food we served them..."

"Slug food?" she asked. "What's slug food?"

"It's just a mixture of decaying organic stuff, like garbage. But the worst part was that their high acidity destroyed the soil for growing anything—the soil was dead. At night we would sometimes find the creatures roaming around out of their area so we had to put up barriers to keep them from contaminating the other beds. We still don't know if we were successful, but if we weren't then we're out of business. That's why we had to destroy them," he said.

The DARPA team took the soil samples, thanked the tech, and went back to DC, where Boris debriefed them. What most of the other people working for Boris didn't know was that the three researchers were part of his Biological Warfare Defense team and carried out all their classified studies on a need-to-know basis. That's why the others weren't aware of their trip or the results of their inquiry. But my dad was told all of this by Boris—I learned they kept in contact quite frequently—and that's how I eventually found out about Boris' team.

After the debriefing Boris immediately brought in security and initiated a classified project file. Only Boris, the three researchers, and a few other people on Boris' team were to have access to their work, which was to further investigate the weaponry aspect of the slugs. Of course they knew that their work had to be couched in terms of suspecting that *unfriendlies* may be developing a biological weapon from mutant slugs. But they were a team hand-picked by Boris' chief chemist, Dr. Elizabeth Munsing, and they had no qualms about developing biological weapons of mass destruction if they could be used to destroy either Islamic fundamentalist regimes or other enemies of the state.

I was frightened when I found all that out, but by then it was much too late for me to do anything about it.

———

Back in Ann Arbor we were telling everyone how much we were looking forward to being in DC over the summer. The semester actually ended in April, but we weren't scheduled to leave for DC until June 1.

"You saw Strangelove himself and he offered you paid summer internships? It must have been Charlie. Your little Dutch-boy looks and *Frankenslugs* wouldn't get to him as much as Charlie's HI-MEMS battery would. What did you do to deserve that?" Gerry asked when the two of us were in our office on the following Monday.

"It must have been our great presentations, but what really got to us was their lab. Gerry, you wouldn't believe all the equipment they've got in there! We'd have our own space and all the apparatus that either of us wanted. With that kind of support, we could cut our research time by a year. Especially Charlie. I'm still stuck with the slugs' reproductive cycle, and I need to examine a few more generations. But even that could be accelerated with the kind of equipment and controlled climate chambers they'd supply me."

"You sound really psyched, George, I'm happy for you. But don't trust those bastards too much. Remember, they're looking for offensive weapons, and if they're that hyped about you two then there's got to be a catch. Watch out."

"Don't worry, Comrade Defender-of-the-realm, I'll be extra careful, especially if I see them attaching little torpedoes on my slugs' feet," I said with a Russian accent.

Gerry smiled, but I could see he was serious, so I stopped being funny and changed the subject to his dissertation defense next year. "You got it all together?" I asked.

"Yeah, mostly crossing T's and dotting I's, but we'll have a nice demo ready for my defense. It's the writing part I hate. I'm a lab rat and would rather just tinker with my toys than write. But it's got to be done even though I've got four publications out there. Anyway, this is Michigan and tradition rules." With that last mild protest about the dissertation process, Gerry went back to work.

Gerry was right about one thing: I was psyched. And so was Charlie. We'd be on our own in DC. The lab had some guy that would find us a nice apartment we could afford while we were there. We talked with him over the phone, telling him approximately where in DC we would like to live, even though we knew nothing at all about the DC area.

Later, when we were back in the apartment, I asked Charlie if she'd feel more comfortable having the civil marriage service sooner rather than later. We agreed that having the civil service first would be better, but we hadn't picked a date. I told her, "Honey, I would love to marry you today, you know that, but I'm just as willing to wait until after we meet your folks. Whatever you're comfortable with is cool by me."

She was looking at a letter as I was talking.

"Look at this," she said, handing me the letter. It was in Chinese, so I just stared at it and handed it back to her. She looked really troubled when she said, "They want to come and visit me in DC this summer." She was completely lost as to what to do. She loved and respected her parents and their traditional values—which included couples not living together before they were married—and didn't want to hurt them unnecessarily. She also knew that it was her life and that her parents had lived in the West long enough to understand her wishes as well.

"We'll get another apartment; since DARPA is giving each of us a living allowance, having another place won't be a problem. They can stay with you and things will be fine," I offered.

"No, I'm tired of being afraid to tell them that we plan on moving in together. I think it's time I told them the truth. I'm twenty-four and I should be able to talk to them like an adult. I love you, George, and want to be married to you forever. I'm going to call them this weekend and tell them that we're planning on getting married and that we will be living together in DC. And that I truly look forward to them meeting you!"

"That might not go over too well. Look, let's have a small civil service with just my family and a couple of friends next month. Then when they come to DC, we can tell them that we've decided to wait on having a formal wedding until after they've met me, and we can plan the event for either here or in England, or wherever they're comfortable. How's that for a plan?"

"That may work...I'll tell them that's what we plan to do when I call them. When do you think we should have the civil service?"

We looked at our calendar and picked Friday, April 15—tax day—for the service in Ann Arbor, and then we'd have a small party at my parents' house in Warren on Sunday. Charlie knew that April 15 was tax day in America and that everyone was uptight about not having their taxes in on time, and that suited her for our wedding day. Charlie had a droll British sense of humor sometimes.

"Wow! That's only three weeks from now. That's a quick romance, don't you think?" I simply grabbed her and kissed her and we were off to the bedroom for more "elicit" sex. Soon it would be legal and it may not be as much fun.

We picked up the license on Thursday and made arrangements to be married by a magistrate who did marriages only on Fridays in Ypsilanti. We needed two witnesses, so I asked Gerry and Charlie asked her friend Nicole. Both were delighted to do it. It was actually a lot of fun. There were two other couples having the so-called "solemnizing service" with us, and everyone was joyful and smiling a lot, including the magistrate. He told us that this was the most fun part of his job and he really enjoyed seeing young people like us getting married. He encouraged all of us to live morally decent lives and to care for others, and suggested we have a religious or cultural service at some other time as well. He pointed out that those couples that do the most in the way of a marriage ceremony are often less likely to split up.

After the brief service in Ypsilanti, we went off to our traditional Friday Happy Hour celebration at the Grizzly Peak back in Ann Arbor. Many of our friends from school were there and wanted to wish us well. When the pitchers of beer arrived, Gerry stood up and toasted us. "Here's to Charlie and George. May they have long life and much happiness, and may their science education put them in jobs that will always be dedicated to peace and love for all people." I guess he took his cue from the magistrate.

"Here, here!" everyone shouted, and then the drinking got serious.

When we got back to my apartment—now it was *our* apartment—after midnight, we were both exhausted. We were a little high, but not really drunk because we ate so much. Actually, we were high on being married— you might even say euphoric. We were giggling and laughing at the silliest things, like my Michigan cap that I said I'd wear at the ceremony, but didn't.

"Wasn't that magistrate a great guy," Charlie said, a little more serious now as we got into bed.

"Yeah, he was…and Gerry, I've never seen him so serious. Hard to believe that I really just met him this year and yet I feel like I've known him all my life," I said.

"And what about me?" Charlie asked, "You just met me this year too. Do you feel the same about me—knowing me all your life?"

"You, my love, I've known since the beginning of time. I knew you and loved you in all my previous lives. Our marriage today is just a continuation of what we've been doing for eons and eons," I said, and with that Charlie started to cry.

"I hope we've done the right thing. I hope we haven't rushed into something too soon," she sobbed. "I'm so worried about what my parents may think—oh, George, did we do the right thing, getting married like this?"

I was a little bewildered by her crying, but I just assumed it was because of all the emotional things we were both going through now. Our jobs in DC, the way our research was going, her parents coming in this summer—I must admit I felt a little like crying too. I put my arms around her and held her close, gently kissing her cheeks and not saying anything. Soon the crying stopped and we quietly fell asleep.

———

We arrived at my parents' house on Saturday planning to spend the whole weekend with the family. My folks had briefly met Charlie one weekend in March when they came up to take us out for dinner. I knew they liked her instantly, but I think they were really surprised at how fast our romance unfolded, and now all of a sudden we were married. I explained it all to them, about Charlie's parents being so traditional, and they understood. But I also knew they were concerned for Charlie's family and probably thought that we should have waited to get married—and that maybe what we were doing was a little disrespectful.

In any event, it was done, and they knew that in a year or so we would have a formal wedding with ministers and all the other trappings that middle-class morality required. Mackie, on the other hand, was thrilled. She loved Charlie, and now she'd have the sister she always wanted. She couldn't wait for us to get there, and she greeted Charlie far more affectionately than she greeted me. She fixed up my room for the two of us, adding some feminine touches, like a new (adult) bedspread and matching curtains that she knew Charlie would enjoy. Mandarin red geometric designs were outlined in charcoal and woven into a mostly gray background. Plus, she had a gift for Charlie: a pair of fantastic earrings that were both contemporary and yet traditional. They had a uniquely modernistic oval shape formed in brushed sliver with a small jade stone placed off-center in each one. She said that they were made for Charlie because she was that way: modern and traditional.

On Sunday around three in the afternoon, the guests arrived. It was just very close friends and family, around twenty-five people in all. Gerry and

Nicole came in from Ann Arbor, and to our surprise so did Margie and Sy! It was nice introducing them to my family; I really felt honored that they came. Gerry and Nicole also brought Mike Lasky with them. I kind of invited everyone not really thinking they'd all drive down, but here they were. Mom outdid herself, making hors d'oeuvres and all kinds of baked goodies, and Dad served champagne. There were toasts by my father and Mackie welcoming Charlie into the family. I saw that Charlie was about to cry again, so I held her close and made her feel at home and that everything was all right with our world. What surprised me a little was how much I saw Gerry and Mackie together. It appeared that they were both very interested in what each other had to say. They had to be talking tech-talk for Gerry to hold Mackie's interest that long.

"So the two of you will be in DC this summer," Mike Lasky said to me, a glass of champagne in his hand. "I don't know if you heard, but I'll be there too. I've been doing some of my ongoing research in Boris' lab, and I've spent the last couple of summers working there."

"That's great, Mike," I said and then called Charlie over to tell her the news. It would be great having him there, I initially thought, and comforting to know that someone from the college would be around if anything academic came up that we needed an answer for. After all, Mike was on Charlie's committee, and he was interested in my dissertation as well. However, by the same token, I thought that it seemed a little incestuous that three people from the same Michigan lab would be working in Boris' lab all at the same time. I had hoped that we would expand our collegial base, but now that Mike would be there I thought that might be harder than I had first anticipated.

———

I learned later that Boris worked closely with Mike; he had the necessary security clearance to work on Boris' biological warfare projects. Because of his background, Mike totally distrusted and hated the Russian government. He was not at all worried or concerned about using bio-weapons on specific elements of the current Russian federation, especially if those projects meant that essentially nonlethal weapons could be used to overthrow the regime and replace it with supporters of a more *democratically* elected government (even though, at that time, the United States and Russia had cordial relations under the Putin administration). To say he was politically naïve would be an understatement. Mike thought that because of his Russian heritage he fully understood Russia's foreign policy. But just because he had a PhD and was born in the old Soviet Union, it did not automatically make him a Russian policy expert.

Boris wanted Mike at the lab that summer to keep a close eye on all our work, making certain that what we did was replicated by his team. He wasn't really interested in Charlie's work on the battery, but he was determined to get his hands on my slugs to see if they could be the biological silver bullet that Boris had been searching for. Mike would do that for him and honestly believed that if Charlie and I were also privy to the military intelligence surrounding the Russian government, we'd be more than happy to help too. But he also knew that in order for us to get our degrees, we had to be working in the open. He thought that maybe once we finished, we would be willing to talk about working for DARPA on their classified projects. How completely wrong he was about that as well.

chapter 5

In mid-August Charlie's parents arrived in DC to visit her and, by default, meet me, their new son-in-law. The weather, like any August in Washington, was abominable: hot and humid. All my new in-laws wanted to do was stay in our air-conditioned apartment while Charlie and I went to work. They did do a couple of Smithsonian tours, taking air-conditioned cabs to air-conditioned buildings. Charlie's dad—I called him Professor Chen right up to the time they left since he never asked me to call him anything else—loved the Air and Space Museum. They took in all three IMAX shows in one day, had lunch, and didn't get home till five. When we asked if they liked the films, Professor Chen said one word: "Hot." I didn't know if he meant the weather or the shows.

Most of the conversations were in Mandarin with a Beijing dialect, or so I was told, because the family originated in an urban area around Beijing. Since I didn't speak a word of Chinese in any of their languages, let alone dialects, I was out of it most of the time. Charlie would occasionally interpret her conversations with her parents for me, but it did irk me because I knew they both spoke perfect English, and they knew that even with their British *dialect* I would understand them. Occasionally they would speak English, but it was mostly greetings and the like: "good morning," "thank you," "please." We never had a substantive conversation about me, or my work, or the fact that I was their son-in-law!

At night in bed, I would ask Charlie what the evening's conversation was all about. "Just family stuff," she would answer, but I knew it was about me and our marriage. I felt certain they were telling Charlie that they didn't approve of me, but I had no basis for that feeling. They never seemed to be disagreeing with each other or acted irritably—maybe I was just being para-noid since frequently they would smile at me and say something that made Charlie smile too.

Finally after two weeks, they had to go back because the fall semester would be starting soon and Professor Chen had to get ready for his classes. It was the end of August, and the temperature was moderating a little—just high eighties—at night. When we were at the airport, Professor Chen pulled me aside and said, "George, I'm sorry we didn't talk as much as we should, and the time seemed to fly by. I know that you were busy with your project, and I really didn't want to disturb you too much. But I am happy for you and Charleen. Why don't you call me *Ba-ba*, or just *Ba*," he said with a smile.

Mrs. Chen came up to me too and told me to call her *Ma*; then she gave me a big hug. She was a beautiful woman and still very fit. I had heard that if you wanted to know what your girlfriend or wife would look like down the line, look at her mother. I was pleased with what I saw. I felt a little sorry that they were leaving now that we were finally finished with the formali-ties. I think I would have enjoyed getting to know my in-laws better. I also realized that in the last couple of days we did have some conversations about our work together at DARPA, and they did seem truly interested. I guess I should have made more of an effort in initiating conversations and not been so uptight about meeting my in-laws.

Back at our apartment that evening, I told Charlie about wanting more face time with her folks. She said in a preoccupied manner, "Don't worry, you'll get to talk with them again soon. They want to have a formal wed-ding in April—April fourth, to be specific—because that would be the most auspicious time for me to marry. It would be on the same day as the Spring Festival in the Year of the Dragon. They also expect us to observe Maitreya Buddha's birthday next January twenty-third, before we are married." We were sitting on the couch while Charlie related all her conversations. She con-tinued, "They agreed to have the wedding here in the States because of your family since it would only be Ba and Ma coming in from England; it would be better all around. I'm supposed to make all the arrangements—Buddhist priest and everything. That's essentially all we talked about when they were with us." She smiled wistfully at me, and I put my arm around her. After a brief pause she asked, "Do you think it would be all right if I asked Marike to help me?"

"Are you kidding? She'd love it! Why don't you call her now and ask her." I added, "In April, you say, almost a year after our first wedding. I think that's cool. And by the way, who is this Maitreya Buddha guy?" I said, pleased to know that her folks had in fact accepted me almost from the beginning. Then Charlie gave me that look that only a Chinese woman can give and get away with—sort of a cross between dragon-lady and angel.

I went online and Googled Maitreya Buddha while she talked on the phone with Mackie. I found out that the Maitreya Buddha festival was celebrated on the Chinese New Year. *Of course we'll celebrate,* I thought. *I guess her parents want me to respect their culture and get to know their history.* I should have realized this much sooner and started my research. It's amazing when you think about it: Western culture is taught to us from the time we're born, but we know nothing of the East. *How "inscrutable" is that?* I thought, making fun of the fact that Westerners use *inscrutable* as a pejorative term for Easterners.

When I finished Googling Chinese customs to start my research on my family's background, I came out of our bedroom—that's where I kept my laptop—and saw Charlie get her violin out of its case and start playing. I hadn't even known that she brought it with her to DC. I didn't say anything but sat down and listened while she played the most beautiful and forlorn music I'd ever heard while never once looking at a piece of sheet music. I was certain that at times she was crying while she was playing since I could see tears on her cheeks. When she finished and put her violin away, she simply said to me, "I promised the folks I'd practice."

———

Our summer work went very well, and when we were back in Ann Arbor, both Sy and Margie were really surprised by how much research on our slugs we accomplished at DARPA over the summer. I was in Margie's office early in the fall semester showing her my work when she said, "George, I think you're ready to write something with this. You've been able to document and codify almost three full generations of those slugs. I think it's publishable and will serve as a major part of your dissertation. After you've written this up, then it's on to the investigation into the possible causes of the mutation and how the DNA recombined to get to that slug you discovered. You'll be using Chaos models for that part, won't you?"

I had been working with Sy on some computer-based modeling with Swarm, a software platform used for simulating complex systems. We both thought that agent-based models would work well for my research. Margie called it "Chaos," which is the more popular term used to describe my approach. I'd been computer literate and a programmer in a number of programming languages for a long time, and it was for that reason that Sy said I didn't need to have an undergraduate engineering degree. I looked forward to further honing my computer skills to solve what I thought was a very complex problem on mollusk mutations.

In early October I was talking with Sy in the HI-MEMS lab when he said, "Margie tells me you're working on a paper about the physiological aspects of your slugs. Good idea. Getting an article or two under your belt will help considerably when writing up your dissertation." I could tell by his smile that he was pleased with my progress. I also felt that somehow Boris might be pleased too.

Charlie's work also went well that fall. Her slug bio-battery was past the demo stage and was now in full development. She was working out all the details: power density, discharge rates, sustainability—all the things she needed to fully demonstrate that a full-scale project was viable both from a theoretical and an engineering standpoint. We worked closely on the project because she needed my work to fully understand the slugs' peculiarities, and I needed her work to fully understand the slugs' metabolism.

The work Charlie and I were doing together, along with my auditing that EECS class, Introduction to MEMS, kept us very busy over the fall semester. Gerry, as usual, was helpful in getting me through some of the engineering elements. For the most part, I had no problems with the science or math and enjoyed the fact that I would be up to speed with my engineering colleagues on the various MEMS projects by semester's end.

Charlie and Mackie were in constant contact about the wedding arrangements. They found a hall and a Buddhist priest (who lived in Ann Arbor), and our own Lutheran minister from Warren agreed to do a traditional Christian wedding ceremony after we held a small Buddhist service first. Mackie also found—and tried out—a real Mandarin Chinese catering company in Detroit that promised to put on a traditional Chinese wedding feast. It would be a small wedding by local standards—around sixty-five people—but on Charlie's side it would be only her parents and a small group of around ten Chinese students from Ann Arbor whom she had met and kept in contact with since coming to Michigan. Then there would be our friends and my family in Warren. For the Lutheran portion of the service, Mackie would be the maid of honor, and Gerry agreed to be the best man.

"Of course I'll be best man at your wedding—I'll be that anyway, by definition," Gerry said in his phony, pumped-up way when I asked him. But I knew he appreciated it. Gerry followed up by saying, "And it will finally give me the chance I've been dreaming of for over two years now: getting to kiss Charlie." His grin and pointy beard made him look like the Joker in Batman.

"You're such a schmuck, Gerry. I don't know why I put up with your silly shit. It's probably because you're Polish and I've always admired Polish scientists." In some sense I had the feeling that his scientific work on protein engineering would somehow cross paths with my own research, but I wasn't sure how that would happen. The fact is, I appreciated Gerry's friendship. I had never met anyone like him, and it was nice to have some of my preconceptions about computer geeks challenged and proven false.

Gerry stood up and gave me a big bear-hug, saying softly, "Congratulations, George. As I said at the civil ceremony, I know you and Charlie will do just great."

The semester went by quickly, and before we knew it, it was Christmas. Charlie and I went home to Warren and stayed at my folks' for the holidays. I think that Charlie was more excited about being with Mackie than spending the holidays with me. The two were getting really close and talking almost daily on the phone. Even though Charlie was two years older than Mackie, Mackie often played the role of older sister. Mackie explained everything in American culture that Charlie either didn't know about or could care less about, having been raised in Birmingham, England. But most of all they both enjoyed violin music, even though Mackie didn't play. Mackie played the guitar and the harmonica and loved folk music, but she loved to listen to violin solos even more.

"Charlie, I got tickets for the Wednesday matinee—just the two of us—to hear Sarah Chang at the Music Hall in Detroit. Girls' night out! It's your Christmas present a little early. I couldn't wait to tell you," Mackie announced when we walked into the house on the Friday before Christmas.

"Oh my gawd—you didn't...you didn't!" Charlie shouted, and the two of them ran off to Mackie's room before we even unpacked.

"What's that all about?" Mom wanted to know.

I explained to her that Sarah Chang was Charlie's favorite contemporary violin virtuoso. She was only around thirty and already had a worldwide following.

"Well, I could see why Charleen would be excited then. Another Chinese woman making good in the West should give her a boost," Mom said.

"Sarah Chang's an American, Mom, and her ancestry is Korean—but, yes, another person of Asian descent making it in the West is nice to see," I said, submitting to one of my mother's more harmless stereotypes.

"Anyway, it's nice that she and Mary get along so well. More sisters than sisters-in-law," Mom observed.

Dad came home from work a little early, and he was delighted to see us.

"Charlie, I was telling some people in my lab about your bio-battery and they would love to hear you make a presentation. Do you think you could do that next week sometime?" Dad asked while pouring his evening Scotch.

"Dad, we're here on vacation. I think we'd like to get away from work for a few days..." I began.

"Of course I would, Dad. It will have to be very informal because your son wouldn't let me bring any work with me, but I can do it off the laptop. But any day except Wednesday—Marike and I have a date," she said, flashing her beautiful smile at Mackie.

"Good, good...then, uh...let's say Friday," Dad said, looking at his DayMinder. "Yes, we'll do it on Friday because that's when we have our office party. George can come after your presentation for the party and the two of you can meet my staff in a more informal way. It will be a nice time."

Christmas Eve and the next day were very quiet with just the family there for the holidays. We all enjoyed our presents, and my parents made a big to-do over our gift to them. It was just a framed photograph of us in our nice clothes with a warm greeting penned on the picture: "To Mom and Dad with all our love, Charlie and George." We gave Mackie a new twelve-hole, Hohner chromatic harmonica and neck support that we purchased at a guitar store in Ann Arbor, and she was thrilled. We had a fire going and sat around talking about past Christmases, filling Charlie in on family history and folklore.

"Uncle Hans was really a horse thief—that was no myth," Dad said.

"Stop it!" Mom said. "Tell her about all the good people—the engineers and doctors in your family, not the horse thief."

We all laughed and felt very warm about our family and the rest of the world—at that moment.

The week went by quickly, and Charlie's presentation on Friday went off like clockwork. Without any written notes, she was able to put on a thirty-minute show and answer questions for another thirty minutes. Finally, at around 2:10 in the afternoon, Dad cut off all the questions and announced that the office party was starting. I walked in around 2:20 and there was still a crowd around Charlie, asking her all about her battery.

"Do you think you'll ever be able to make your battery compact enough to fit into an all-electric or hybrid vehicle?" one engineer asked.

"What about safety? Does any hydrogen byproduct leave a potential hazard hanging around?" another asked.

Charlie fielded those and many more until Dad said, "Okay, people, that's enough for now. Why don't we let Charleen enjoy the party with her husband? And here he is—this is my son George, who discovered the slugs that Charlie's using in her work," he said loudly with his arm around my shoulder. A number of Dad's staff approached me, introduced themselves, and said how glad they were to finally meet me. Shortly after five in the afternoon, most of the people had left, so we politely made our good-byes. Dad told the few people still hanging around that he'd see them all tomorrow night at their annual party, and with that we went home.

New Year's Eve was quiet; Charlie, Mackie, and I stayed home and watched the ball drop on Time's Square from the comfort of the front room—Charlie and me sat on the couch and Mackie sat on the floor in front of us. Mackie could have gone out, but she said she'd rather be with us. What surprised me was her interest in Gerry. To the best of my knowledge, she'd only met him a couple of times: at our marriage party earlier in the year and one or two times in Ann Arbor. For someone who was not usually interested in men, she seemed to want to know a lot about Gerry.

"He seems really smart," she said. "Is that just my reading of him or has he actually got brains in his head and not just in his pecker?"

Charlie and I laughed. I'd never heard Mackie talk about men that way before.

"Well, I can't speak for his pecker, but he does have a good brain in his head. In fact, he's helped me a lot in understanding the engineering elements of my program. Why all this interest in Gerry?" I asked.

"Nothing special. We've been e-mailing occasionally, that's all. Technical stuff," Mackie answered. Both Charlie and I noticed that she seemed to be blushing, so we didn't push it.

The rest of our end-of-year vacation went by way too fast. We went back to Ann Arbor on Tuesday, the third of January, and got right back into the grind. Our dissertation research was well underway, and both of us were anxious to produce more articles for publications. We both scheduled our committee meetings in March so we'd have that out of the way in time for the wedding in April. Gerry was busy getting ready for his defense in March. He wanted to have his degree by graduation in May because he had accepted a position with IBM in New York starting in June. We didn't talk much when we were in the office together, and I never got to ask him about his relationship with my sister, even though I knew it was probably none of my business—but after all, Mackie was my sister.

———

Back in DC, Boris' team had developed their black operation—known to CIA and other intelligence insiders as a black-op—inside one of the larger climate-controlled rooms found throughout the main DARPA laboratory. It had a controlled entry system that allowed only those cleared to work on the project inside. The staff hung a sign on the door that simply said "DOG" as an inside joke. Most of the DARPA staff knew that DOG was shorthand for a *black lab*, and you don't ask about it or try to get into it. Some of the staff joked that actually Boris was dyslexic and he thought it said GOD, which was his real title. Dad had found this out and told me about it years later. From his description I was able to put together how Boris was so familiar with my slugs' physiology and behavior.

It would seem that with the help of Mike Lasky's unquestioned access to our lab last summer, some of our slugs had found their way into Boris' project. They were being nurtured for Boris' real purpose of developing a new, nonlethal but nation-destroying weapon. Using the knowledge they gained from Mike's relationship with Charlie as a member of her dissertation committee, and other notes and papers from my work that Mike also had access to, they were able to engineer a newer, leaner, and meaner slug: a slug with an even higher acidity level—a pH slightly less than two—and a shorter incubation period. By selectively breeding those slugs with the traits they needed, they were soon in a position to mass produce the creatures and even test them out on some select government-owned farm plots in Virginia. If I thought my original slugs were Frankenslugs, then these babies were truly the *Brides of Frankenslugs*.

What Boris envisioned was that the engineered slugs would totally destroy a country's farmland, leaving the soil dead. They could accomplish this because they were much more robust and could withstand and actually continue to propagate in northern winters. Destroying the arable land would in turn cause the country infested by the slugs to collapse because of its inability to feed its population. Then the United States, or an ally, could step in to feed the people, destroy the slugs, and bring the land back again. But the United States would do it only if they had a say in who would run the country after their intervention.

They still needed to work out the problem of controlling the slugs— they needed to know how they could destroy, or neutralize, the slugs once the action was complete. That was why they needed my help, but by the time I was informed, it was already too late for me to help.

———

Charlie and I were formally married in April. The Fu symbols—signifying the Chinese God of Happiness—that were hung all around the hall did their work for us, as the sun shone on that Wednesday, April 4, 2012, in Warren, Michigan. We had the Buddhist ceremony first, and both of us wore traditional red Chinese gowns with gold and silver embroidery that Mackie found online. You could feel the happiness from Charlie's parents when they saw how we were dressed and how respectfully we (me, in particular) acted when the Buddhist priest performed the simple service.

After that service there was a pause in the program while Charlie and I went off and changed into our Western clothes for the Lutheran service. The attendees regathered in the hall, and as the violin trio played Mendelssohn's "Wedding March," all eyes were on Charlie as she walked down the aisle. She was unbelievably gorgeous in the dress that she and Mackie picked out together. Like other things she wore, it was both modern and traditional. She wore a short, simple lace veil and an antique white off-the-shoulder gown with a brocaded floral pattern along both sides. Her dress was fitted and flared out at the bottom, which accentuated her stunning, delicate figure. She wore the silver earrings that Mackie gave her and a simple string of pearls that her father had given her years ago.

But the real surprise was Gerry: he had shaved his beard! He looked so young to me since I had never seen him without a beard. His hair was cut neat, and he had on a new suit. Mackie was beautiful too, in her maid of honor dress that beautifully complemented Charlie's gown. It was also an antique white, off-the-shoulder affair, but instead of brocade it had a simple, yet elegantly stitched pattern. The two of them made a handsome couple standing beside us at the altar. Charlie's parents were beyond proud as they met her halfway down the aisle and walked her back up to the altar. When the minister asked, "Who gives this woman to be married to this man?" Ba stepped forward and said with tears in his voice, "I do."

My parents couldn't have been happier. This was probably one of the most joyful days in my whole family's life up till now—thanks to Fu.

We hadn't seen Gerry in the last couple of weeks due to all of our busy schedules and didn't know that he had cleaned himself up for his defense last month, which we heard (from Mackie) that he passed without incident: no changes, rewrites, or edits needed. He just had to bind it and submit the required number of copies and it was a done deal. He was now officially Dr. Gerald Kolaczki, with all the rights and privileges the University of Michigan could bestow on one of its newest PhDs.

At the party both Charlie and I noticed how Mackie and Gerry seemed to be getting along. We knew that they were seeing each other (just friends, according to Mackie), but it appeared that they were acting like more than "just friends" now: lots of hand holding, giggling, and whispering, and I think I even saw them kissing on the sly. Mom knew something was going on long ago. She noticed something about their chemistry at our wedding party last year and asked me if I knew what was happening with them. Naturally, I didn't. With both Mackie and me living away from home now, our parents didn't get to see our dating habits and most of our new friends like before, but they were still very interested, and Mom always asked about our social activities when the occasion rose.

The party was now in full swing; we were all served tons of food, and we occasionally got up to dance or make a toast. Gerry and Mackie danced every dance, and we all knew something was going on by the way they looked at each other. Even Dad commented on their behavior: "What's with Mary and your friend?" he asked me.

"Beats me," I said, but he was not satisfied, so he posed the question to Charlie, knowing that she'd be more upfront than me.

"I'm not sure," she answered, "but they do seem to be acting like they know each other better than I was led to believe." That seemed to satisfy Dad's curiosity, and he asked me to tell him more about Gerry's academic background. When I told him, he seemed to be satisfied that his daughter was attracted to this man who could be her intellectual match.

The family sat at the head table, which was slightly elevated, and people kept coming up and wishing us all kinds of happiness and luck—very Chinese. During a lull in the activities, Mackie said, "Shall we tell them?"

"Tell us what?" I asked.

"Gerry and I are engaged!"

"What!" my father said. "And when were you going to tell us this news?" he asked, trying to act somewhat perplexed but smiling just the same.

"Today," Mackie said. "We didn't want to take away from Charlie's wedding by announcing it earlier, so we decided to tell you now, after the service and everything when everyone was feeling good." You could see that she felt somewhat guilty about not filling the folks in earlier but was relieved that it was finally out in the open. Mom just sat there staring at Gerry and Mackie with a look that said, *Yes, I know, but I wish you had told me sooner.*

"When are you planning on getting married and what about your degree? Where are you going to live? And—" my dad was asking when Mackie cut him off.

"Enough, Dad! Everything's cool. We've worked it all out, and we'll explain everything later, but, first of all, yes, I'll finish my MS at Lawrence Tech. Now can we continue enjoying Charlie and George's party?"

I looked at Charlie, my parents looked at us, and Charlie's parents looked at all of us, then Charlie's father picked up his glass of champagne and eloquently said to just us at the head table, "Here's to the happily engaged couple, Gerald and Marike. May they find love and happiness just like George and Charleen have."

It was a fitting way to end the meal and put everyone in the spirit of goodwill and friendship. With the wedding now over, Mackie and Gerry's engagement announced, and the future looking very bright for all of us, it was time, once again, to focus on our work and careers. However, in retrospect, had we known then what was happening in DARPA with our slugs and the socio-political situation going on in other parts of the world, we might not have had such high hopes for the future.

PART II
INFESTATION
Winter 2014

chapter 6

IT WAS JANUARY 2014. A lot had happened in the world over the last three years. The uprisings in the Middle East that started in 2011 had culminated in a completely changed political structure throughout Egypt, Lebanon, Tunisia, Yemen, Jordan, Syria, Iraq, and Iran. They formed a new alliance similar to the old United Arab Republic of the last century but not centralized in Egypt like the previous union was. Noticeably missing from the pact were Saudi Arabia, Turkey, and some smaller Islamic countries, but these independent countries, especially Turkey, for the most part, were openly sympathetic to the new regime.

The regime was essentially a decentralized group of supposedly autonomous states with separately elected governments. However, the major political parties (and in reality, the only ones) that dominated the alliance were the Muslim Brotherhood in close affiliation with Hezbollah. Both groups claimed to promote democratic societies in the amalgamated countries, but any candidate not supported by the political alliance could not run for office. The political parties' primary organizational headquarters were located in Egypt and Lebanon to give some semblance of regional recognition.

The food shortage in the Middle East caused by the severe droughts of 2010 had already left most of the poorer Muslim countries there in turmoil. Prices had skyrocketed and jobs were scarce. Some observers suggested that the rise of the Egyptian-Lebanese coalition was, in part, due to the high food costs. Basics, like bread and animal feed that depended on cheap grains like wheat, were no longer cheap. Other economic issues, like the lack of international trade agreements, added to the crisis. But that mattered little to the

Muslim Brotherhood and its extremist partners when it took over the sitting regimes.

The general populations in the regions were not necessarily overly religious, but they were willing to let extremist elements of the Islamic world take over if those parties could bring some stability and economic relief. It mattered little to them that they may have to give up a significant amount of their personal freedom and that the coalition's brand of democracy was essentially the people's right to vote for whomever the party said they had to vote for. As long as the poorer citizens and their families weren't starving, they just didn't care.

After Gerry defended his dissertation in 2012, he went to work at IBM's Watson Research Center in Yorktown Heights, New York. Gerry had been working there for a year, and his long-distance courtship with Mackie while she finished her MS was not the best arrangement. But they survived with lots of weekend trips and short vacations together, and their long wait was finally over.

Mackie and Gerry were married right after she got her MS in the summer of 2013. It was a beautiful, warm Sunday on that June 16, and Gerry's folks, along with some other family members, came in from New Jersey. I was the best man this time, and Charlie was the matron of honor. The wedding was held at the same hall that we had been married in a year or so earlier. However, this time Mackie got a great Polish caterer from Hamtramck to do the wedding dinner, and Gerry's family was delighted. Gerry danced the first polka with Mackie while everyone urged them on with whistles and shouts before joining in. It was truly a classic Polish wedding, except that Mackie wouldn't let people pin money on her gown, which was an older but still practiced Polish tradition in Hamtramck.

As things quieted down at the reception and we were able to talk while Mackie was running around being a great hostess, Gerry told Charlie and me, "When I heard that this woman played guitar with a harmonica strapped around her neck, I knew I had to meet her. I didn't tell you when we actually started dating, George, because I was worried you wouldn't approve of me."

"Now why would you have thought that?" I asked sarcastically. "You've already told me how you two met at our first wedding party and that Mackie thought you were very interesting...looking, that is," reminding him of his beard and long hair. We all smiled, enjoying our reminiscence of Gerry's and Mackie's early time together.

Charlie told Gerry that when she found out about their engagement, she was thrilled for Mackie because she had always liked Gerry. She said that she never thought of him as a nerd, but she knew that I did. She also noted that she could see that the two of them were deeply in love and true soul mates, and that made Gerry smile and brought a few tears to his eyes.

After they got married, Mackie was hired by IBM to work along with Gerry's team because of her expertise in neural networks. IBM had a policy of hiring spouses if they filled a need, but they also hired lots of engineers with backgrounds other than computer science, and Mackie fit both those criteria. The newlyweds took up residence in New York and had been living and working there for almost a year when Charlie and I graduated.

Around the same time that Mackie and Gerry got married, I was told that Boris had the following conversation with his boss, the new director of DARPA.

"No, no...my slugs can't kill or even physically harm people; they're simply an agent for mischief, not mass destruction!" he said emphatically.

"But they are biological weapons, and you know that under congressional edict we're not allowed—"

"They are NOT weapons. They cannot kill anyone in any way whatsoever. In fact, one could even argue that they could be a food source—sort of an exotic escargot if one took the time to clean and cook them."

Boris was not very convincing on that last point. He then continued in a calmer manner. "Look, all I'm saying is that historically the CIA, with our help I might add, has devised and used a variety of programs that caused mischief in regimes that we wanted toppled. The hope, of course, was that such regimes would be replaced by ones that were friendly. Remember some years ago when the CIA messed with the food production programs of North Korea? That project almost worked, had we stayed the course on it."

"Yes. But it didn't work and they became even more anti-American than before we ever started that stupid program," the director noted.

"I can assure you all my researchers have concluded that would not happen here. As long as the coalition countries are all economically linked and do not depend on, or even want, outside intervention, any trouble one country would have in surviving would put a strain on the whole coalition. That could lead to their downfall if we were ready to act when it happened. I can further assure you my program can create that kind of trouble in one or two marginally self-sufficient countries such as Iran and Syria. If their food supply was disrupted, they would need a significant amount of outside resources to survive—resources that would strain the coalition and ultimately cause it to break down," Boris said with authority. "And, I can with certainty assure you that our program's mechanism would not take even one human life in the process."

"What *mischief* are you talking about here?" the director asked wryly.

The new director of DARPA was the twentieth person to head the agency. She had her doctorate in bio-chemistry and, like her predecessor, came to the government from the private sector, where she had been the CEO of a think tank engaged in bio-engineering research. She was sympathetic to Boris' plight for nonlethal weapons that could change a nation's, or region's, geo-political climate to one more favorable to Western interests. However, she was not pleased with the term *mischief.*

Boris explained, "You recall that a few years back there was a serious drought that led to that new strain of rust that killed off much of the Middle Eastern wheat crop? Syria, Turkey, Iraq, Iran, and Lebanon lost major amounts of their crops, and they're just now recovering from that damage. I'm suggesting that we deploy our slugs in the northern Iranian and Syrian wheat fields. With CIA help we can do that through Iraq. In a year, or even less the way our new slugs have been engineered, there will be total loss of the vast majority of their wheat crop. They will initially attribute the loss to the weak condition of the land that's still recovering from the drought, but when they do find our slugs, they won't know that we did it. They'll probably attribute it to an infestation caused by the long drought."

"And how will this cause the regime to fail?" the director asked.

"I don't think that event, in and of itself, will cause the failure. It will, however, begin to strain the coalition's ability to feed these two populous countries. Once that happens, we go back in with the slugs and destroy the barley and rice crops; and then we hit Lebanon's and Egypt's crops with the slugs. When that happens, the coalition will no longer be able to replace the lost crops, then Syria and Iran—as well as Egypt and Lebanon—will ultimately have to seek outside help. And that's when we must be prepared to step in."

The director then asked, "From what you've told me about your slugs, how do we stop them from destroying all the crops in the entire Middle East once you've turned them loose?"

"That too is the beauty of my plan. We not only offer them food, we offer them our technology to get rid of the pest that's causing the problem in the first place, just like we did when we offered them rust control technology based on our agriculture programs at Kansas State," Boris said with a victorious smile on his face. "You realize, of course, that we would have to place significant strings on them for our involvement," he added, "like having a more open society and making them sign a permanent peace treaty with Israel."

"Lots of luck on the last one…but it could come in time if the diplomats play their cards right," she said.

———————

In the fall of 2013 I was wrapping up my dissertation research and explaining my findings to Margie. "In the mid 1960s a company named Deiotron built a radar testing facility on the outskirts of Ann Arbor, Michigan—actually in Ypsilanti on that plot of land that I used for getting my slug samples. The facility was designed to measure the radar cross-sections of a large variety of military vehicles and aircraft. A radar cross-section is an electronic measurement expressed as an area—usually in meters-squared—that can help distinguish objects that are being targeted by a radar system as the object rotates through various angles of incidence. I recently learned that even though the radome was large—it was actually just a large inflatable structure and not a true radome—it wasn't large enough to house most of the vehicles and airplanes that were being analyzed. In addition, I found out that highly classified Soviet missiles and US reentry vehicles and warheads were also scheduled to have their radar cross-sections measured there as well."

I had learned about Deiotron from an old, retired electrical engineering professor who used to consult for them back in the sixties. He kept an office in the EECS building, and I found out about him through my latest research on microwave-induced mutations.

"Because of size limitations and security questions regarding the movement of large weapon delivery systems—both ours and Russian—wooden models of the various weapons were built as stand-ins for the real devices and sprayed with a metallic paint in order to reflect the radar beams. These models had to be small enough to fit into the various anechoic chambers located throughout the structure and were typically sized at around one-twentieth scale. Because they were models, the testing radar frequencies also had to be scaled appropriately in order to obtain the correct radar cross-section profile. Since most of the long-range radar detecting systems operated at L-band—a specific radar frequency range—then the scaling frequencies would have to be in the X-band range."

It appeared that I was still in the habit of blinding people with science. I continued, "X-band radar operates at around ten gigahertz, or equivalently, at a wave length of around three centimeters, which is roughly an inch. Not small enough to cause anyone's cells to be ionized like X-rays can, but still small enough to heat stuff—like in a microwave oven—by causing the molecules of nonmetallic substances, like living organisms, to vibrate at high rates of speed…and that's how, I think, all the trouble started."

I guess I could just as easily have said to her, *"Margie, the slugs' mutation was probably caused by them being exposed to high frequency radar waves."*

———

By 2013 the continuing drought in the Middle East had eased somewhat, and some semblance of stability seemed to be emerging in the region as food crops began to get to market at more reasonable prices. Trade between the coalition countries, as well as travel and cultural exchanges (within well-defined limits), was open without export licenses, visas, or even passports. Simple identification cards issued by the ruling parties allowed the citizens from the coalition countries to move freely from one state to another. It began to look like one big regional government on the scale of the European Union, and all they needed to be further united was to have a common currency, which was currently under consideration.

The fragile economy, once again, gave rise to the extremist element in the coalition calling for the annihilation of Israel. They claimed that Israel was the usurper of Arab lands and they wanted to install an Islamic republic in its place. The new Islamic Republic of Palestine, as they referred to it, would of course be a member of the coalition as soon as all the "hated Jews" were evacuated to Europe, the United States, or anywhere else, but they couldn't stay there. They didn't call for killing off the approximately six million Jews in Israel because they didn't want to engender a negative world opinion—after all, it was the Nazis who exterminated around six million Jews during the Holocaust. But if some died during transportation out of the region, well, that was "just too bad," as some of the coalition leaders had said publicly.

At the end of March in 2014, I was in our apartment supposedly getting ready for my dissertation defense, but I was watching the news instead. I was stressed out by the whole process, and I was shouting to no one, since I was alone in the apartment, "I don't know why we were so dumb as to think that both of us defending within the same week would be a smart thing to do—one big party, less aggravation. Stupid, stupid!" We had scheduled our defenses for early April—mine would be on Tuesday, April Fools' Day, and Charlie had hers scheduled for Thursday, the third. How could we not have known that the last-minute changes, anxiety, and just pent-up frustration would make us both crazy? We'd hardly talked to each over the last few weeks. It was obvious that we were taking our problems out on each other, and our overworked nerves were frazzled. And to top it all off, the international news was also feeding into my worries about our futures.

Charlie asked coldly when she came home, "Shouldn't you be rereading or going over your presentation? Why are you just watching the news again? Nothing's changed since yesterday. You have absolutely no control over the situation over there anyway, so stop worrying and finish whatever it is you have to do for tomorrow."

She left me in the front room watching TV while she went off into the bedroom to work on her presentation for Thursday. She was not planning on being at my defense because she knew it would make me even more nervous than I already was. The TV news was still reporting about the situation in the Middle East. The United States State Department was getting very nervous about the new alliance. They knew that once there was some semblance of stability within the countries, like there appeared to be now, they would definitely organize into one massive military machine ready to take on Israel—and even the United States if they felt they needed to.

The Muslim countries would have nuclear weapons from Iran and their trading partners in North Korea and Pakistan. Such weapons would be huge bargaining chips in any war that they hoped to keep limited to the Middle East. It would be a *don't mess with us or we'll use the bomb* approach that was similar to the so-called Mutually Assured Destruction (MAD) strategy of the United States and USSR in the Cold War era.

The saber rattling had already started with some countries in the alliance, notably Syria, calling for the destruction of Israel. Israel, for its part, had remained silent about the alliance and had even offered to enter into discussions with various agencies in the countries under the regime. Also, with Israel having strategically poised atomic weapons and not being opposed to taking a preemptive strike under its own motto of "Never Again," the situation was at best very tense.

I turned off the TV and started in again on my defense. I couldn't help but think about the news, though, as I tried to come up with answers to some hypothetical questions that might be asked. By the time I went to bed, I was totally exhausted. Charlie was already in bed and it looked like she was asleep so I didn't bother her. I laid there with my eyes open for a long time, not sure what was worrying me more: the Middle East or my thesis defense. I decided it was my thesis, which didn't help me get some sleep before morning.

By 9:10 the next morning, my committee and I, along with a number of visitors, were all in one of the beautifully ornate, large conference rooms in Rackham for my presentation. There were coffee, doughnuts, and bagels on a side table. Most of the people helped themselves to some coffee and rolls before we started. Sy motioned to me to take something to eat too, but I just wanted my water bottle in case I got dry-mouth, which I heard was not unusual.

Sy was smiling. "Ready for your big day, George?"

I casually smiled and nodded yes, trying not to look as nervous as I really was. Sy was talking to Margie most of the time. I think they were probably going over their routine on how they would conduct the defense—who would question me first, whether I needed to make one or two presentations, and how formal they would conduct the overall process.

At around 9:15 Sy asked everyone to take a seat so we could begin. My committee of four faculty members sat at the conference table with me, while everyone else sat in some very large, comfortable chairs by the elaborate leaded windows on the south side of the room. I put my laptop on the table and connected it to the projector, which was displaying the first slide. It read:

A MUTANT VARIANT OF *ARION DISTINCTUS*:
SOURCES AND CAUSES OF DNA RECOMBINATION
AND ITS IMPLICATIONS TO ENVIRONMENTAL BIOLOGY

by

George Fredrik Brachmann

A dissertation submitted in partial fulfillment of the requirements
for the degree of Doctor of Philosophy in The College of Engineering
and the School of Natural Resources and Environment in
The University of Michigan
2014

Sy started out by welcoming everyone and making some brief comments about my work at EECS in the HI-MEMS lab. He pointed out that I had already published two articles on the topic and I had another currently under review, all in peer reviewed journals. He introduced the rest of my committee to the few outsiders in the room—Margie first, as cochair—giving their titles and affiliations. He then introduced me and asked that I make a brief presentation of my work followed by a period of questioning from the committee and then general questions from the observers, if there were any. With that I took a quick swallow of water and started in on my presentation.

Once I started talking, I began to relax. I knew my slugs better than anyone else in the whole world (or at least that's what I thought then) and was totally comfortable talking about them. I then described the mathematics of my complexity model that could work backwards through the DNA chain and present the most probable cause of the mutation in the first place.

I finished my presentation by saying, "In conclusion, I feel that my model clearly demonstrates that a high-frequency electromagnetic field, similar to wavelengths found in the centimeter range, caused and sustained the physiological changes in the slugs I described earlier. The change occurred over one generation through long-term exposure to the maturing organisms that survived the initial radiation." I had already related my anecdotal knowledge of the radar facility in the area over fifty years earlier as the most likely source of the radiation.

I then took a deep breath and sighed, which brought smiles to the faces of my committee members. The presentation took exactly twenty minutes, putting us near ten o'clock. The room was booked till noon, so there was plenty of time for questions.

Sy offered everyone more drinks and rolls, and a number of people took him up on the offer. Once back in their seats, the questions started. Margie went first.

"George, can you give us more detail on why your original idea about using the slugs for land-use preservation was not viable?" she asked.

After I answered Margie, the rest of the committee asked their questions, and since it was only Sy who was not on the SNRE faculty, most of the questions centered on the environmental elements of my work.

"You say they completely killed the soil. How did they survive all these years on our experimental plots in Ypsi?" one member asked.

"Their life cycle in Michigan essentially killed most of them off in the winter and the eggs that survived each spring lived on the detritus that had been in the soil for many years. It seems that they had reached some kind of equilibrium there, but the land had been definitely degraded due to their presence and would probably not be able to support future generations indefinitely. Remember, most of the organic material on the plot was placed there by failed building projects and would eventually run out too. I suspect that without Ms. Chen's battery program and similar efforts for utilizing their unique properties, this transient subspecies would eventually become extinct."

Sy asked some questions about the computer model I developed from the Swarm Chaos platform and its impact on future energy research and computer science in general. All of them wanted to know about my future research plans and where I was going next.

"My wife—Ms. Chen, who is defending her dissertation on Thursday—and I have been offered tenure track positions at MSU for the fall and we've both accepted," I told them.

By then I was completely relaxed because there seemed to be no more specific questions, nor were there any concerns expressed about my work. At around 10:45, my guests and I were asked to wait outside in a wide, lavish, and comfortably furnished corridor while the committee deliberated my fate.

In less than fifteen minutes, I was called back in and informed by both Sy and Margie that my dissertation had been accepted; there were a few minor typos that needed to be corrected, but there were no substantive changes or corrections required. And with that Margie got up, hugged me, and gave me a kiss on each cheek. The other members shook my hand, and for the next twenty minutes or so we just talked about my future. I was finally relaxed enough to have a cup of coffee and a bagel.

Two days later Charlie defended her dissertation in a nicely furnished conference room in the EECS building. She had a larger group of observers than I had since many of the HI-MEMS grad students wanted to see her defend. Sy was also her chair, and Mike Lasky with two other EECS faculty members rounded out her committee. Margie was there too and so was I. Charlie was a lot more confidant than I was and had no qualms with me coming to her defense. In fact, she insisted on it.

The process was essentially the same as mine, only Charlie had some very nice demonstration models on display, with all sorts of instrumentation wired up to them. Her presentation was slick, demonstrating how the bio-battery, under various configurations, could supply energy for a variety of tasks. She even had a miniature model house wired up, showing how a future bank of batteries would work along with the electric utility's grid system to run the house and even charge the electric car.

Sy pointed out that she too had been published prior to her defense and that her work was an integral part of a federal program on alternative energy sources. He also gave me credit for finding and analyzing the bio-source— our Frankenslugs—for the project. The questioning period was relaxed since everyone seemed to know it was a forgone conclusion that she had passed.

When her passing was finally official, we celebrated with a couple of bottles of champagne that we brought with us. It was a small party in the lab with lots of congratulations and best wishes for us up in East Lansing that fall.

"Well, Dr. Chen, how are you feeling now?" I asked back in our apartment later in the afternoon.

"Well, Dr. Brachmann, I'm feeling very nice. What would you like for dinner?" she asked lazily.

"You," I replied. "Just you."

As we lay in bed that night, I could only think about having all that time off until the fall with no responsibilities. Our appointments at the lab would end soon, and my family, including Gerry and Mackie, would be coming to Ann Arbor for our graduation. They had strict orders from Charlie's parents to take lots of pictures and put them up on Flickr—an internet photo sharing site. I just lay there smiling while Charlie was in a deep-sleep mode that often comes after a long and tiring work period.

What I found funny, or rather odd, while I was lying there thinking was that I had heard nothing from Boris in over a year. I had the impression that he was really interested in our slugs, but we received no more offers of summer internships, nor were we in any way contacted about our work. I assumed he was just not interested in the slugs or Charlie's battery anymore.

Mackie and Gerry flew in for graduation at the end of April and stayed over for the party the following Saturday in May. After the party the four of us were just sitting around talking while my parents were cleaning up and putting things away. We all offered to help, but the folks insisted that we just relax and enjoy ourselves because the four of us didn't see each other very often anymore and Mom and Dad felt it would be nice for us to just sit and talk.

"So what interesting work are you two up to?" I asked as we sat comfortably in the living room.

Gerry and Mackie filled us in on their work in the computational biology group. They worked with a multi-disciplinary team on a project designed to cross the boundary between traditional computer science and bio-transmitters—designing processors based on biological neurotransmitters rather than electronic transistors. They said that they were in on the ground-floor with protein engineering. It was fun to see how excited they were about their work and how they talked with such enthusiasm about working for IBM.

"You can tell she's psyched about it," Gerry explained with a smile on his face.

Mackie then said, in a somewhat blasé fashion, "In fact, in a month or so—end of June, right, honey?—we're off to Israel to work with some IBM partners at the Technion, Israel's technical university, where they're developing the same kinds of technology...can't wait!" She said it like it was perfectly normal to be going to the Middle East when there was so much turbulence over there.

"Israel! Wow, that should be some experience. But aren't you a little anxious about that given the current political situation? And have you told Mom and Dad?" I asked, with a whole lot of butterfly activity in my stomach all of a sudden.

"We talked about it," Gerry said, "but decided that Israel seems pretty safe—at least for now, since it appears that the Muslim Brotherhood revolutionaries seem willing to avoid any kind of war at this time while they're trying to get worldwide support for their client states. And, no, we haven't told your parents yet. We were hoping you'd help us out there."

"Yes, but how long do you think that stability will last?" Charlie asked, noticeably anxious. "And how do you expect us to help you tell Mum and Dad?"

Gerry answered, "Just, sort of, support our decision. You know—stand there smiling and acting excited for us to have such an opportunity, that's all. As for trouble in Israel, nobody knows, of course, but I do believe that Middle East peace is really at hand now for the first time in years, and it will all work out in the long run. After all, the Brotherhood, with all its saber rattling, is bringing some semblance of democracy to their people." Gerry hesitated for a second. "That is, unless some assholes in our country try to step in there now and make matters worse. Remember Dr. Strangelove and your Frankenslugs? I'm glad that he didn't take more of an interest in them and that you guys got stuck with the good side of the project. Who knows what kind of shit he could have done with those critters."

The four of us were quiet now, thinking about the world situation. For some reason I was very uneasy. The current situation in the Middle East seemed ripe for another major conflict that would surely require United States intervention this time, even if no one wanted to get involved. I guess that after listening to my brother-in-law for four years, now I, too, was a little paranoid concerning our own leaders' ability to act with restraint in tough situations.

After a while my parents came in to join us, and Gerry and Mackie told them about their plans. Temporarily disregarding our emotions, we stood by smiling and acting excited for Gerry and Mackie just like they asked us to. We could see that Mom and Dad were not too thrilled but simply hugged them both and wished them success in their work.

———

By the time Charlie and I graduated in 2014, Boris' mischievous slugs—they weren't mine anymore after all the bio-engineering Boris' team did to them—were field tested and readied for action, even though there was no proven method for controlling them on a large scale. The feeling was that the worst possible scenario would be to employ the available cyanide compounds to eradicate them. They also knew that the slugs were self-limiting in the sense that once they killed everything else in the soil they too would soon die off from starvation and cannibalism, not necessarily in that order.

However, the weapon had not even been tested on a tract of land in a moderate climate like the Middle East. Some of Boris' researchers feared that

the slugs could literally run amok, taking over all the land they initially established a presence on as well as the land they simply came in close contact
with. But the idea that a technical fix was imminent led Boris to disregard
the warnings of his staff.

Boris had been around long enough to realize that the so-called "technical fix" offered up for solving politically related issues using modern technology rarely came into fruition. Surely he knew that after sixty years a technical fix for safely storing nuclear wastes had yet to be accomplished. That
same overconfident engineering attitude would also hold true for destroying
out-of-control Frankenslugs. But in the slugs' case, going through sixty years
of uncontrolled growth...well, then the world as we knew it might no longer
exist.

chapter 7

I STAYED IN close contact with Gerry and Mackie after they left for Israel. Mackie would e-mail me often with updates from her journal that she kept on their international adventure. Her first entry detailed their arrival. She wrote that they were ecstatic when they arrived on Sunday, June 29, 2014, at Ben Gurion Airport outside of Tel Aviv. After studying conversational Hebrew in New York for two months, they found that everyone they'd met so far spoke English. After going through a rigorous customs check, they booked a *sherut*—a shared mini-van—to take them to Haifa and then on to Technion City. The fifty-mile drive took two hours because the sherut had to make a couple of stops along the way, and traffic was a little heavy once they entered the city of Haifa.

"Will we stop for a falafel?" Mackie asked the driver in her practiced Hebrew, and to see if she could be understood with her Midwestern accent.

"*Lo*...no, no stopping," the driver answered her, at first in Hebrew then he switched to English. Mackie guessed he was not impressed with her language skills.

There were two other people in the van with them who were going to Haifa, but they were not inclined to converse either in English or Hebrew with Gerry and Mackie, so the ride north on the relatively boring but modern Coastal Highway 2 was mostly silent. When they reached Haifa, the other two passengers were dropped off at the central bus terminal. Then the driver took Mackie and Gerry to Technion City—the university campus—around three miles east of Haifa's city center. Mackie said that Haifa city, along with its magnificent port, was a beautiful place—one of the oldest cities in Israel, with winding streets passing through hills and alongside the hiking trails leading up to Mount Carmel. It was hard to believe that they were less than twenty-five miles from the Lebanese border in the north.

The driver knew exactly where on the sprawling campus to take them without having to be told. It seemed all visitors to the campus were dropped off at a central reception center, and they guessed he'd done this before. It was before noon when they arrived, and after a quick call by a receptionist, their host soon greeted them: Professor Avi Gittleman from the Quantum Information Processing Laboratory, where they'd be working for the next year.

Mackie's journal pointed out that Avi was short for Avraham—the Hebrew name for Abraham—and they felt they had known him for years. They'd been in contact with him for some time now, so they knew about his work and he was familiar with theirs. Avi was a tall man—maybe six-foot-four—and around forty-five years old. He was wearing a white dress shirt that was unbuttoned at the top, cuffs rolled up, and no tie, a pair of khaki trousers, and brown loafers. His hair was pitch-black and he wore it long and flowing over his whole head. His olive complexion gave him that healthy look that many people from the Mediterranean are gifted with. Mackie said that you would not know by looking at him that he was one of the world's preeminent scholars on the development of protein-based computer nanoprocessors.

"Shalom, shalom…welcome to Israel and welcome to Technion City, and you of course are Marike," he said as he put his arms around Mackie and gave her a big hug. Then reaching with one hand over to Gerry and pulling him in close as well, he said, *"At long last, my young brilliant colleague Dr. Kolaczki—Gerry, so good to finally meet you in person."*

They couldn't help but smile and hug the big scientist; it was like meeting family. Avi brought transport with him and took them and their luggage over to their apartment in the university's visiting faculty housing facility. He never gave them a chance to unpack—just a few minutes to freshen up—telling them that there would be plenty of time for unpacking later.

Mackie wrote that they were so hyped-up by now that they had no time to be tired, but what struck them as odd was that it was Sunday, yet it looked like any *other day of the week. Avi explained, "In Israel the campus shuts down on Friday afternoon, just before shabbos, and then reopens on Sunday."*

Avi couldn't wait to take them over to the Taub building of Computer Science. Their station—"station" was sort of like a program designation—was called the protein engineering computing station and was essentially brand-new.

After a quick tour and introductions to key staff and fellow researchers, Avi decided that his guests had seen enough for their first day, so he took them back to their apartment to get settled in and to rest up for tonight. They would be having dinner with his family and he would be picking them up at seven thirty.

From Mackie's journal we learned that Avi and his family lived in a lovely house located on the third, or upper, tier of the city. It was off-campus and had fantastic views all around, including the harbor and Lebanon to the north. Lights from both could be seen from their front yard. Mackie and Gerry were awed by the scenery and ancient history associated with Haifa.

"This is just magnificent—I've never seen anything like it or felt such a biblical awareness of any place I've ever been to. Avi, you say that some scholars put the age of the city at over thirty-four-hundred years? That is truly unbelievable," Gerry said.

"That's true, but other scholars say that the city itself is only about half that age. In any case, we know that people have lived in the area for many centuries because of its climate and access to northern and southern ports. I'm delighted you like my city," Avi said. "Come in now, meet the family. They're probably wondering what I've done with you."

They walked into the Gittlemans' modern house that was furnished in Israeli décor, quite similar to Danish modern only with brighter colors and more outré designs. The simple but elegant blond wood and oriental rugs that complemented the modern furniture seemed made for their home. Once inside the house, Avi introduced them to his family.

"This is my wife, Tikva, and this is my son, Ben, who will be a Bar Mitzvah this winter, and this is my brilliant daughter, Avigail. The Kolaczkis have heard me talk about you two kids so often, they've been dying to meet you," Avi told the children. He then said with much delight, "Family, meet Marike and Gerry—you finally get to see them in person and not from the blurry pictures I've taken off the Internet."

Meeting the Gittleman family was an enchanting experience for them on so many levels. Tikva was a blond, blue-eyed beauty and, unlike Avi and the children, she spoke English without a hint of an Israeli accent. They found out later it was because she was an American whose English name was Hope Anderson—*tikva* translates to hope in Hebrew. It was not unusual for many new Israelis to exchange their names for Hebrew ones. The children were a remarkable amalgamation of the two, having their father's complexion and his flowing dark hair, but they had their mother's more delicate features: smaller noses and, in Avigail's case, even her blue eyes.

The meal was spectacular with many Middle Eastern dishes: hummus, baba ghanoush, a variety of salads, and the main course: Israeli-style lamb chops. Almost everything had parsley, mint, and olive oil on it—Mackie's favorite flavors. During dinner they learned that Tikva was majoring in music (with a minor in fine arts) at Boston College in 1993 when she met Avi, a young engineering student from MIT. She graduated in 1996, and Avi stayed on for his PhD in computer science. Needless to say, the beautiful Norwegian-American woman fell in love with the tall, exotic-looking Israeli, and the two were married in 1998 right after Avi graduated.

From Boston they moved to Technion City, where Hope Anderson became Tikva Gittleman and their two very talented (just ask their parents) children were born. Tikva played piano and flute, wrote poetry, and gave music lessons in her spare time, and, like many other mothers, she balanced work and family with equanimity.

After dinner they sat around drinking Turkish coffee and snacking on Elite Chocolates. Tikva arranged to meet with them the next day, Monday, and show them around the area—where to shop, what to buy, what restaurants to go to, and the whole shebang. They were looking forward to it, but not as much as they were looking forward to just getting some sleep.

Mackie's journal related that she and Gerry showed up at Avi's station in the lab early Tuesday morning. "Are you both fully indoctrinated Israeli scientists now?" Avi teased them as he showed them to their work cubicles. In no time at all, the three of them were talking tech and laying out their year's research agenda. They were hoping to have a functional processor at around the same petaflop benchmark rating as the IBM Blue Gene series of super-computers. If they could reach that threshold, then they'd have accomplished a major breakthrough in bio-chemistry computer engineering.

Avi had placed a sign over their cubicles that read, "WATCH YOUR P's AND QUBITs," making a pun on the quantum relationships called qu-bits that would be fundamental to their processor.

Mackie and Gerry loved their work, and over the next few months they got to know everyone in Avi's lab. In a sense they were all like family as well as colleagues. Israelis are not the kind of people who stand on ceremony, and it takes outsiders some getting used to. But they soon realized that Israelis think of each other as family, and in your own family you don't stand on ceremony.

On occasion some senior IBM people traveling through the Middle East stopped by and visited them, expressing high hopes on the part of the company for their work.

"You two realize, of course, that the future of computers as we know them is in your hands. We're looking for great things from you guys, so keep it up," a senior VP once told them.

After he left, Mackie said to Gerry, "That's a little scary, and why did he say 'you guys'? Do I look like a guy? Like he was telling us the whole world of computer science was on our shoulders—I don't think so."

Gerry smiled, kissed her, and said, "Hey, if they think we *guys* are that important, who knows what kind of perks we can get from IBM once we're back in the States?" Gerry stopped being cute and said, "Essentially, hon, I think he was just trying to say that with all our projected advances in the field of high-speed computing, we can finally see that cures for a variety of cancers, AIDS, as well as many gene-related illnesses are now a reality. If that's true then who knows, solving world hunger might even come next. We may have broken the petaflop speed a few years back with solid-state proces-sors, but with our bio-processors those old supercomputer systems will look like Model T's. You know those MBA *guys* aren't very good at expressing themselves," he said, smiling once again.

He then reminded her that they were having a music party at Avi and Tikva's that night. Mackie and Tikva had started playing some great du-ets with her flute and Mackie's guitar and harmonica ensemble. They loved going to those music sessions and were planning on playing some original pieces at Ben's Bar Mitzvah in December. Their life in Israel was going very well, and they knew that when the time came for them to leave, they would hate to go.

———————

The months seemed to fly by, Mackie noted, and it was in the fall when it happened. I found out about the event and all the details from officials at the Technion later. It was on Sunday, October 5 when the worker walked into the lab wearing a long gray technician's coat, carrying a box like he was going to deliver it to someone. It didn't seem unusual at first because packages and other equipment were delivered to the lab with some regularity. But before anyone could challenge the worker, he blew himself up, taking out most of the lab with him. The devastation was total. Avi, his researchers, techs, and staff were killed instantly. The explosion also destroyed most of their working models and research notes, as well as the computer processors they were developing.

But the greatest loss to me was my beloved sister Mackie and her remarkable husband Gerry. My life would never be the same after that day.

Our two families and all our friends were devastated. Funeral services were held in both states, Michigan and New Jersey. There were also many funerals held for the others lost in Israel.

My brain was numb for a long time—I could not accept her death. There were many times I would wake up at night crying inconsolably, and Charlie would hold me and cry with me without ever asking why I was crying. I had terrible fits of anger, and at times no one wanted to be near me. There were many other times I thought I would never recover, and it was months before I could go even one day without crying. But, eventually our lives went on, and after the first of the year I found myself occasionally smiling again.

I also kept in touch with the Israeli authorities that were trying to piece together exactly how it happened. It seemed that a terrorist had been planning the attack for some time. He carried it off on the day after the Muslim feast day *Eid-al-Adha*, the day of sacrifice. That holy day actually commemorates Abraham's willingness to sacrifice his son, Isaac, and according to the Bible, as well as the Koran, God intervened, replacing Isaac with a lamb.

Why the terrorist chose that period of time to sacrifice his life and the Israeli scientists is not clear. Then again, a terrorist's motives are never very clear.

The Technion was one of the most liberal institutions of higher learning in Israel, having students and scholars from all over the Middle East, including many Arab countries. They had been warned on numerous occasions that security could easily be breached with such an open campus. But the administration believed that an open campus that shared scientific and engineering knowledge with everyone could only lead to better understanding and peace. Now, once again, in the long struggle for Israel's survival, innocents were sacrificed for the misguided ambitions of the fanatics. Maybe fate had picked the day after *Eid-al-Adha* and not the terrorist.

My parents' suffering was unrelenting, and I couldn't get over how much older they looked when we visited them over Christmas break. Mom was so skinny she hardly cast a shadow, and Dad just looked gaunt. They were even more devastated when they learned that Mackie was about two months pregnant. They seldom smiled, and we really didn't celebrate the holiday like we had in past years. There was the obligatory tree, but our gifts were more ceremonial than practical or something we could delight in. We all missed Mackie and Gerry so much that it was hard to get into the spirit of the season. But we talked and reminisced about the old-days—how Mackie and I would spend hours in the lab doing our own research projects, Mackie's performances in the school plays, and all the happy times we had. That even included the "robust" dinner conversations we had with Dad.

We didn't talk about the "attack," as it was called, because that only brought tears and questions of why. Why would they want to kill people who worked for peace and understanding? Why would they think that a suicide bomber could accomplish their goals? There was never any answer to these questions, so we stopped asking.

However, a few years later I learned from Dad that there might have actually been a motive for the attack—and in a way I was indirectly involved.

While growing up, I remember thinking that the Israeli-Palestinian problem was fairly clear-cut. I thought that the Israelis were intransigent, the Palestinians were essentially anti-Jewish, and there would never be peace between them. But as long as Israel stayed united and militarily strong, then they would survive. After all, they had a nonaggression pact with us, so even if they weren't able to defend themselves, the United States would come in and save them.

However, after our own drawn-out wars in Iraq and Afghanistan, it was obvious that even the United States, with all its military power, couldn't guarantee another country's security. When the Egyptian-Lebanon union formed, we were certain that Israel's existence was threatened, and this time we were all really scared—well, those of us who were pro-Israel. Anti-Israeli feelings had been building up for some time in the United States with the belief that Israel was the bully in the Middle East. Some United States observers of the Israel-Palestine problem actually thought it was about time things got evened out over there, and now maybe Israel would be more reasonable when dealing with its Arab neighbors.

However, the extreme fundamentalist wing of Islam still insisted on the complete and total eradication of Israel as a Jewish state and that all people of non-Muslim faith had to be expelled. Sadly, this obviously racist and intolerant attitude is apparently acceptable to many parts of the non-Muslim world as well. This makes me wonder what it will take to make people wake up to the fact that something has to be done to make the radical elements realize that such an attitude is not acceptable—that a new generation of Middle Easterners is out there that has demanded freedom, equality, truth, and open access to worldwide information. Even now, nearly four years after the so-called *Arab Spring* revolutions of 2011, we still haven't been able to deal with such a massively destructive force as religious and racial hatred.

It wasn't until early in 2015 that I was able to talk at some length with Tikva via Skype. Mackie introduced us to the Gittlemans over Skype last fall, but now, even though we shared similar grief, we could discuss the three—Avi, Mackie, and Gerry—without breaking down uncontrollably. Yes, we cried often, but we also exchanged our thoughts and feelings, which was good. It was through these conversations that I learned much about my sister's life in Israel. I knew that one day, when we were up to it, Charlie and I would go and visit the place that made Mackie and Gerry feel so good about their work and their life.

It became sort of a regular thing, "keeping-in-touch" after our initial conversations about how we were coping with the death of our loved ones. "How are Ben and Avigail doing now? Are they settling down and getting into the rhythm of school again?" I asked.

"The kids are remarkably resilient. Of course, they still cry a lot and tell me how much they miss their *abbaleh*—their dad—but they're doing as well as can be expected."

"I understand. And you know that if they'd like to come here during summer break, Charlie and I would love to have them. East Lansing is nice in the summer. It would give them a chance to see a new place and maybe help—"

"Thanks, George, that's really sweet of you," Tikva said before I could finish. "But I think it best that we stay close together for a while longer. We have lots of friends and family here for support, and that's kept us strong. Anyway, thanks for the invite. I'll keep it in mind for maybe some future time." We paused, staring at our computer screens for a moment, then Tikva said, "By the way, I'm still going through things in Avi's lab that were not lost in the attack, and I came across a thirty-two gigabyte flash drive with Gerry's name on it. I'm mailing it to you because I know the lab has all his technical papers, and I saw that most of the files seemed to be personal notes. I'm certain he'd have wanted you to have them..."

"That would be great—thanks, Tikva. I'll take a look at it and remove anything of a personal nature, and either I'll send the rest on to IBM or the lab, depending on what it is. As you said, I'm certain that they have the work-related stuff, but just in case. Will that be okay with you?" I asked.

"That'd be fine, George."

Then I asked her, "How's the political situation over there? Is the Muslim coalition affecting you? Will you be all right? I've been reading that the Syrians are demanding your...I guess *demise* would be putting it kindly."

"George, this is Israel. We've been living with crisis after crisis for over sixty-five years now. We'll survive. But thanks for asking. Love to Charlie and let's talk again soon."

I closed my Skype connection to Tikva and went into the living room.

"How are they doing?" Charlie asked when I walked into the room. I filled her in on our conversation and told her about the flash drive that would be coming in the mail.

"Interesting," she said. "I wonder what Gerry could have been saving on a flash drive. With all their computing power and need for storage, I would suspect that most of their work was stored off-site anyway—the flash drive couldn't be that important, I should think," Charlie said.

"With the processors they were developing he just may not have wanted to store everything in the cloud, and, who knows, some of it might just be personal stuff anyway. We'll have to wait and see what it is when it gets here."

It had been cold in East Lansing that winter. There were numerous snowstorms when the semester was just getting underway, and even though it was a very rare thing to do at MSU, classes were actually cancelled one day. It made me think about Ben and Avigail and the fact that they probably had never seen an old-fashioned Michigan-style snowstorm. I bet they'd love it. Maybe I'd invite them to spend a winter here instead.

I was smiling thinking about it, and in a sense I was also worried. I silently prayed for Tikva and the children's safety as I lay in bed thinking that night; I couldn't get the constant threats of annihilation out of my mind. It now seemed more probable than it had since the Six-Day War back in 1967, when the world thought that the Egyptians would conquer Israel under their UAR banner. After forty-eight years, Israel was once again in peril of being wiped off the face of the earth. I felt very helpless and slept fitfully that night, if at all.

When the Muslim Brotherhood came into power and aligned with Hezbollah, renewing its call for the annihilation of Israel and its Jewish population, we all finally realized that Israel's paranoia was real all along. The first two years of the pact seemed to quiet things down, and the saber rattling against Israel seemed to cool off. Maybe they realized the political reality of the situation and backed off of their demands for the destruction of Israel, or maybe the drought and subsequent food shortages kept them preoccupied. But it had been pointed out in articles in the press and over the Internet that the Muslim Brotherhood was anti-Israeli even twenty years before Israel existed, and they weren't changing now. The calls for the obliteration of Israel picked up once again in Syria and Iran in spite of UN and Western objections and warnings that the world would not accept such an action.

Then a strange thing happened in Syria and Iran. It seemed that they were once again inflicted with major wheat crop failures, but this time it was of biblical proportions and not related to the drought of a couple of years earlier. Their entire northern wheat fields were decimated, and, in addition, the land seemed to be totally useless for growing anything after the loss of the wheat crop. It appeared that they were suffering under some kind of an infestation and blamed Israel for it.

Their agronomists discovered that a nonnative species of slugs had been introduced into their fields, and they automatically assumed that it was Israel. They likened it to how the Jews inflicted plagues on Egypt thousands of years earlier just as the Old Testament (and the Koran) tells it in the Passover stories. In fact, many world leaders actually believed it to be true too, even though Israel unequivocally denied that they had anything to do with it.

When I read about the physiology of the slugs, I knew immediately it had to be Boris using my now hyper-engineered slugs. I cried when I read about it on the Internet and felt sick to my stomach when I finally came to the realization that they were mine—but they had to be a highly modified version of the original ones I discovered. My slugs could never have inflicted that much damage in such a short period of time without some very selective breeding. Because of what I read and deduced from what was known about the pests, I assumed it had to be DARPA—that is, Boris—who reengineered them as a destructive weapon. I could think of no other organization in the United States capable of such a bio-engineering feat.

Gerry was right: the bastards were going to use my work for weapons and there wasn't a damn thing I could do about it. When I realized what had been done with the slugs, I promised myself that I would try to somehow right the situation. The thought that my original work could be used to starve innocent people and endanger Israel even more and add to its suffering was something I just couldn't live with. *But what could I do?* I wondered... and then it came to me.

chapter 8

My APPOINTMENT AT Michigan State was in the Computer Science and Engineering (CSE) Department, where I worked in the Digital Evolution Research Laboratory. We developed computer models for something called a *digital organism*. With the use of some Chaos models and statistical methods, we recreated the organism's evolutionary history in a way that was similar to the methods I used in my dissertation on how the mutated Frankenslugs recombined their DNA.

"So, what do you think, Yancey? Would you work with me on this if we can get an internally funded research grant?" I asked my colleague, Associate Professor Yancey Stetson, III, who taught agronomy in the Department of Biosystems and Agricultural Engineering.

"Sure, I would—it sounds like something I've wanted to do since my sabbatical. You say we would be mutating mutant species to bring them back to their original phylogenetic state? You think we can do that?" Yancey asked in his mellow, Kansas drawl.

Yancey was a flaxen-haired, lean, tall, and square-jawed man, born, raised, and educated on the western plains of Kansas. He attended Kansas State University in Manhattan, where he received his doctorate in agronomy. He would have preferred doing what five previous generations of Stetsons did—growing wheat and other food crops on the fertile Kansas plains—but modern times caught up with his family, and he knew, like his brother and sister knew, that their parents would be the last independent farmers on their land.

Yancey's family sold the majority of their fields and equipment to a large corporate mega-farm, and the money was used, in part, to send him and his siblings to college so that they could do something else—preferably something other than farming. But Yancey, the oldest of the three siblings, still wanted to be involved with the profession in some way, so with over 120 years' experience in farming (that is, his family's experience), he became an agronomy professor.

Yancey came to MSU in 2007, and I first met him seven years later in 2014, when he had returned from his sabbatical leave—he spent a year as a visiting professor at the American University in Beirut, Lebanon, serving on the faculty of Agricultural and Food Sciences. When he returned from his sabbatical, he gave a departmental talk about the concern in the Middle East over a new strain of slug that had been discovered first in Syria and then in Iran that was decimating their wheat fields. I went to his talk, and afterwards I introduced myself to him and told him about my work and how I thought that the nonnative slugs he saw in Lebanon might in some way be similar to the ones I found in Ypsilanti.

When I talked with Yancey that first time we met, I didn't go into all the details about DARPA and Boris. I simply related my work on how I thought the mutation occurred and on Charlie's work for using them as a sustainable energy source. He was definitely interested in our research, so we met a couple of times after that to discuss the possibility of working on some common projects.

After I realized, or at least strongly suspected, that the Middle Eastern slugs were from my original Michigan strain and that the Syrians were trying to blame Israel for introducing the slugs, I knew that I had to destroy, or neutralize, them. But I needed Yancey's expertise as an agronomist and an expert on the Middle Eastern variety, and I knew that this was where we should team up. I also knew exactly how we could do that: neutralize the slugs by mutating them back to their evolutionary parent species, *Arion distinctus*.

I was relieved when Yancey said he'd work with me on the project if we got the funding, not only because of his agronomy expertise, but also because he was senior faculty and had a number of grants under his belt already. I thought that might enhance our chances of getting funded. But aside from all the practical reasons, I had just liked the guy from the first time I heard him speak. He seemed so well grounded and sure of himself that I couldn't help but think that I wanted him to mentor me through my early years as a junior faculty member even though he was not in my department.

As it turned out, I couldn't have made a better decision in my whole life.

It was early February when we both received letters from the vice president for research notifying us of our grant. We hadn't talked much about the project since I first broached the subject to Yancey in January. After getting the grant, we were looking forward to working with, and getting to know each other better. I was pleased to be working with Yancey, a senior faculty member with a great reputation for scholarship and honesty. Also, I could see by the way he was smiling when I came into his office with our notification letter that he looked forward to working with me as well. A few days before we received our grant, I did bring Yancey up to speed about Boris and DARPA. I filled him in on how interested Boris seemed to be in my slugs, but I thought it was strange that he never got back to me. In any case there were all these physiological similarities between Yancey's Syrian slugs and my Frankenslugs that led me to believe the two varieties were at least cousins.

After receiving word that our grant was approved, Charlie and I were invited to the Stetsons' for dinner and to talk shop.

As someone who grew up with a father who was involved with city planning and mostly urban environments, Charlie was excited about meeting some real American farmers. She had never met any people who actually worked the land and had always wondered what they were like. She also had to admit that she had a number of preconceived notions about them— such as that they were ultra-conservative, Christian fundamentalists—even though she knew that had to be a stereotype. Based on what I had told her about Yancey, she was looking forward to having her prejudices dispelled. After all, MSU started out as Michigan's agricultural college, and now that she was on the faculty, she knew she should get to know more about her university's aggie roots.

It was cold and snowy when we left our apartment for the Stetsons' house that Friday the thirteenth evening. I was finally feeling a little better about my chances of redressing the misuse of my discovery that was further endangering an already much endangered world. I was anxious to get working on our project, and my supportive wife was also anxious for me to get started. Since Mackie and Gerry's assassination, I'd found it hard to stay focused on anything other than my hatred for the Muslim terrorist who killed them. Maybe I could turn that hate into something more constructive now.

"That was such a great dinner—thanks again, Noreen," I said, as Charlie nodded an enthusiastic agreement.

Noreen Stetson could best be described as the salt of the earth. She was Yancey's high school sweetheart, and they were married right after her high school graduation. He was a junior in college at the time, but in that part of the country marrying young was not uncommon. After all, the families had known each other for literally generations, growing up on farms near Garden City, Kansas, and going to the same schools. In fact, they had many relatives in common since there hasn't been a population influx to that part of Kansas in over sixty years. However, like most modern families, they were far more sophisticated than people from other parts of the country gave them credit for. And just because Noreen never formally attended college did not mean she wasn't educated.

When they moved to East Lansing and were raising their family (they had two daughters, ten and thirteen), Noreen started sitting in on classes in political science and economics—she loved those subjects. And by the time Yancey got his sabbatical to go to Lebanon, she was probably as knowledgeable about the Middle East as any college graduate majoring in poly-sci. Noreen was a comely woman in her early thirties with brown hair and hazel eyes. Her Irish ancestry provided her with pleasant features, and after two children she looked a little plumper than she did in various family pictures I saw around the house. But she was still quite attractive and was dressed nicely in a simple floral patterned pullover dress.

"We call beef stew, biscuits, and canned corn old-fashioned down-country winter fare," Noreen said with a warm smile. Yancey and the girls were clearing the table, and we were sitting in their den by an inviting fire while Noreen told us about their house. "Yancey put a gas Heatilator in shortly after we moved in. I don't think it's as nice as the wood-burners we have back home, but it's more efficient and lots more heat gets back into the house as opposed to going up the flue."

"It seems that winters in Michigan require significantly more heating to stay warm than in England. I think East Lansing is colder than Ann Arbor, am I right?" Charlie asked.

"Why is the weather always the topic of conversation in Michigan no matter where you live?" Yancey asked as he came into the den. "I heard from the day we got here that in Michigan if you don't like the weather, wait ten minutes." The girls had gone to their room so it was just the four of us now.

We mused about Yancey's comment for a while, making other small talk as we relaxed in the den. Yancey offered us after-dinner drinks, so I had a cognac with him, but Noreen and Charlie passed.

Charlie asked, "Yancey, George told me that you were in Lebanon on your sabbatical last fall. How was the political climate for you...I mean, as an American?"

It was Noreen who answered. "Actually, we were all supposed to be there for the summer, but I came back with the girls after only a month. I found the 'climate,' as you put it, intolerable, even though I knew what to expect. Yancey was at the American University and was very much insulated from the people of the city. But we had to interact with them every day, and I can tell you there were times when I was actually frightened."

"Were you threatened? Did someone threaten you or the girls?" Charlie asked with real concern.

"If you mean were our lives in danger, then no...no. It was much more subtle. We had made contact with a Maronite church in Beirut and had hoped that we could do some missionary work with them. We're Methodists and outreach is part of our religious calling. However, we found the atmosphere very disconcerting. The lovely people we met at the church felt like they were under siege from the fundamental Islamists. They were constantly being watched for any breaches of Islamic customs—like the girls had to be completely covered and needed to wear a veil and long sleeves even though Lebanese women didn't. But because they knew we were working with the Maronites, they would harass us all the time about such things. I couldn't take it any more. We only planned on being there over the summer, but we left early."

Yancey said, "I was committed to teach at the American University, so I stayed on and pretty much lived on campus for the whole academic year. As Noreen said, I wasn't worried about their physical safety as much as their mental safety and agreed they should go home."

Noreen added, "I also felt that it would be safer for the Maronites we were working with if we left because our presence really posed a true physical danger to them—more so than to us."

Noreen then went on to tell us about how Hezbollah had taken over the government; and even though they ran clinics and schools and fed the poor, it was all done under their own version of *Sharia*, strict Islamic law.

"The majority of the people in Beirut were not fundamentalists and many were Christians. But they don't bother with them—they bother foreigners who they think might be proselytizing and trying to convert Muslims, which is certainly not what we did. We only worked with Christians and had no work-related contact with Muslims. In reality that would be a capital crime under their law, but they just constantly harass foreigners, like they did to us, until we left."

We talked more about the stifling religious conditions in the country and about politics in general. Charlie was pleased to learn that Yancey and Noreen, unlike most of their relatives and friends in Kansas, were liberal Democrats. Yes, they were Christians and did practice their faith, but they were far from religious zealots and had as little use for extremists in this country as they did for those in Beirut. Yancey told us that the atmosphere was different at the American University because they never discussed religion or politics. "You never knew who might be listening," he told us with a wry smile on his face.

He then confessed that the reason he was so interested to work with me on the mutant slug problem was not only because of the agronomy implications, but that when he analyzed the Syrian strain, he and his colleagues had all realized that they were probably engineered. Some of his colleagues did think that it might be Israel, but Yancey believed that it would not be like the Israelis to destroy food crops. He believed that hungry people are ripe for revolution, and the last thing Israel needed was another revolution with the possibility that an even more fanatical regime may step in.

Yancey said, "It really bothered me recently when I heard that the Syrian government was blaming Israel when all of the evidence was to the contrary. I guess I knew that if anyone would do something that stupid it would have to be one of our own black-ops groups, but I never expressed that to anyone. When you, George, more or less confirmed that for me, I knew I had to work with you."

Yancey then said with measured seriousness, "Tell me, George, do you think we can really do that—mutate them back again, and by so doing replace the current subspecies with the original? I've never heard of any subspecies reverting back to its parent species either by the action of some agent or spontaneously. I hope you have some solid underlying theory for how we're supposed to do this," Yancey said in his unique, easy-going manner.

Noreen and Charlie were staring at me, waiting anxiously for my answer. "I'll go over the methodology with you next week and in more detail than we've outlined in our proposal, and we'll see then if my approach is valid," I answered. "I not only think we can, but we *have to*—and before it's too late for Israel and maybe even the world as we know it. I doubt if Boris' people have developed a control program for their creation, so it's just a matter of time—what, ten, twenty years?—before they're all over the world. And then what? I also don't think we can eradicate them without doing irreparable damage to the earth's environment. No, I think our approach is the only viable answer."

We sat there quietly thinking about the implications of what I just said. I had never really verbalized my concerns about a worldwide infestation like that before, even to myself, so when it finally came out, I must admit I was really frightened.

I had received the flash drive in January that Tikva said she would send to me, but I hadn't looked at it yet. I didn't know if I could deal with the contents emotionally, knowing that Gerry and Mackie's stuff was on there. But over that cold weekend in February, I made the effort. It was mostly text files and some spreadsheets, working papers on their research, but there were also some personal Word files that I opened and read. One was Gerry's diary—I never expected that. It was fairly boring, with entries like, "Played bridge with Avi and Tikva last night," but every now and then there would be a reference to Charlie and me.

"George and Charlie would have loved that restaurant we went to last night, *Chez Meesh*, with all the Michigan crap on the walls. We'll have to take them there if they come to visit." I had to smile when I came across those little references, and then I would start to cry again.

I looked at some of the other files and noticed that a number were programs Gerry had written for their new systems. It took me a while—I wasn't nearly as competent as Gerry was in writing native code, and especially if it's been written for a bio-processor—but I finally figured out that the systems they were developing would be operating at unheard of speeds. I could see that there were multiple instructions carried out simultaneously and that simple binary logic would not cut it. I wondered if IBM had all these files or if Avi's lab had them. I assumed so. After all, they funded the project, so they should have them.

I also realized that if IBM had high-speed quantum computers that were operational and if we had access to them, then it would cut a lot of waiting time off our work on the slug project. I was thinking that I would have to ask Yancey if he could schedule time on one of the supercomputers that MSU had access to. If that were so, then I was confident we could come up with a solution in time to stave off WW III and save the world's food system. It sounded like a great B movie in my head—*George and Yancey Save the World*—but sadly enough this time it might be for real.

"Okay, George, explain to me in layman's terms—I'm not as computer savvy as you are—how this process of yours is going to work," Yancey said when we met to work on our project later in the week.

"At our digital lab, we use all kinds of complex computer models to create evolutionary profiles. Some are based on Chaos theory—you know, nonlinear dynamical systems—and some are based on Bayesian statistical procedures like the ones used in medical research. I want to combine those two elements and then use a backward chaining inference method to come up with a process for essentially starting with our Frankenslugs' DNA and then work backwards through their evolutionary history to the original organism," I explained.

"Backward chaining, like they use in artificial intelligence programs?" Yancey asked.

"Right, exactly. I think that's our best chance to remutate—if there is such a word—these guys back to the relatively harmless critters they once were. Do you think that's a worthwhile approach?" I asked.

Yancey thought for a while and then said, "I have no problems with the broad approach, but like my father used to say when I had all these great ideas on how to make our farm more environmentally friendly, 'Good idea, but you know the devil's in the details,' and that's sort of how I feel now."

"How's that?" I asked.

"As I understand backward chaining, it's like you have the answer, now what's the question? Unfortunately, there could be a huge number of questions that have the same answer. And then you have to take it from there for each possible question, going on and on until after an infinite amount of time you come up with the original question. Do I have that right, George?"

"Sort of, but with the right programming modules—some of which I've already developed since my dissertation—and the added statistical procedures, we can do that much faster so we don't need an infinite amount of time. Maybe half that," I joked.

Yancey smiled. "Okay, I'll go along with that. You write the programs and do the analysis so we can see what DNA changes are needed to get from point Z to point A," Yancey said. Then, looking quizzically at me, he asked, "What do you expect me to do? Now, don't tell me you expect me to come up with the mechanisms needed to reverse all those steps in the same order they occurred originally to finally get back to *Arion distinctus*. I doubt if can do that. If I could do that I would be in line for a Nobel Prize."

"Actually, Yancey, that was exactly what I was hoping you could do. Look at it this way: if you do do it, then you can thank me later when they give you the Nobel."

"I was afraid that was what you wanted. I guess I knew when we first started on the proposal that I would be expected to make that happen. After all, I'm a Kansas farmer and people have been expecting miracles from farmers since time began. So what else is new?"

I was getting to like Yancey more every time we talked. He was really brilliant and had that farm wisdom that comes from experience and a sense of self-worth that allowed him to accept any challenge he was given. He was an outstanding engineer, having been one since he first drove his dad's 1980 John Deere combine (purchased new the year before Yancey was born) out of the barn before he was even thirteen years old. He knew how to handle explosives, shoot firearms, and do all kinds of engineering-related procedures like keeping the farm equipment repaired and running. I couldn't help but think how much fun he and Mackie would have had if they had ever had the chance to know each other.

We had started working in earnest by early March, laying out a work plan for both of us. We co-opted one of the CSE's clerical staff to work for us part-time, setting up our accounts and doing all the standard clerical things that are needed to run a small research project. We then looked for a grad student who wanted to do the kind of interdisciplinary research we were involved in, and Yancey found one in his own department: a first year doctoral student from India, Barindra Padawal, who was on scholarship after doing his bachelor's and master's degrees in computer science at The Indian Institute of Technology, Bombay. He wanted to get his doctorate from the Biosystems and Agricultural Engineering Department, and with his background he seemed perfect for the job.

"You say you come from a family of farmers in Goa. I didn't think they did much farming there anymore, Barindra—did I pronounce that right?" Yancey asked while we were interviewing the grad student.

"Please, call me Bobby—that's much easier to say than Barindra, and I'm used to that nickname. And, yes, my family has one of the largest farms in Goa where we grow rice and some other smaller fields of food crops. But that's about to change since the land is becoming more expensive and will probably be converted for tourism. That's why I'm interested in biosystems engineering—I would like to keep on farming and still be able to use the land for the tourism industry."

"And your undergrad and master's are in computer science, right, Bobby?" I said, looking at his application. "Do you think that you'll need to use your computer knowledge to run the family business?" I asked, making conversation.

Bobby gave us a long explanation of how his knowledge of computers tied in to current modern farming practices, land management, and business. We were impressed and hired him on the spot.

"By the way," I said after he had been hired and was smiling broadly at the opportunity to work with us, "you said that you're used to the nickname Bobby—where did you get that nickname?"

"In England—I have relatives in a place called Handsworth Wood, just outside Birmingham, that I often visited over the summers. It's much too hot in Goa then, so England is a nice respite. The locals there started calling me Bobby and so it stuck."

"Interesting, my wife is originally from Birmingham. You'll have to meet her; in fact, she's on the CSE faculty, and you might even want to take her graduate seminar."

His eyes shone and he smiled broadly. I was pleased that we hired him.

It was before the summer break started in May, and our work was progressing slower than I had hoped. It seemed that Yancey may not have been that far off when he said it would take an infinite amount of time to do the kinds of analyses I planned. He kept himself busy working with our mutant slugs since we couldn't get any of the real trouble makers out of Syria. Charlie was a great help in that department since she had been farming them for her battery program, and Yancey's farming expertise helped her out in that department as well.

She was about to give up on her slug battery because she thought the slugs were an unsustainable product. They required too much in outside resources to survive; plus, the slugs would eventually destroy everything. But Yancey was helping her out in trying to create a renewable environment for the slugs to work in. They had taken over a portion of one of the bio labs for their research, and they got along well together. In the meantime, while I was developing the *remutation model*—that's what we were calling it—Yancey knew that if he had to develop a mechanism for accomplishing the required backward mutation steps, it would have to be through organic enzyme chemistry.

He was an expert in protein engineering, and had already created a number of new enzymes useful for a variety of food industry products. He had been experimenting with ways in which he could introduce those enzymes into a living organism—such as an egg cell—to change the characteristics of the creature in a known and predictable manner.

He and Charlie were working together in the lab when he told her, "All I need now is for George to tell me how he wants our slugs to evolve backwards and I can start a program to try and make that a reality."

"You know, Yance," Charlie responded, "what you're doing is so much more important than my battery; I feel bad when you take time out of your project to work with me." She had started calling him *Yance* a while back, and he never asked her not to. His siblings called him that when they were young, but they hadn't called him that in years. Yancey later explained to me that he liked being called Yance by Charlie because it made him feel like Charlie was his little sister, and he said it was a nice feeling for him. In fact, Charlie liked Yancey too as the big brother she never had. She also knew that if we ever—or, more realistically, when—we had children, Yancey and Noreen would be a great surrogate aunt and uncle team for them.

In the meantime Bobby and I did some calculations and realized that for our models to get us anywhere near where we wanted to be, we would definitely need a much faster computer. At the rate we were going and using the fastest computers available to us, it would probably take years to get any meaningful results. Our complexity programs required a large number of iterations, and it didn't help that we were being slowed down by statistically analyzing results along the way. That further created delays that we hadn't seen earlier.

Bobby's expertise from working on a compiler project in Mumbai was a tremendous help. His knowledge of processor efficiencies and how to calculate the time for them to accomplish specific instructions was invaluable.

"You see, George, we can't use standard benchmarks to estimate our processing time because those benchmarks don't take into account the multiple operations you're performing using machines with quad-processors," Bobby said in his own inimitable techie fashion.

"Can you come up with a better estimate?" I asked him.

He tilted his head quickly to one side, which was his way of telling me that he most certainly could. After his analysis I knew we needed access to a supercomputer. Yancey had tried to get time on machines that were available to MSU, but they were all booked for the next five years by externally funded projects. Internally funded projects, like ours, had the lowest priority for getting access. But I had an idea for how we might get a supercomputer for ourselves, and we all agreed it was the best way to go: get IBM to give us time on one of theirs.

chapter 9

ALAN WACKFIELD WAS one of IBM's top VPs; his title was vice president for international cooperation. He had visited with Gerry and Mackie last year on a trip through the Middle East. Mackie had told me about that visit and how she didn't like being referred to as a "guy." She did tell me, however, that he was very impressed with their work but may have been a little too dramatic in characterizing what they were doing by saying, "The future of computers as we know them is in your hands."

When I called him to set up our meeting, he told me how he had described the potential impact of Gerry and Mackie's work. But after their murder and subsequently hearing about what they had accomplished with Professor Gittleman in such a short time, he felt he might actually have been making an understatement. He was looking forward to meeting me, Marike's brother, especially when he heard that I had a flash drive full of program notes written by Gerry.

It was mid-June when Yancey and I arrived at IBM's corporate head-quarters in Armonk, New York. The facility was about fifteen miles or so south of their Yorktown research center where Gerry and Mackie had worked. We were on a one-day trip so the airfare for the two of us essentially blew our modest travel budget, but we felt that it would be best if both of us met with Wackfield to convince him that giving us computer time on an IBM Blue Gene series supercomputer was in their best interest.

"Come in, come in," Alan Wackfield said as he led us into his elegantly appointed office with high, very dramatic windows looking out onto an almost park-like area of the building's grounds. The whole facility was almost monumental—like a national park that surrounded a presidential landmark—a veritable symbol of IBM's status in the business world.

"It's George, right? And you must be Professor Stetson," he said as he shook our hands and directed us to the large conference table located in an alcove on the east side of his office. The furniture was Herman Miller modern, and his own Aeron chair complemented the lesser distinguished chairs and furnishings located around the table and against the wall.

"You have no idea how much we miss your family, George. They were both remarkable scholars and truly global citizens," he said, being once again a bit too superlative in his description, "but I'm sure you don't need me to tell you that." He then asked Yancey, "Did you know them, Professor Stetson?"

"No, but from what I've heard I'm truly sorry I never had the opportunity to meet them. But knowing George, it doesn't surprise me how you should feel that way about his family. And please, call me Yancey."

"Well then—George, Yancey—can I get you some coffee or something else to drink? And please call me Alan."

Alan was the picture of a corporate VP. He was impeccably dressed in a dark blue, summer weight suit, white shirt, and rep tie. He was a trim man, probably in his mid-fifties, with slightly graying hair at the temples. His hair styling looked like it cost three hundred dollars—at least it did to me, but I'm not the greatest judge on the cost of haircuts.

After some small talk about the smoothness of our flight into White Plains and the drive to Armonk, coffee was brought in and we got down to business.

"You say you have a flash drive that belonged to Gerry and Marike that you think I should look at; is that right?" Alan asked.

"Yes, here it is," I said, handing him the SanDisk 32 gigabyte drive. "I've taken the liberty of removing his personal Word documents…notes to himself and some personal family stuff. I hope that was all right."

"Of course it was," Alan said as he plugged the drive into his laptop, which was sitting on the table, and began quickly comparing the files and folders with a list on a pad near the laptop. After a few minutes he turned to us. "Sorry to be so boorish, but I'd rather do this with you here than later after you left. As I suspected these are all files we have on record from their project. As you know, he and Marike stored their work off-site and we, as well as the Technion, had access to those files. I was curious to see if they had produced other work that we didn't know about yet and would have wanted to share that with you now. Obviously as one of their relatives, you would have some interest if that was the case, and you should know that immediately."

He then removed the drive from the laptop and gave it back to me, which surprised me. "Don't you need that? I mean...I think that as their employer you people would own it," I said.

"Their work is in the open literature like the vast majority of IBM research. No, I think that since you were given the drive by Professor Gittleman's wife, it's rightfully yours. You should keep it, if for no other reason than to appreciate the brilliance of your sister and brother-in-law. The Technion is continuing with Professor Gittleman's research station, and work has already been started on advancing the bio-processors Gerry, Marike, and Avraham were developing," Alan explained. "But, thank you very much for giving us the opportunity to see the list."

We sat there for a minute, nodding at each other and not knowing what to say, and then Yancey broke into the conversation.

"Alan, I'm not sure if George has told you much about our work at MSU, but I think you might be interested since it too has global implications, and I think IBM might just be interested in getting involved," Yancey said in his low-key way.

When Alan confessed that he was not aware of our project, Yancey filled him in on the whole situation, including the political dynamics in the Middle East and the immediate need for neutralizing the slugs' impact. He didn't leave out any technical issues but presented them in a way that an MBA would understand without having to talk down to him. I was impressed.

"Yancey, if what you're saying is accurate then I think you're telling me that global peace is being threatened and you may be able to keep that threat from coming about—is that correct?" Alan asked.

We told him that that was our understanding as well. However, we had no proof that the world would go to war and that the slugs would actually destroy the entire world's food crops—all that was conjecture. But we felt that either or both of those events might be a logical conclusion to the slugs' ultimate damage. We didn't tell him that we thought DARPA was behind it, but we just stayed with the fact that the slugs existed and had destroyed crops in the Middle East. We thought that should be enough to pique his interest.

He sat there quietly for a while and then said, "Write me a brief one-page proposal on MSU stationary asking for Blue Gene computing time to develop an evolutionary model for mutant slugs. Don't ask for a specific amount of time based on our commercial rates but simply request an unspecified amount for your project's duration. Attach a copy of your current in-house proposal with it. Can you get me that ASAP?"

"It will be in your e-mail by the time we get on the plane later this evening," I said.

We thanked him for his time and his understanding. He nodded, but then he warned us, "Look, you two, I have no doubt of your sincerity or your ability to conquer this threat, but if any heroic press accounts arise—like, *MSU faculty members get IBM's latest supercomputer to try and save the world*— we'll deny that we knew anything about that element of your work. You can understand that, can't you?"

We assured him we fully understood that the press, the Internet, Facebook, and all the rest of the news networks were the last places we would want to go. Officially, our research on remutation was just that: pure research for an old aggie school's concern over sustaining food crops and controlling destructive pests. He smiled when I said that, telling us that he did his MBA and undergrad work at Texas A&M, another old *aggie school*.

———————

We were out of Alan's office by early afternoon and on our way back to White Plains in the hopes of getting an earlier flight out to either Lansing's Capital Region Airport or Detroit Metro. In the car I drafted the one-page proposal and showed it to Yancey at the airport. He offered some minor changes, and then we attached our MSU proposal and e-mailed it to Alan. We told him in the e-mail that the official proposal on MSU stationary (with the appropriate departmental signatures) would be mailed out to him on Tuesday. We were pleased with ourselves for what we had accomplished at

IBM and celebrated by having a drink at the airport while waiting to board our flight back to Michigan.

"I just hope that this is the breakthrough we've needed to get this job finished in time. I'll have some better ideas now on how we might proceed with our enzyme bullets once I know what I'm shooting at," Yancey said. He frequently used firearms jargon when describing his approach to things.

"With the IBM Blue Gene we'll be able to speed up our work a thousand fold. If Bobby's calculations hold true, we should start seeing some results that you could *aim your enzyme gun* at by July or August. How's that, *pardner?*"

Yancey smiled at my feeble attempt to mimic him. We both had warm smiles—maybe from the Scotches we drank—as we boarded the plane back to Detroit Metro. We knew we'd be home by nine and that, too, made us smile. We looked forward to telling Charlie and Noreen about our good fortune with IBM after we called them on our cells to let them know when we'd be home.

Noreen had developed a doomsday forecast for us similar to the one used in the journal *Bulletin of the Atomic Scientists.* That journal had a clock pictured on the upper left corner of each issue's cover with hands showing the time before midnight. The closer to midnight, the closer the world was to annihilation by either an atomic war or some other man-made disaster like climate change. The big hand had been anywhere from around three to seventeen minutes before midnight since 1947, depending on what was happening in the world with wars, peace treaties, and civil unrest.

Noreen's clock was just focused on the Middle East, and each Wednesday at our weekly staff meetings, she'd give us a time and a one-paragraph summary of what she saw happening. The summary for the week of June 15 was the following:

> <u>THREE</u> Minutes to Midnight: The Egyptian-Lebanese collation is getting more tolerant of Hamas and Hezbollah accusing Israel of destroying food crops. Syria and Iran are threatening independent action against Israel, and the coalition may be forced

to go along with it. There has been some mobilization in Israel that they claim is just precautionary, but it's causing the Western alliances some anxious moments. There's fear that the crop losses will greatly exceed the drought losses of five years ago, causing food prices and unemployment to once again rise, creating further instability in the coalition countries.

"Not a very rosy picture, honey," Yancey said when he read her report. "Three minutes left on the clock—could you put that into months, or preferably years, as to when all hell will break loose over there?"

We—that's me, Yancey and Bobby—were in our project office, and Noreen continued, "I don't know—it's all relative to what it's been like since we started the project in February. But if I had to guess, I'd say that if the food shortage gets as bad as you say it's going to get, then it's definitely months, not years. Remember, in February I just picked five minutes as a reference point and have gone up and down from there. But you know this is the closest I've come to putting it at midnight. I'm scared, Yancey."

Noreen knew her subject because she pored over all the news, Internet feeds, and foreign press that she could handle in a day. She would carefully analyze her data based on solid political theory and historical precedents; she knew what she was talking about.

We were all pretty gloomy after hearing Noreen's forecast even though we had the good news about getting the IBM computer to talk about.

"Do you think I should call my father and tell him what's happening?" Bobby asked.

"No, Bobby, I wouldn't do that. I'm sure that like everybody else in the world your family is monitoring the Middle East situation as carefully as we are. Because our work is so closely connected—in some way—to the situation, we're just more sensitive to the problem. I don't think you should unnecessarily alarm them," I said.

I then went into our morning agenda and asked Bobby—mostly to take his mind off Noreen's clock, "Bobby, you have the Blue Gene performance standards. What's your estimate now of when we should start getting some positive results?"

"I already did that even before you guys left for New York. I should think that our current algorithms will start bearing fruit, so to speak, in a week or less after we start running them. When do you think we'll get access?" Bobby asked.

I told him we expected to hear from New York by the end of the week. I also told him that we requested travel funds for him to go there to learn how to efficiently make use of their proprietary Objective-C libraries, and he was psyched by that. We also told him that IBM was supporting our project as a pure research effort, and it had nothing to do with the Middle East situation, so he should keep that in mind when talking with anyone about his work with us.

Yancey filled us in on his newer approach that employed enzymes for modifying the slugs' DNA. He would use it on the slugs' eggs rather than the slugs themselves in order to alter their DNA and make them revert back to *Arion distinctus*. He just needed those DNA patterns from us before he could get started in earnest. He was already doing some preliminary work to test his process, but it would be slow at first until he could start growing new generations in a sequenced manner. He felt that he'd be ready with his test sites in about two weeks, or around July 1.

We hoped that our timeframe would give us the results we needed to start the final project and still have enough time to hold back any attack on Israel—or for that matter, hold Israel back from any preemptive strike against the coalition countries. We also felt that we were attempting an impossible feat—that we would never have enough time to develop the process, implement it, and make enough progress to calm everyone down before irreversible damage was done to the world. But we were determined to give it our *best shot*, as Yancey was inclined to say.

After Bobby returned from his IBM training in New York, we were given secure remote access to one of IBM's Blue Gene systems. We cranked away at our model for almost two weeks. We had no final results yet, but we could feel it coming from the data that we were getting. It was mid-July, and we were getting antsy. Noreen's updates hadn't gotten any rosier, and even though her timeframe was still three minutes to midnight, the situation was definitely getting tenser. Charlie was now teeming up with Yancey full-time on the enzyme approach. She put her own research aside to help with our project on an unfunded basis. Since she didn't have any summer funding anyway, she was willing and able to give all her free time to the project.

"I think Yance and I have a good chance to do this. In our experiments we were able to change some base pairs of the DNA chain, and then by catalyzing them with Yance's *enzyme soup*—that's what he calls it—we changed the pairs back to their original structure. I think that's truly magic, don't you?" Charlie said to me in her lab.

"I think you two will get the Nobel after all. I teased Yancey about that a while back, but now I think it's a real possibility," I said.

Charlie confessed, "You know, George, if this work wasn't so damned serious I'd really be having fun on this project. I must admit that in all honesty once I'm working I forget about the real problems we're trying to solve and just concentrate on the academic work. Then reality hits me when I think about Noreen's updates, and I start to feel guilty about loving my job. Do you think that's normal?"

"Of course it is, honey," I said. I then sat down on one of the stools in the lab and, taking both her hands in mine, explained, "I hear that medical doctors would go insane if they were constantly thinking about their patients' pain and suffering. I guess they've developed a way of coping—in some sense—by knowing when to divorce themselves from that element of their job, and we probably should do the same. Once we have a working product in place, there'll be plenty of time to feel more politically involved, but right now why shouldn't we enjoy our work? After all, that's what we've been trained to do," I told her.

"I'm glad you keep me grounded. Have I told you lately that I love you?" she said with her enchanting smile and gently kissed me on my forehead.

I just smiled, got off the stool, and hugged and kissed her, and we both went back to our work.

———

It was the last week of July when I heard Bobby shout from his cubicle, "I think we got it! Look, look!" He was showing me the sequences for the DNA changes that would take us back from *Arion d. distinctus* to *Arion distinctus*, our original slugs. I looked carefully at the sequencing to make sure it worked. The way we determined if our model was valid was once a particular backward sequencing was suggested, we tested it by taking it forward again. We'd had close calls in the past where a sequence seemed to work, but then when we chained it forward again, it didn't give us our Frankenslugs. But here was a sequencing that did work. After trillions and trillions of iterations, statistical testing, and numerous false alarms, we hit it.

We couldn't wait to tell Yancey and Charlie. I grabbed a screen printout of our monitor with just enough data to show them the results, and we both literally ran down the hall.

"Look at this!" I yelled, as we ran into their lab. They both stopped what they were doing and came up to meet us. They knew immediately what we had and couldn't wait to see. The printout was not the complete picture of course, but enough was there to show them that we had solved the riddle.

"Nice work, you two!" Yancey said as he looked over the data and quickly scanned the sequences to see how he might replicate the process in his slugs' eggs. Just knowing the right sequencing wouldn't necessarily solve our problems. We had always suspected that it was microwave radiation that modified our garden slugs' DNA in the first place, as I had posited in my doctoral dissertation; we also knew that just irradiating the slugs again wouldn't necessarily reverse the process. But an engineered enzyme working in the egg sac could do it, and now all Yancey and Charlie had to do was engineer the magic dust that made the transformation.

The four of us went back to our project office after our initial jubilation quieted down. We realized all the implications of our discovery and talked about the next phase. It would still be a long process. First of all, if the eggs hatched while the Frankenslugs were still around, then in all likelihood the offspring would be eaten. It might take many generations before the high-acid slug population would decrease sufficiently to allow the new breed of slugs to survive. But it was important to do it this way so that the soil would come back to life again, which is what we really needed in order to grow new crops once the Frankenslugs died off.

What was even more difficult was that once the right recipe for Yancey's *soup* was discovered, it would have to be manufactured in huge quantities. The enzymes would then have to be distributed over vast land areas at the life cycle intervals for the slugs that existed in that region. And of equal importance, the *soup* had to be bio-friendly and not negatively impact the biota of the region. It would take time and lots of money to do all that—and we had neither.

We were becoming a little depressed when Yancey said, "Well, my gosh, you people look like we just lost World War Three when we still haven't finished attacking the enemy. We're not giving up now." He put his arm around Charlie's shoulder and continued, "Look, Charlie and I still have to develop the recipe for the soup, which will take—who knows—maybe a month? Could take more or even less, but we're still going to work on it anyway no matter what happens." Charlie smiled in agreement, and then Yancey said to Bobby and me, "In that time you two will have to come up with a strategy for manufacturing and distributing the stuff in enormous quantities. Think you could do that?"

"Do we have a choice?" Bobby asked.

"Not if you want your PhD," Yancey joked.

"Then we'll get started on it right away, won't we, Professor Brachmann?" Bobby said to me with a mischievous smile on his face.

I immediately e-mailed Alan Wackfield at IBM and told him about our success and thanked him, once again, for the use of IBM Blue Gene technology. I also told him that if we hadn't had their computer and were still using our old equipment, we might have gotten the solution in around another four years and seven months.

Later that day Alan called me. "George, well done young man, well done! I'm delighted that we were able to help, and from what I can figure out there may be a whole lot of commercial uses for your methodology. Let's plan on talking soon and see if we can come up with some kind program that would be mutually beneficial to you and IBM, okay?"

I really felt good after talking with Alan and went back down to Yancey's lab to tell him about the conversation. He and Charlie were already deep into discussions on the type of enzyme they would have to engineer, but there was no doubt that they felt confident about their approach.

After filling them in on my talk with Alan, Yancey said, "I just talked with Noreen and she wants to make dinner for us tonight. Tell Bobby to come too and to bring a date if he wants."

Yancey was pleased to hear that we may get some personal reward from IBM out of this endeavor, other than just saving the world from total destruction—at least that's what Yancey told me.

It was a hot late July evening when we all got together at the Stetsons' for dinner. Noreen planned barbecue chicken that night, but remembering that Bobby was invited, she changed the menu to barbecued tandoori chicken with curie rice and some other Indian side dishes. The meal was superb, and Bobby, who didn't bring a date, was most appreciative that his dissertation advisor's wife would be so thoughtful. He brought a bottle of Goa Feni for the dinner, which was hard for him to find in East Lansing.

"This bottle is from my family's distillery and is still not widely available, but I did find it here in Lansing and thought you might enjoy it," Bobby said as he gave the bottle to Yancey.

"I don't think I've ever had any of this. How appropriate for tonight's dinner—shall we open it now?" Yancey asked.

"Please, by all means, let's do that," Bobby said, and so Yancey opened it and we all started to drink the potent Indian wine before dinner.

We didn't know the power of Feni, and that combined with the heat and our empty stomachs made us all very loose by the time we sat down to eat. It was a nice family-like setting, and all of us, especially Bobby, enjoyed the ambiance. I think we all felt that this was like the beginning of the end, and if we just held our breath we might be able to pull this whole cockamamie project off in time.

After dinner the Stetson girls went inside to help clean up while the rest of us stayed outside, enjoying the late summer weather. A breeze off of a nearby lake kept the mosquitoes down. We were quiet for the most part, just sipping an after-dinner drink and occasionally commenting on a meteor and the stars in general.

"Back home in Goa, we also have beautiful nights like this. But in the summer, it's much too hot to stay inside, so we frequently sleep outside. We would get the off-shore ocean breezes at night, which made it tolerable, but I don't think I could live anywhere else in the world," Bobby said.

"I thought you went to England in the summer," I said.

"Yes, for a number of summers, but not all of them. I do like England, but I'm most at home in Goa."

"George tells me your relatives in England live in Handsworth Wood. That's near the Perry Barr campus of Birmingham City University where my father teaches. Are you familiar with the school?" Charlie asked Bobby.

"Yes, I am. My cousin took her jewelry program there and is doing very well as a jewelry designer in London. It is a small world indeed," Bobby said. And then almost as an afterthought, he added, "Yes, so small that a rogue slug could destroy the whole thing—England, India, the United States…our homes; we can't let that happen, can we?" Bobby asked in a heartrending way.

"We won't let it happen, Bobby. Not with all of us working to prevent it. I guarantee you here and now, we won't let it happen," Noreen answered him, and the way she said it with such conviction I knew right then and there she was right.

It was then that Bobby told us he had lost his mother last year and was worried about his father's mental state. His father had lost his will to work and looked like he might be fading away. Bobby wondered out loud if our project could in some way use his father's expertise. That would give him something to live for.

"You know, Bobby, I think that a Goan farmer like your father may have just the expertise we need for a very special purpose. Let me think about it for a while and I'll let you know what I'm proposing he do, okay?" Yancey said.

We were all a little surprised by Yancey's comment to Bobby but had little doubt that he was serious and not just trying to make Bobby feel better. As it turned out, Yancey was right-on about our need for Mr. Padawal.

chapter 10

THE PROBLEM THAT Yancey and Charlie were having had to do with the way the eggs absorbed the enzyme. It's very hard to pass something alien through an egg's outer shell even though it's porous. The egg has many layers of protection to prevent foreign substances from penetrating down to the cell nucleus. It could be done, of course, by direct mechanical insertion one egg at a time, but that was totally impractical. But Charlie's expertise in biochemistry came through, and by early August they had cracked the problem by placing their special enzyme in a colloidal suspension with a protein that the nucleus accepted as friendly.

Using a climate-controlled greenhouse that accommodated a sustainable population of Frankenslugs, Yancey and Charlie found that their remutation success rate for the enzyme application was almost 100 percent. Not all the eggs that hatched were normal *Arion distinctus,* but the abnormal ones didn't survive and a slightly higher number than expected were not even viable, but they were greatly encouraged since none of the hatchlings were *Arion d. distinctus*—my original Frankenslugs. Yet even more encouraging was the fact that the Frankenslugs did not try to eat their offspring! They couldn't figure this peculiarity out, but it didn't matter. This would greatly reduce the time for total replacement.

When Yancey and Charlie discovered that their enzyme approach would be successful Charlie related to me her conversation with Yancey. He asked her how long or how many generations it would take to completely replace the sub-species.

Charlie explained that currently it took six weeks for a new generation, and each generation could survive on average nine generations. She told me that we could make the place colder to reduce that time but that wouldn't be of help in the Middle East.

She told Yancey, "To play it safe, we should plan on applications every six weeks for eighteen months to take us out to the three sigma level. That's a long time to wait, but if after that time all the sub-species members are eradicated and only the common garden variety is left and the soil is on its way to restoration, that would be a major accomplishment."

I said, after hearing Charlie's analysis, "I only hope that during the treatment period we can prevent a war from happening."

———

Yancey announced at our project meeting on Wednesday of that week, "Well, as you all have heard we've developed a successful enzyme. Now, have you two come up with anything new on your manufacturing and distribution task?" he asked Bobby and me.

"Not really," I said. "I think we're in need of outside experts on this one. I'm not that knowledgeable about that end of the business world. I was thinking of calling Alan again to see if IBM would be interested in taking on the task, but..."

It was then that Yancey said, "Bobby, isn't it true that your father has that manufacturing expertise as well? I think now would be the time to bring him on board the project. How does that sound to you?"

"My father is *indeed* an expert in that area," Bobby said, smiling while recalling Yancey's promise from last month. "I think that would be a great idea. My father is a farmer who has lots of experience producing large quantities of liquid agro chemicals, which would be of great benefit to our project."

"And it would be coming from a country outside the United States, giving more credibility to our project as internationally based. I like that aspect. How soon do you think you could do that, Bobby? That is, talk with your father about our real work and get his input on the issue?" I asked.

"I'll set up a teleconference with him tonight so I can show him my work—he'll like that—and then get his input on the enzyme production," Bobby said.

"Bobby, I have to remind you that you have to explain to your father that what we're doing is in the strictest confidence, and he cannot share it with anyone else. Will that be a problem?" I asked.

"Are you kidding? My father's an Indian businessman—he'll share nothing with anybody, unless it is to tell them that his son is a genius," Bobby said with an impish smile.

"George, I would think Dad would be the one to ask about product distribution. After all, he's working in transportation, and didn't we talk about this before? We weren't sure where he might come into the project, but now I think this is the place," Charlie suggested.

"Okay, we'll talk with Dad this weekend when we go into Warren," I said to Charlie, and then to the others, "I think he'll be pleased at what we're doing and may be in a good position to help out. GM has a number of partners in the farm equipment business—like giant fertilizing systems—and Dad's connections could certainly help us there."

"Okay, then it's settled," Yancey said. "You two should work on how you'll bring your fathers into the fold, and Charlie and I will continue refining our product, making sure that it can be produced consistently in large quantities. We'll meet again next week—that is, if the world is still here next week," Yancey said with a faux grimace.

We arrived at our house in Warren around noon on Saturday, August 8. My parents were expecting us and waited to have lunch until we arrived. They looked so down when Charlie and I first came in but started to perk up when we sat down at the big table in the dining room.

We were fairly quiet for the most part during lunch, just making small talk. After lunch Charlie helped Mom clean up and put away all the leftovers—there was enough left for the whole week.

I asked Dad to come down into the lab with me, saying I had something to show him. When we went down to the basement, I could tell that no one had been down there since Mackie and I worked on the slugs almost five years ago. Everything was covered with dust and the work tables looked like they could use a good washing down. Most of the equipment, including my microscopes, was protected with dust covers, but they too looked like they could use some work. The place looked sad, and I could tell that Dad felt uncomfortable, since it was mostly Mackie's place.

"I do all my photography digitally now so I don't use the darkroom anymore," he said as a way of explaining why the place was so unkempt.

"I know what you mean. I don't think anyone does photography with film anymore. Maybe you ought to redo this place into a den or rec room," I offered.

We sat down on one of the benches at the work table and Dad asked, "So what is it you wanted to show me?"

"I need your help, Dad," I said, and followed that with, "the world needs your help."

After I explained the whole problem to him, leaving out nothing, we just sat there for a while. Dad was deep in thought, but I could see that he was greatly troubled. Maybe I shouldn't have hit him with such a heavy burden. He and Mom were still trying to get over Mackie and Gerry's murder, and now to drop this on him was totally unfair.

"You know, George, we've been in contact with Professor Gittleman's family since the, uh...the tragedy," he said. "You have no idea how helpful they've been to us—they were Mary's family while she was there, and they truly loved her. They've shared so much about her—things we didn't know about, like her love of hiking around Mount Carmel and how excited she was when she found out she was expecting. She was finally certain of it enough and was going to tell us..." He paused, and I could see he was choking up. I wanted to hug him, but we were not that kind of family, so I just waited until he could start again.

"I've come to love them in a way no one could really understand— maybe because when I talk with them or write them e-mails, I feel I'm still in touch with Mary. Can you understand that, son?"

I didn't answer him; I just nodded and let Dad talk.

"And it's because of them—and maybe your sister—that after what you've told me, I will do my best to help out with your project. I could never sit by and watch the destruction of Israel, even before Mary went there. And maybe some day I'll be able to explain why. But now with Mary's adopted family—and in some sense, my family too—still there…there's no way I can sit and do nothing. I'm not exactly sure how I can help yet, but give me some time to work on it and I'll get back with you. You know GM no longer makes farm equipment, even tractors. But we do make some trucks for both military and civilian special purposes. But that's the easy part—from what you tell me you're going to need much, much more than a couple of trucks to distribute your enzyme and—"

"Hey, you two, are you going to be down there all day?" Charlie shouted from the top of the stairs.

"We're coming up now," Dad yelled back, and so we did.

While Dad and I were talking downstairs, Charlie was briefing Mom on what our conversation was about. She didn't bore Mom with all the technical details that I explained to Dad, she just told her enough so she too could understand the gravity of the situation.

Mom looked into Dad's eyes when we came up from the basement. We had been down there for over an hour. "Will you help them, Pieter?" she asked, already knowing the answer.

"I will try my best, Mimi, that's all I can do."

———————

Later that night back in East Lansing, Bobby called me to relate his earlier conversation with his father.

"Hallo, Papa, es iz Barindra," Bobby said, opening the teleconference with his father Sunday morning. He was speaking in an ancient form of Yiddish that his father had learned growing up and working with the Jewish merchants of Goa. He taught it to Bobby so that they might be able to conduct business in secret—so to speak—since it was highly unlikely that other Hindis understood what they were saying. Bobby told me how they got into the habit of speaking in Yiddish whenever they wanted to talk about things that they didn't want others to know about. As soon as Bobby's father heard him say hello and tell him in Yiddish that it was Barindra calling, he knew it was serious.

They were using teleconferencing because Bobby wanted to show his father some technical documents that he couldn't translate, but he knew his father would understand them. Bobby explained the whole project and how they were now at the point of having to produce millions of gallons of the enzyme mix that they planned on spreading like liquid fertilizer over the infected fields. He told his father the basic recipe for Yancey's soup and asked if he could produce it in the quantities they needed.

Yadu Padawal—Bobby's father—explained, "Barindra, I'm a farmer and a producer of spirits, I fully understand the problem. But even more important, after what you've told me, I also understand the need for the strictest of confidentiality in this matter. Let me think about it. I'll download the documents you've shown me and get back to you." He then added, "My son, I'm very proud of you, just like your mother would have been if she was here—but you already know that." Bobby said his father had a noticeable sadness in his voice, but he could tell his father felt better now that he would have something to help take his mind off his loss, and that made Bobby feel better too.

Bobby was satisfied with the conversation and had the feeling that his father had already solved the problem and would produce the soup. All he had to do was wait for his father to call him, so he could relax for the rest of the weekend after calling Yancey to fill him and Noreen in on his conversation. He also wondered how I was doing with my father and if I was having the same success so he called me too.

Maybe it's universal, but whenever I felt burdened beyond my capabilities, when I shared that burden with a close family member, like a parent or my sister, the problem would seem to melt away. I think Bobby must have felt that way too because both of us were quite relaxed and in a good mood on Monday when we further shared our certainty that our fathers would take care of our manufacturing and distribution problems. We should have realized that the expectations we had for our parents were a little too impractical and that the reality was far more complex. But at that time, we just wanted to believe that our problems were solved and that our dads were taking care of us once again.

———

Boris Bethelheim was in his DARPA office on Monday, August 10, when he got the memo from the vice president for research about our program and the current status of our remutation efforts. The VP kept Boris informed about a number of contracts that Boris funded to MSU for nonspecific faculty research grants. I also later learned that Boris knew he had to get me and Yancey involved with his program. The next day he notified us through his office that arrangements had been made to fly us to Washington for a proprietary conference on mutant slug remutation.

We weren't told who else would be at the conference, but Boris knew that we would come because our VP could not say no or even ask why we *had* to be there. We could have refused to attend, knowing that we would probably be getting funding from IBM—once the world was made safe again—but we still felt obligated to go to Boris' conference since he did pay for our original research. Also, as responsible faculty we knew that DARPA funding was much too important for MSU's academic research program; it was also nice for MSU that DARPA picked up the tab for Yancey and me to attend.

"I guess I'll finally be able to meet Dr. Strangelove after all," Yancey said on Tuesday when we were told about our trip to DC. "You've worked with him, George, what do you think this is all about?"

"With Boris it's hard to tell. I'm just curious as to why after almost seven months into our project he's asking us to attend some conference. You'd have thought if he was so interested in our program he would have called to talk about what we're doing long ago," I answered. "I don't like it. I don't trust him and I'll bet everything I own that it was one of his classified projects that initiated that highly engineered version of *Arion d. distinctus* found in the Middle East."

"Well, the only way we'll find out is to ask him when we see him," Yancey said.

"Are you okay with all of this?" Charlie asked me that night as we lay in bed.

"Actually, no. Why didn't he invite you too? He should've known that you're an integral part of our team. What's his problem?"

"George, you know I'm not officially part of the team. Nowhere in the university is my name associated with the project. Boris probably doesn't even know I'm involved, so stop being so paranoid about him."

I knew she was right, but for some reason I didn't quite know why. I felt that Boris was getting his information from another source, like maybe GM. But I had no reason to suspect that Dad would keep Boris up-to-date on our work. But still, Gerry had implanted distrust for Boris in me a long time ago, and I'd never forgotten it. I finally fell asleep with a million scenarios running through my head about what I would do in DC. I barely slept at all Tuesday night.

It was hard to concentrate on anything else Wednesday morning at our project meeting. Noreen presented her update on the political situation in the Middle East, warning us that the area was extremely close to some kind of confrontation, but she still kept her clock at three minutes to midnight.

Bobby and I both talked about the success we thought we had had with our fathers to get Yancey and Charlie's enzyme solution in the field.

"Sounds good to me," Yancey said, "but let's wait till we hear back from your parents before we do any celebrating. Getting their support is one thing, but actually getting the job done is another. In any case George and I leave this evening to attend some kind of *proprietary*—whatever that means—conference about our work. Any words of wisdom, Bobby, Charlie, Noreen?"

"Ask him why they did it—why they poisoned the soil. Did they think that it would destroy the coalition or maybe save Israel? Ask him *why*," Bobby said with a passion in his voice that I had not heard before.

"I think the first thing we need to ask is *if* they did it. If they deny it then any follow-up like that, Bobby, would be useless," Yancey answered.

"But if they don't deny it then will you ask Bobby's question?" Charlie inquired.

Yancey answered her like he had already played that scenario out. "Probably. But first I think we should find out if they're able to control their slugs; and if they're not, then I think we should offer to help them out through our project. Once we get to be part of the solution, then we can ask all kinds of policy questions. But first, let's see what the hell this is all about. Does everyone agree to that?"

We all nodded in agreement, and after a pause Noreen joined in on the debate.

"You know there's a history of scientists and engineers getting involved in policy decisions at the highest levels of government with mixed results.

On occasion rogue science-based agencies cloaked in secrecy and having a perceived technological or scientific fix on a pressing, usually vital, issue have made pacts with other clandestine agencies, like the CIA. In many cases the agencies initiating the so-called *fix* had little oversight from the nonmilitary government agencies, and so they were able to carry out their own policy solutions to problems they had no business, or the authority, to get into in the first place."

We listened attentively to Noreen since she was our policy expert.

"I think that this might be the case here. I think that DARPA—or more specifically, Boris Bethelheim—worked out some arrangement with either the CIA or some other highly-trained military black-ops group to distribute the slugs. I don't think he'll tell you the truth on this one. If I'm right about the genesis of the project, then he can't tell you."

"You got that one right, Noreen," Yancey said. "However, I think we're all in agreement on this one: stop the slug infestation first, then argue about policy later…if we can, okay?"

———

It was hot and humid, and it looked like thunderstorms were on the horizon when we arrived at Boris' lab at DARPA's headquarters in Arlington, Virginia. Things looked pretty much the same as when I was there four years ago, though not as new. As we walked into Boris' office at 8:30—the time he told us to be there—I was surprised to see a copy of my dissertation on his desk.

"Come in, come in, George, so good to see you again. And Professor Stetson, finally getting to meet you. Come, sit here by the table. The conference doesn't start until nine," Boris said as we sat down at his small table. "George, I've been rereading your dissertation; and Professor Stetson, I've also read your report to the State Department on the slugs you analyzed from Syria. That was a couple of years ago when you were in Lebanon, right? I think you two are our foremost experts on the problem we need to discuss over the next couple of days. That's why I wanted you here for the conference—to be perfectly frank, if you two couldn't make it there would be no conference."

"Could you be a little more specific as to how you see us participating in your conference?" Yancey asked.

"Of course. We've been asked by the State Department to come up with some way to neutralize those slugs you discovered in that region of Syria and Iran. Failing that, then we've been asked to eliminate them in such a way that the land would become fertile again. Based on your knowledge, we thought that you two could help us out."

"How do you think the slugs got there in the first place?" Yancey asked. He was, as always, direct and right to the point.

"We don't know. State's been working on that end of it—and that's not our concern actually. We didn't create the problem, but as it frequently happens in these cases, we've been asked to solve it." Boris paused here and, looking directly at me, said, "They think it might have been used as a weapon by some country, or some group, and since our job is to understand how weapons work, we've been picked to solve it."

I got the distinct feeling that Boris was not being totally truthful, but for some reason he seemed concerned that I believed him. I found out from Dad years later what that reason was.

"What makes you think *we* can solve it?" Again, Yancey got right to the heart of the matter.

"Hmm, interesting that you should ask. After looking at your work, I think you two are the only ones who *can* solve it. I should also think you would know that. We know that the slugs are *Arion d. distinctus*, and that's the same sub-species that you found in Syria. We also know that George's dissertation describes how the mutation of those particular slugs occurred. And, we also know that you two are currently working on a remutation of the mutated slugs. No one else, at least that we know of, has your expertise." Boris paused. "I sense you're having some trouble here, Professor Stetson, am I right?" he asked with a noticeable sourness in his voice.

"To be perfectly frank with you, Dr. Bethelheim, I am concerned. I honestly believe that the United States is the only country capable of pulling off that kind of operation. Professor Brachmann and I have been working on a project that would hopefully neutralize—to put it into your words—the mutant slugs. We are willing to help in the Middle East for the purposes of saving lives and hopefully preventing a regional war. But we want your assurance first that our government was not responsible for that infestation."

"I can't give you that," Boris said. "Do you have any idea how many various governmental agencies are involved in nation-building projects? I'm sure you don't. And any one or some combination of those agencies was capable of putting together some kind of policy assisting program. I'm not privy to that kind of information. But I can assure you that the people you'll meet today are not responsible for the crop losses, and they want to help rid the world of this crisis as much as you do. Look, if you don't feel comfortable working with us on this project, then forgive me for inviting you and making you the centerpiece of the conference. It's your choice. Will you help us?" Boris asked. He looked down at his white coat and brushed off some crumbs in such a nonchalant manner that I could tell it was important to him that we stay. "By the way, Professor Stetson, please call me Boris."

"We would be willing to help out since we agree that the problem is apparently at a crisis stage," I said, "and we certainly believe that we should do whatever we can to resolve it. Do you have an agenda for the conference?"

"Yes, it's right here," Boris said, handing us an agenda. While we looked it over Boris said, "George, I never had the chance to tell you how sorry I was to hear about your sister and her husband. I know that you'd want to do whatever is in your power to see to it that those people who attacked her will never do that again. I've spoken to your father and assured him that the country will do everything in its power to prevent another attack like that."

———————

There were about fifteen people in the large conference room where we would be working for the next day and a half. I didn't recognize anyone from my previous work there except for a chemist who turned out to be Dr. Elizabeth Munsing, a bio-chemical engineer and Boris' senior researcher. I recalled briefly meeting her when Charlie and I first arrived there in May of 2011. Everyone who was attending the conference was already in the room when Yancey, Boris, and I entered shortly after nine o'clock.

"Welcome, everybody, glad to see that you are all here for this most important conference," Boris said. He then introduced Yancey and me and had everyone else go around the table and introduce themselves and tell us what their area of expertise was. He also explained the reason why this was a proprietary meeting—because there were possible commercial interests involved for some attendees—and requested that we all abide by the rules of confidentiality. Before he left he turned the meeting over to his senior researcher.

Boris, looking at his watch, acted like he had other things to do, but I think he left because he didn't want to have to lie to us about his involvement in the slugs' infestation anymore.

Dr. Munsing was a tall, skinny, plain-looking woman with brunette hair that was slightly graying. She looked to be in her early fifties. She wore a long, white lab coat with her name and title embroidered over the upper pocket—just like Boris' coat. Under her coat I could see that she was neatly dressed, having on a simple gray, pinstripe suit with a plain white shirt. I thought it was a bit odd that she seemed so overly dressed for August in DC. She was officious as she read out the order of the presentations and how the conference would be conducted. When she was finished with her instructions, she called on the first presenter, a liaison officer from the State Department who would spell out their concerns.

Yancey and I weren't scheduled to talk until late in the afternoon under the section titled "Solutions and Mitigation." Most of the talks were well-prepared and expertly presented, but, with the exception of the State Department's briefing about the greater threat of war in the Middle. East, we learned very little new information about the slugs.

During lunch we talked with a number of the people in attendance. Most were from Boris' lab and the others were from other federal agencies that were asked to participate in the forum. Yancey and I would speak last, including time for a short Q&A session today. Tomorrow's session would be strictly Yancey and me going into detail about how we thought the slugs could be eradicated and what would be needed from the government or civilian contractors to get the job done.

We both felt comfortable with the way the conference was going and were impressed with the attendees. They all seemed like committed government employees who wanted to do what was best for our country and its foreign policy. Yancey and I both sincerely believed that Boris was right, that these people had no part in introducing the slugs. However, as it turned out that was not true.

The meeting started Friday at 8:30 a.m. sharp. Again, Dr. Munsing took the podium and summarized yesterday's session, spending a lot of time talking about Yancey's and my upcoming presentations. She explained that the rest of the morning we would be working as a team to come up with a viable program for the slugs' eradication. She emphasized that Yancey and I would chair this session, and she would simply control the meeting to make certain we stayed on point. Again, lunch would be brought in, and the meeting would officially conclude before lunch in case people wanted to leave early.

Yancey and I had told them yesterday about our work and how we were attempting to neutralize the slugs by mutating them back to a relatively harmless species. We immediately opened the floor for discussion on our approach.

"Why don't you just sterilize them?" an attendee asked.

Yancey smiled when he said, "To the best of my knowledge, it has not been tried using radiation on a hermaphroditic animal. When sterilization was used in other pest eradication programs, we focused on the males in the hopes that the sterilized ones mated with the females first, which would discourage the females from mating with the fertile males. It's not clear that we can do that with these animals to achieve a zero population outcome."

"What about hormones?" Dr. Munsing asked, her first time speaking at the conference as a participant. "I understand that hormones, when applied judiciously, can have the same effect as rendering the species infertile as if it was done by radiation. Have you considered that approach, Professor Stetson?"

"Yes, I have, and as a farmer I can tell you that the amount and type of hormones that would be needed to effectively render them sterile would make the soil as poisonous as the slugs did. Our enzyme is totally biodegradable and soluble, hormones aren't. I wouldn't want to raise any food crops for people or animals in soil having that much hormone product distributed on it."

Dr. Munsing neither agreed nor dissented; she listened politely, took notes, and let the discussion continue. After a few hours of good discussion with offers of help from the State Department to implement our program, if it was approved, we all congratulated ourselves on a fruitful and productive conference. While a sandwich lunch was being brought in, Dr. Munsing declared the conference over and thanked everyone for coming. She especially thanked Yancey and me and asked that we hold off from lunch there and join

Boris over a debriefing lunch in his office. We said our goodbyes to everyone, promising to stay in touch with those we would in all likelihood be working with in the future—*if our project was approved*—and left.

When we went back to Boris' office, he had a private lunch set up for just the three of us at his conference table.

"I took the liberty of having our meal sent here. I hope you don't mind. I know you're taking the five-twenty back to Lansing, and I wanted to have a chance to talk with you before you left. Is that all right? I promise to have you out of here by three."

It seemed someone had kept Boris fully informed of our talk, and he just wanted to make certain he fully understood what it was that we were doing.

"Do you think that it would be wise to have GM and that Goan Indian company do the manufacturing and distribution end of your project? How do you expect to get the support of Syria and Iran to let them in their countries to do that?" Boris asked.

We made it clear that we weren't completely settled on that end of the project, but with our contacts and Yancey's colleagues still in Lebanon, we felt we could do it.

"Let me tell you as an old government bureaucrat that what you're proposing will be quite a task for a nongovernmental agency to take on. You know it's wrought with danger, and if you fail—"

Yancey cut Boris off and said, "I'm not sure our own government is in any better position than us to pull it off. The distrust on the part of the coalition towards the United States will not be easy to overcome. Also, the lead time you guys need on something like this is just too long. We have to start now."

"You may be right. Let's just leave it at that for now, and may I just offer you the services of my office if at any time along the way you run into difficulties in carrying out your program. Can you accept that?" Boris asked.

I said, "Yes, we can, Boris. And let me thank you for your offer. We know that our work is not going to be easy, and we'll take all the help we can get down the line. We feel that many of the people we met these last couple of days would be able and willing to help, and with your permission we may contact some of them."

I didn't want to make an enemy of Boris now. Not until I was certain that he was not part of the problem. Yancey caught my meaning and joined with me in thanking Boris.

We got to the airport early and decided to get a drink and discuss that last meeting with Boris. The bar was not crowded, and we took a table near a window overlooking the tarmac. The weather was breaking, and sun could be seen streaking out from behind a fair-weather cloud.

I broke the silence, saying, "I hope it was all right for me to placate Boris at the end there. I know you were intent on having him admit he planted the slugs, but as Noreen said, I think he came as close as he could without giving it up. At least he admitted that it could have been one of our agencies. And as for his telling us that no one in the room was responsible, that might have been true...after he left."

We had been sitting there looking out the window at the variegated cloudy sky, pretty much wrapped up in our own thoughts. Yancey listened to me, and after a couple of minutes he asked, "Were you upset when he reminded you that it was Middle East terrorists that murdered your sister?"

"Not really. Unlike him I don't blame every Muslim for what happened to Mackie. If you're asking me if I want to get even...well, Yancey, you should know by now that I'm not made that way." I was playing with my napkin and realized how tense I was after Yancey's question. I relaxed a bit and said, "But I wonder what the fuck the policy advantage would be from such a stupid act—destroying food crops?"

"I would think he was hoping that the US would step in, solve the food crisis, and then get them to change their policy of hate and distrust towards us and Israel," Yancey answered.

"I can't believe he would be that naïve. If history is any teacher then he should know that buying a country's loyalty is not that easy. At least, not in these modern times when a ploy like that would immediately point the finger at us for creating the problem in the first place."

"You're right. But the problem now is to stop the slugs, and he can't do that. I think it was his intent to also stop the infestation while offering food, and since he couldn't control the slugs, he's looking for outside help. And that's where we come in," Yancey said.

"Do you think if we stop the slugs Boris will try to push his policy agenda to higher offices?" I wondered.

"To tell you the truth, I think if we can control the slugs and get the food supply back on track, Boris will be completely marginalized—and if not Boris, then whoever it was that planted the slugs in the first place will be out of the loop."

"Which begs the question: can we do it without Boris' help?" I asked.

"I don't know the answer to that one yet," Yancey said, "but I guess I'm not opposed to getting some help from Boris if there are no other options. What you're asking me is if we should make a pact with the devil to do God's work. That's almost biblical, and I'm not much of a Bible scholar. My gut tells me to do whatever it takes to get the job done. After we do that then we'll see what it is the devil—or in this case, Dr. Strangelove—wants for payment."

"Yancey, you are always so practical, and I feel that you're right on in this case, but..."

Yancey said, "Like the man told us, if we want out simply say so. Nothing's easier than that. I think I might have gone too far in casting him in the role of the devil. I think his love of country is unbounded. I also think that he's arrogant and full of self-importance, and it's that that makes him so dangerous...but he's not the devil. I'm sorry I led you to believe I felt that way."

"Then you're saying we should get his help?" I asked.

"Only if we really need it, but as I've said before, let's not get ahead of ourselves. Let's stick with our plan for now until we know for sure that we can't do it ourselves, and then we'll bring in Boris and the big guns."

Our plane was announced for boarding, and as we walked down the concourse to our gate, I couldn't help but feel uneasy. I guess I knew deep down that Boris was right, that depending on GM and Bobby's dad to carry out the plan would be too much to ask. I knew, as Boris suggested, that it would take an organization the size of a government to get the job done. Maybe Yancey felt that his Lebanese contacts were that government, but if that was so he never mentioned it.

PART III
TREATMENT
Fall 2015

chapter 11

THE SUMMER OF 2015 flew by, and we were well into the fall semester when we finally had to admit the obvious: we had made little progress on our project. The in-house project funding was for all practical purposes gone. We only had enough money to continue Bobby's research appointment, but that would end in January. The department continued to fund our lab space and support the few slugs we had left for research purposes, but it was made clear that if another faculty member received any kind of funding and needed our space, the project would be closed down. Noreen had moved the hands to two minutes before midnight and said that unless something was done soon, war between Israel and the coalition was all but inevitable. To say we were totally discouraged at our weekly meeting in late October would be putting it mildly.

It was my turn to open the meeting (Yancey and I would alternate running the meetings), and I said, "I suppose I could get Wackfield at IBM to support my recombinant DNA programs, but that wouldn't be enough to keep this project open at any level worth mentioning."

Charlie had been in contact with Dad about the trucks, and she said, "Dad was very discouraged about getting any support from GM. It seems that GM doesn't see it as humanitarian aid, and without knowing exactly what it is their trucks will be spreading around, they're noncommittal about wanting to get involved. They also don't think their trucks would work. They claim that special purpose farm equipment would probably be needed, and they don't manufacture any. I think we've struck out there. But Dad insisted on continuing to pursue the delivery system any way he could."

"Maybe we should tell him to back off for now until we know for sure we can get the enzyme solution. What does your father say, Bobby? Are we still in business?" I asked.

"I talked with him yesterday, and he's not sure he can manufacture our solution. It's not the technical element of the problem, it's the cost. He simply can't afford to build a facility to manufacture the product in the quantities we would need. His estimate places the cost at over one hundred and twenty-eight million dollars, and that doesn't include labor costs. He was wondering if we could come up with the funds somehow."

"Ouch!" Yancey said. "I kind of suspected that it wouldn't be cheap, but I didn't think it would be that expensive. In any case, I'm certain that we couldn't get it done cheaper anywhere else. I think we have to pull the plug on this one unless we can come up with the money and resources to get it done."

"What about your contacts in Lebanon?" I asked. "Could they in any way help out on this?"

"Unfortunately, they're like our fellow academics everywhere else in the world: they have great ideas and noble ambitions, but they don't have any money. I suspect their government contacts are like ours—namely Boris—and they would have to get in bed with them to get the job done. Like us, they don't want to form that kind of a relationship with their own home-grown ideologues either."

"There's been a huge build-up of military personnel on the Egyptian-Israel border," Noreen said. "And we're seeing military activity in Syria and Iran at levels we've not seen before. Also, the rhetoric about Israel launching biological weapons of mass destruction on their lands is getting more intense. I've never seen anything like it on Al Jezeera before—I think this is it!"

"How long do you think they have before they launch a full-scale war?" Yancey asked her.

"You know I can't predict that, but my best guess is that it's weeks, maybe a couple of months at most. I think they would like to launch a winter attack so their troops would be back in time for planting and harvesting the few crops they expect this year. They're brazen enough to think that a full-fledged attack on Israel would last only days, and then it would all be over with just mopping up and taking over control of Israel in time for spring."

"Can they do that?" I asked incredulously.

"No. Israel will in all likelihood launch precision air strikes and even tactical atomic weapons, which will completely muddle the situation for the rest of the world. In fact, it wouldn't surprise me if Israel launched strategic atomic weapons—ballistic missiles—in a preemptive strike if they think that an attack is imminent. And if that happens..." she said, leaving her thoughts hanging.

We were all silent after that, not knowing what to say or even what to do. Needless to say we were all fairly shaken up for the rest of the day, and none of us could do any meaningful work. When we left in the afternoon, we went home not knowing who we could turn to, or if we were even in the game anymore. At dinner Charlie and I hardly spoke, but as the evening wore on I concocted a plan. It wasn't developed enough to talk about yet, but a plan was there and it was growing.

On a beautiful fall Tuesday in early November at exactly noon Jerusalem time, missiles exploded in the troposphere over Cairo, Damascus, Beirut, and Tehran. But instead of a nuclear holocaust, leaflets fell from the sky. It took a long time for the leaflets to reach the ground, demonstrating that if it had been nuclear warheads instead of leaflet delivery systems, given the height of the initial explosions the bombs would have completely wiped out the cities. The hundreds of thousand of leaflets in each missile carried the same message, written in Arabic and English:

ISRAEL DOES NOT WANT WAR.

URGE YOUR LEADERS TO PULL THEIR ARMIES BACK. LET THIS
HARMLESS MESSAGE BE A WARNING THAT IF ANY COUNTRY
IN THE COALITION LAUNCHES A WAR, ALL THE COUNTRIES
IN THE COALITION WILL SUFFER. IF THIS MESSAGE HAD BEEN
A TRUE RESPONSE TO A WAR STARTED BY YOUR LEADERS,
THEN WHOEVER CAN READ THIS LEAFLET WOULD HAVE
BEEN SERIOUSLY HARMED.

ACT NOW TO PREVENT TOTAL DESTRUCTION
OF YOUR COUNTRY.

The United States satellite missile-tracking stations reported spotting the simultaneous launches from four silos in Israel and the high-altitude explosions just a few minutes after the launch. The sequence was such that no response could have occurred in time to prevent a warhead from detonating if that was what the missile had carried.

The next day, at our November 11 meeting, Noreen gave her take on Israel's motive for the leaflet attack. "The height of the deployment could not have been missed by the coalition. They would have realized that if they attacked Israel, it would be a mass suicide mission. Even if they knew where all of Israel's silos were located—which they probably don't—they couldn't wipe them out in time. They would also know that the amount of time, even though it was literally just minutes, that it would take for them to launch an attack on Israel would still give the Israelis enough time to annihilate them."

Noreen also told us that there had been calls for sanctions against Israel by the coalition and their allies in the UN for their unprovoked act of war and the threat of nuclear extinction. The United States and our allies passed it off as a simple and realistic fair warning to the coalition for its vast arms buildup with only one target in their sites: Israel. They also noted that nowhere in the warning was nuclear weaponry mentioned. They also threatened to veto any sanctions imposed on Israel for a simple warning and said that, if anything, sanctions should be considered against the coalition for considering acts of war on its part.

We learned much later from Boris that what wasn't known by the UN at that time was that both the United States and Russia had privately told the coalition that the promised food shipments to replace their lost crops would not be forthcoming if they continued their belligerent actions against Israel. After a few more days of saber rattling and denouncements against Israel, Egypt began pulling its army back from their border, and military buildups in Syria and Iran seemed to ease off. Also, the rhetoric against Israel cooled down for the most part. However, Syria and Iran continued their harangue against Israel with little or no effect.

"I see that your clock is back to three minutes," I told Noreen at our meeting the week after the leaflet attack. We were still meeting on Wednesdays even though there didn't seem to be much to do anymore. But we continued to pursue our project and would do so until the Ag Department threw us out of our space.

"Yes, I think the Israeli warning was effective—at least for now. The hostility is still there, and unless something changes it's not going to go away. I personally feel that if the food shortage continues and if prices and unemployment continue to rise at their current rates, then eventually the coalition may risk the suicide option just to gain back their control of their own population. That's why my clock is at three minutes instead of, say, four or five."

Yancey said, "So we're still between the proverbial rock and a hard spot. The farm lands are not in any condition to farm yet, and the slugs, although many have been wiped out by conventional pest control methods or simply died off from their own nature of killing the soil, are still out of control on the periphery. They still could continue to do serious damage, and if they travel out of the area," he warned, "then all bets are off. We have to carry out our project to save the soil. But if we do that, we may just strengthen the coalition to the point that once things are under control, they may once again want to take up arms against Israel."

"It's all moot," Charlie said with a resignation in her voice that concerned me. "We simply don't have the funds or the clout to save the land. Maybe we could mount a massive Facebook campaign, but I don't think that would work anymore. In fact, it may even prove counterproductive. I'm at the point where I just want to get back to my own research on green energy programs and leave these massive international issues to be resolved by the fucking politicians. Enough!" And then she started to cry.

I put my arms around my wife and held her tight. Bobby discretely left the lab, saying he had a class, while Noreen and Yancey hung around quietly while Charlie regained her composure. It was then that she told Yancey and Noreen that she was pregnant and that her hormones seemed to be taking control of her emotions. We had known for over a month now that we were going to have a baby but had decided to wait until we could tell everyone.

I didn't mention my latest idea, and under the circumstances I knew it could wait. Noreen was all over Charlie, hugging her and kissing her cheeks and wishing us both much happiness and good health. Noreen promised us

138

that she had two outstanding babysitters just waiting for the opportunity to work for us. The two women hugged and kissed each other again as tears streamed down Charlie's cheeks.

Yancey, with his Midwestern grounding, laid it out for me in simple terms: "Congratulations, old man. I know there never appears to be a time in history that seems right to bring kids into this world, but we all do it anyway." We were all smiling by then and feeling good. There would be time enough for more tears later.

"Hello, Dad? It's me, George."

"George! It must be important for you to be calling me at work. Is everything all right?"

It was Thursday, November 19, when I called my father. My plan was beginning to gel, but I needed some confirmation that I wasn't completely off my skull before I broached it to the rest of the team. I knew that Charlie was planning on calling our parents either that night or the next day to tell them the news about our baby, and I wanted to talk to my father before he got all emotional on me.

"Yes, everything is okay, I just have something I want to run by you, and I wanted to do it before the week was over. Is it all right, or are you too busy to talk now?" I asked.

"I'm not busy...what did you want to know?" he asked anxiously.

"Do you think Tikva Gittleman would be willing to help us out on our project?"

"I'm not sure. What kind of help are you talking about?"

I explained how we all knew now that it would take a country to carry out our plan. No single institution or combination of organizations like MSU and GM was capable of pulling off a project on the scale we were talking about. There was only one country in the Middle East that had the technical resources to do that, and that was Israel. I wanted to know if Tikva was in any position to find out if Israel would be willing to save the Islamic coalition.

After I filled Dad in on my thinking, he said, "I know that she's a close friend of the Ben-Isaacs. Professor Ori Ben-Issac is the director of the Technion's Industrial Affiliates Program—that's the program that invited Mary and Gerry to Israel with IBM's participation. I think your plan has some merit and is not as strange as you think it is. And I think Tikva might be just the person to take it on. She's been looking for something to do that would be a meaningful and peaceful response to that monstrous attack on our families. The Technion, you know, has a lot of political influence in Israel, so if they believe in your plan then it is a distinct possibility."

I sensed that Dad seemed to be holding back on something, that he knew more than he was willing to tell me now. "Will you ask her, Dad?" I knew the answer before I even asked.

"Yes, but I should tell you not to get your hopes up. Even if she says yes, like I did when you asked for my help, it's no guarantee that it will happen. You have no idea about the political elements you're facing trying to get Israel to work with the coalition, let alone the skepticism of many people about the threat from the slugs. Even here at GM I've been told that my efforts were considered to be silly by some high level people. Someone close to me, on the inside, said that they referred to my request as 'trying to prevent homeless snails from destroying the earth.' Can you believe that? They called slugs *homeless snails*."

"I've never heard slugs referred to as that—"

Dad just kept on talking. "You know I believe you and support you, but I'm your father. Anyway, yes…of course I'll ask her to talk to Professor Ben-Isaac. But you may want to consider an alternate plan just to be on the safe side." I was about to respond when Dad added, "Oh, and by the way, since that warning from Israel to Egypt and the others in the Middle East, many people are thinking the threat is over. I don't, but I'm not the decision maker here."

All I needed was for Dad to get the ball rolling in Israel to get the plan started. The next day I got a hold of Yancey and met with him at the college—just the two of us. I wanted to run my plan by him before bringing it up at Wednesday's meeting.

I filled Yancey in on my conversation with Dad and waited for it to soak in a little before saying, "Am I off my rocker or do you think we have a chance at it?"

Yancey was quiet. He was sipping a cup of coffee slowly. Finally, he put his cup down and told me, "You know, ever since Bobby told us his father needed over a hundred million dollars to build a plant for our project, I've been thinking about what we were trying to do. I really hadn't given the distribution effort that much thought before. You see, George, in Kansas we have a well-defined method for farming. We know when to plant, when to sow, when to fertilize, when to weed, when to leave some fields fallow—it's a highly technical and exacting business of knowing how much we can farm, when to do it, and what we need to get it done. If we didn't know all those things, we could be broke after one season. When Bobby told us the cost, I began doing some calculations just to see if Bobby's dad might have overestimated the cost, and I came to the conclusion that he actually underestimated it."

"Are you saying we can't do it?" I asked.

"I'm saying that we have to do it right. Simply dumping the enzyme solution over all the farmland is way too inefficient and expensive, and it would take way, way too much time. We have to do it right—we have to do it like farmers."

"How's that?" I asked.

"Look, we know that the slugs are now concentrated at the periphery of the fields, that the center of the fields are essentially dead and there are no viable slugs living there. We have to treat the high probability sites first. Second, the area is so large now, covering cities, villages, roads, woodlands—you name it—we can no longer treat it with one mass delivery system, even if we had the trucks and distributing machinery. What we have to do is come up with the amount of product we need to just cover the land that contains the slugs. We have to have a prioritization procedure for doing that. If we can do that—I guess I should say *if Israel* can do that—then we'd be home."

"So you like my plan?" I yelled out.

"Shhh...calm down. I didn't say that, I just said that—"

"Yeah, I know, you said '*if Israel*'...and it's a mighty big if. But what do you think we need to do just in case Israel is interested in doing it?"

"Come up with a prioritization scheme and a new estimate of product. If it's done right—that is, by the most efficient procedure you can design—then we have a chance for success. We need to do it like farmers." Yancey picked up his cup of coffee, took a sip, and made a sour face. "The coffee's cold," he said with little emotion.

***

Over the weekend Charlie called our folks on both sides of the ocean and told them that they would be grandparents next year. Needless to say there was great warmth and love expressed during those phone calls. All kinds of admonitions about how Charlie should take care of herself and how I shouldn't let Charlie lift anything over twenty pounds (she never did that anyway) made us smile the whole weekend.

On Monday morning in our project office, Bobby was working on some of his other class work when I asked him, "What do you know about the Traveling Salesman Problem?"

"I had that problem in my Operations Research class as an undergrad. We looked at a number of possible solutions—you know, finding the shortest path to go from city to city without going through the same city twice. I can look that up again, if you like. Why do you ask?"

I explained Yancey's observation about being efficient and how the TSP—as the problem is called—might be an approach to getting that prioritization scheme he said we needed. "Do you think you can give us a presentation on it by Wednesday at our meeting?"

"Oh, sure, no problem, George, I can do that," Bobby said with his usual self-confidence. One thing about Bobby, when it came to problem solving using computational methods, he seemed to know them all. I couldn't get over how well-trained Indian computer engineers were. No wonder they took the lead in computational analysis in South Asia and had been challenging the East Asians in that field.

"Get a map of the farmlands in Iran and Syria that have been decimated by the slug infestation. See if you can come up with a list—or a number—of centers that have to be treated. Just get a rough estimate now so we can get a handle on how long it might take to come up with a solution. Will you be able to do that as well by Wednesday?"

"No problem!" That was Bobby's standard reply when asked to do a difficult task. He would say that and then tilt his head to one side, acting like you just asked him to simply erase the blackboard.

———————

When I came home on Monday evening, Charlie was already there. Her Monday schedule was light so she usually got home by three and either worked at home or cooked us a great dinner. I was beginning to feel good about our project again and our ability to get the job done. The semester was half over, and people were already thinking about final exams and winter break. I was thinking how fast time was flying and realized that we probably should be doing some planning for our baby, who was due around mid-June of next year.

Almost as soon as I walked in Charlie said, "I think we should look into renting a house in Okemos. It would be great to be closer to Noreen and the girls; I'd like that very much. What do you think, George?"

"Great idea. I think we can't afford to buy right now so renting would be good. Why don't you ask around at the housing office to see if any rentals are coming up soon? And let's ask Yancey and Noreen to keep an eye open as well." Charlie was tired a lot lately so I didn't push her about dinner. "How about if I make us omelets for dinner?"

"Echh!"

"Still nauseated?" I asked.

"That…and the fact that I have no appetite. Nothing sounds good to me. I thought pregnant women were supposed to crave pickles and ice cream or things like that. I don't have any craving for any food," Charlie answered. "Why don't you just cook for yourself, George? I'll grab an apple or some-thing later."

After I finished cooking my omelet, Charlie peeled and cored an apple, cut it into about twenty pieces, put it on a plate, and sat down to join me for dinner.

"George, I don't think I'll be coming to the meetings on Wednesdays anymore. I hope you don't mind. My teaching and other research is keeping me busy, and I'm always so tired lately…"

"It's okay, honey, there's really not much you can do now anyway. In fact, Noreen won't be coming anymore either. She'll give Yancey an update and he'll tell us." Acting like an understanding husband and first-time future father should act, I took her hand and said, "Being pregnant is no picnic—I know because I've checked it out on the Internet," I said naively. "No need to feel guilty—I'll fill you in on what's going on, and if we need you I know you'll be there." I could see she was feeling guilty, so I added, "It was nice the way all our parents got excited about the baby last weekend. I think we've made them very happy, don't you?" I asked.

Charlie was smiling now as she nibbled on a small piece of apple. "Yeah, it was nice how they responded. You're so understanding, George. You know I really love you," she said with tears in her eyes.

"Hey, cheer up," I said, "I haven't filled you in on my plan yet, would you like to hear it?" I told her all about my talks with Dad, Yancey, and Bobby about getting Israel on board to do the treatment in a more efficient and cost-effective manner.

"That's brilliant, George. It can't miss—I'm so excited for you. I was certain that the project was dead in the water, but now..."

"It's far from a done deal, but at least it's a viable—well, almost a viable plan, and we're all working on it. I'm psyched."

We cuddled up on the couch after dinner, and we enjoyed each other's company physically and emotionally, and that night we enjoyed each other's bodies as well. I had read that some pregnant women became easily aroused, and without having to worry about birth control, we had one of the best nights sexually that we had had in months. I also slept well that night, something I hadn't been able to do lately. When I awoke, I was looking forward to our meeting tomorrow and getting started on the hard work in front of us.

At the meeting I asked Bobby, "Were you able to get all that done for today, Bobby? I know I asked a lot of you on Monday, so what have you got?"

"There's a bunch of methods out there that address the TSP, but I like the modified Branch and Bound method the best because—"

"Can you just cut to the chase?" Yancey asked impatiently, but with a smile.

"Oh, yes…uh, I looked at the maps and I think that there are some-where between two and five thousand centers, and with that many places we should use that TSP method I just mentioned. The problem, of course, is the computer time requirements for getting an optimal solution. It could take hours on our machines, so do you think we can get IBM to let us have time on one of their Blue Gene machines? That would help considerably."

I shrugged and said, "I don't know, but I'll ask Alan Wackfield when the time comes."

Then Yancey said, "Bobby, if you have a little time after the meeting today, I'd like to see how you got those centers. I think you're on the right track, but I have some agriculture maps of that area that might help to nar-row it down even more. The more efficient we are in planning our strategy the cheaper and quicker we can get it done."

We finished up with a few other items and ended the meeting. I wished Yancey and Bobby a happy Thanksgiving and told them that I looked for-ward to next week when we would have a better handle on our approach. I would be in Warren for the holiday and would be talking with my dad about how he made out with Tikva in Israel and would update everyone about that at our next meeting.

"George, you know that even if Israel says yes, we're still going to need our government's support to implement the plan. Have you been thinking about that?" Yancey asked.

"One word: Boris," I said.

Yancey smiled, shook his head, and said, "Good luck!" He was getting up from the table and was about to leave when turned back to me and said, "Oh, almost forgot—found a place for rent on Shawnee Trail that's not far from us. You want me to have them hold it till you and Charlie can see it?"

"That'd be great, Yancey. What's the address? We'll drive by it on our way home this afternoon," I said. I couldn't wait to tell Charlie.

"Which one is it?" Charlie asked as we drove down Shawnee Trail.

"It's 2439…there, that's it on the right," I said. It was a California style ranch home, probably built in the sixties or even seventies, but the neigh-borhood was still very middle-class with neat lawns and well-maintained exteriors.

"You don't think we could just stop by and knock, do you?" Charlie asked.

"No...let's wait until Yancey asks them. This wouldn't be a bad place at all to live. Close to campus and just a few blocks from the Stetsons. It looks great, doesn't it?" I said.

Charlie nodded and had a contented smile on her face. It would be our first house, and I could see the wheels churning in her head—furnishing and decorating the baby's room and buying our first real bedroom set.

It was a typical late November day in Michigan, cloudy and gray. It had snowed last week, and the fields outside of Mason just east of East Lansing were still covered with a soft sheet of snow. It looked so peaceful to me. The flat fields of mid-Michigan and the light early-afternoon traffic made it an easy ride for the first hour or so. But as we got closer to the Detroit area, traffic began to pick up, and the lack of open snowy fields was a little disheartening. We drove into Warren a little after four in the afternoon. Even though it was the day before Thanksgiving, traffic was actually lighter than I had expected. It was already starting to get dark as we drove up to my parents' house.

———

We barely got inside with our backpacks before Mom was all over Charlie. "How are you feeling? Is the baby all right? You look thin—are you eating?" she asked after almost smothering her with hugs and kisses.

Dad was more subdued, as expected, but he too couldn't help but gush a little. "Come in, you two, come in. Here, George, put your bags down, you can put it away later." He quickly turned to Charlie and said, "Let me look at you, little mother." I don't know what he expected to see since she was barely two months pregnant and wasn't showing at all. But he took both her hands into his and, pulling her arms aside, he stepped back to look at her belly. Smiling as if he could actually see the baby through her coat, clothes, and tummy, he then pulled her forward and gave her a big hug. I was glad that we had given the folks something so nice to look forward to—and I think Charlie did too, even though I don't think she was too fond of being called *little mother*.

After settling in we had a light dinner. Charlie gave the excuse that we ate a late lunch and weren't hungry to explain why we hadn't eaten very much. I was starved, but I didn't want to make Charlie the bad guy on this one, so I just let my stomach growl. Of course we knew that tomorrow would be a real Thanksgiving feast, and Charlie would have to come clean with Mom about her eating habits. But it could wait for now.

"How about something to drink, George?" Dad asked after dinner. He didn't offer Charlie anything since she was pregnant, and Mom rarely drinks, so it would be just the two of us. We went into the den where dad had a little bar while Mom and Charlie talked in the living room. Dad's bar was just a modest liquor cabinet with an assorted collection of glasses and snifters—no sink or fridge. "Cognac?" he asked.

"That would be great. Do you still have any of that Courvoisier XO left that you got as a present a couple of years ago?"

Dad smiled as he pulled out the odd looking, teardrop shaped bottle that was still half-full and poured two large snifters around a quarter full. "Do you want me to warm it a little in the microwave?" he asked.

"No, no...this will be fine," I said as I wrapped my hands around the large glass to warm the honey-colored liquor.

"George, you and I will be staying up late tonight. We'll be calling Israel to talk with Tikva around one—is that all right with you?"

"Of course!" I said. "What's going on?"

Dad explained that he talked briefly with her last week after I called, and they planned on talking again this week when I would be in town. "She was impressed with the plan, and she's happy to get involved. She was going to be making some contacts for us and wants to give us feedback as soon as it was possible for the two of us to be together."

———————

"Hello, Tikva—I can see you, but I don't hear you yet," Dad was saying over the Skype line.

After some clicking and adjusting on Tikva's computer, she said, "Pieter, George, I can see both of you and hear you. Am I coming through?"

"You're coming through fine now. How have you been? How are the kids?" I asked.

We hadn't talked in almost a month. The last time we talked was on Avi's *yahrtzeit*—the one-year anniversary of the attack. They had just returned from the cemetery where they held the unveiling of Avi's headstone. I had been reading up on Jewish death and burial practices and was aware that headstones were unveiled at the gravesite around a year after the person's death. In fact, I even lit two *yahrtzeit* candles for Mackie and Gerry last month because they were my family, and they died in Israel—I thought it was just something we should do. We didn't say any prayers, but just the lighting of the solemn candles in their traditional glass container gave us both comfort.

"Everyone's good—thanks for asking. Listen, I've been talking with Ori Ben-Isaac about your plan, George, and even though he thinks you're crazy, he said he would help. Pieter, could you bring George to Israel early next month to meet with Ori and go over the plan in detail? Ori wants to meet you two after I told him all about how you've been trying to get GM involved. I can't promise you anything, George, but if Ori buys into the project then I'll do all the legwork—and trust me, in Israel that will be a lot of work because of this country's outmoded bureaucracy," she said with a knowing smile.

"We'll be there as soon as we can get away, right, George?" Dad said.

"I can't do it much sooner than mid-December because of exams, but that gives us three weeks to polish up our presentation, okay? Really looking forward to seeing you in person and meeting the kids. We'll talk again before we leave," I said.

"Me too, Tikva, I'm really looking forward to this visit," Dad said.

After we signed off, we decided to have another cognac. Even though Dad appeared relaxed, I could tell he was psyched. I hadn't seen him this excited about anything in a very long time. "I wonder if your mother wants to go?" he asked, without actually asking me.

"I was wondering the same about Charlie," I said. We sat there quietly for a minute, and then I said, "I'm hungry—I'm going to make myself a sandwich and go to bed. We'll talk to Charlie and Mom tomorrow, okay?" And with that Dad went upstairs while I went into the kitchen.

We had to wait till almost 2 a.m. to call Tikva, so it was almost 3 a.m. when I finally got into bed. Charlie was fast asleep and didn't even stir when I crawled in. I could hear soft voices from my parents' room, and I knew Dad was telling Mom all about our talk and asking her if she wanted to go. I was thinking of doing the same with Charlie but decided to wait until tomorrow. I think the sandwich I ate was keeping me awake, and I didn't fall asleep until it was almost time to get up. My restlessness was probably due more to what was on my mind than the ham sandwich, but I was feeling good knowing that we were finally doing something positive to get the project back on point.

I had to smile to myself as I thought about eating the *ham* sandwich on kosher rye.

chapter 12

We landed at Ben Gurion on Monday, December 21 during a mild rain shower. I was surprised how cold it was—barely fifty degrees. But I was told that wasn't unusual for Tel Aviv at this time of year. After clearing customs Dad got us a private car, not a sherut, to drive us to Haifa where we would be meeting Tikva at her house. Mom and Charlie were as excited as Dad and I were, but for different reasons—Dad and I for getting Israel involved in the project and Charlie and Mom for seeing the Holy Land. It was late afternoon when we got to Tikva's place in her storied Carmel neighborhood.

"Finally, I get to see you all in person—my Michigan family!" Tikva said when we drove up. She greeted us all with hugs and kisses while Ben, a handsome fourteen-year-old, and Avigail, a beautiful sixteen-year-old, stood behind her with shy smiles on their faces. "Come in, come in...how was the flight? I bet you're all tired and starved," she was saying as we walked into her house. She had the table set and showed us where to freshen up. She explained that she knew we would be hungry but not for a heavy meal, so she just had a bunch of salads and side dishes, like hummus and tahini and some stuffed grape leaves.

But first there were more hugs and kisses all around. We did feel like family, and you could see Mom and Dad looking at everything. I'm certain they were thinking, *so this is where Mackie and Gerry sat when they were here.*

Dad started talking to Ben, asking him all kinds of questions about what he wanted to be, and discovered that Ben—not surprisingly—was interested in science like his father, Avi. Dad then took out an envelope and gave it to him saying, "I'm sorry I missed sending you this for your Bar Mitzvah last year, so will you please accept it now?"

Ben looked at his mother as if to say, *Is it all right?* When Tikva nodded, Ben took the envelope and thanked Dad.

Mom then opened her travel bag and took out a small, nicely wrapped package and handed it to Avigail. "So, I see that you were sweet sixteen in June. Well, here is a little something for you too, and I should like to add that you are a very beautiful young lady," she said, handing the package to Avigail. Avigail didn't need her mother's approval; she took the package and, quickly thanking Mom, ran off to her room to see what it was. Ben followed his sister to see what was in his envelope as well.

"Pieter, Miriam, you didn't have to do that—but thank you for thinking of them," Tikva said, smiling at the folks. "Come, let's sit at the table. We can talk while we eat." She called the kids to come and join us, and the two came in with broad smiles—they must have liked their presents. Ben—like any fourteen-year-old—could always use the extra cash Dad gave him, and Avigail was at that age where silver earrings with little jewels were just what she wanted.

We talked about everything, and particularly how excited we were to be working on ridding Israel's enemies of their slug infestation problem in the hopes of planting a seed for lasting peace.

———————

We didn't stay late—we were exhausted. Tikva called the university, and in ten minutes a graduate student from Avi's department picked us up in a mini-van and took us to the Technion's visiting faculty housing where we would be staying for the week. We all knew it was the same building that Gerry and Mackie stayed in when they were here. The young student, who spoke perfect English, showed us to two adjoining apartments; we knew from Mackie's letters that their apartment didn't adjoin any other, so it was not theirs. I don't know if that knowledge was helpful or not for the folks. I think that maybe deep down, they would have liked to have been housed where Mackie slept when she was here. In fact, the only topic that we didn't discuss that whole day was the murder of Avi, Mackie, and Gerry.

It didn't take Charlie long after we unpacked to conk out. I, on the other hand, had my usual fight with myself over falling asleep. I had a lot on my mind. I felt that maybe we were trying to accomplish too much in just one week. I was also concerned for my parents, wondering how they would handle coming to the place where Mackie and Gerry were murdered. I hoped that they might enjoy their visit to the Holy Land in spite of the torturous memories it might bring. For a couple who were not very religious, they were really psyched about their trip to Bethlehem. They booked it from an agency in Detroit because they knew that the place would be packed with Christian tourists at this time of year, and they wanted to make certain they would be accommodated. In fact, the people on our flight over were mostly Christian tourists who wanted to see Christ's birthplace "before the country is taken over by the Arabs," as one American traveler told us at the airport.

Finally, around midnight I fell asleep, but because of the time change I was up again around four.

The next day Mom and Charlie got ready to explore Haifa. Dad and I were greeted early by the same grad student who drove us yesterday, and he gave us a brief tour of Technion City as we walked over to the Computer Science building. Tikva was already there when we arrived, and she introduced us to Professor Ori Ben-Isaac, director of the Technion's Industrial Affiliates Program (IAP).

"Your facilities are very impressive," I said as we walked toward the conference room just around the corner from the station that Avi Gittleman was working in over a year ago. I could see Tikva tense up as we walked by the area, and I wanted to do something, but I didn't know what. Dad did. He put his arm around Tikva's shoulder and held her close as the two walked together. I was so glad that he was there. I'm sure it was tough on him as well, but I knew he could handle it for all of us, and he did.

Ori responded to my comment about their department. "Yes, we have some of the finest research facilities in the world where people from all over—yes, even people from our enemies' countries—come to do research." He looked sadly at Tikva when he said that. "Our IAP is a model that many countries in Europe and Asia have employed to make it possible for public-private cooperation in the sciences to thrive," he explained with his slight Israeli accent.

Ori Ben-Isaac was a man of modest height, about five-foot-eight. He was in his mid-fifties and was developing a slight paunch, and his dark hair was thinning at the top and graying slightly at the temples. He was a good-looking man, and from the way be carried himself with such a military bearing, I'm sure he was an outstanding soldier when he did his required service in the Israeli Defense Force, the IDF.

I learned from Ori during our visit that when he was a teenager, he wanted to be a scientist and not spend his life on the kibbutz where he was born. He applied for and received a scholarship to Cal Tech in 1982. He got his master's degree in 1983 and his PhD in electrical engineering in 1987. He returned from California with his wife—whom he met at a Hillel mixer in 1983—to be on the faculty at the Technion, where he became the director of the IAP a little over two years ago. I also knew that he was a close friend of Avi's, whom he mentored when Avi and Tikva came to the Technion in the nineties.

The conference room was set up for a meeting, with a speakerphone in the center of the table and a laptop attached to a projector in front of the director's chair. Dad, Tikva, and I sat on one side of the table, and there were two other people from the Technion on the other side. One was a woman I would have guessed to be in her forties, and the other was a younger man who was dressed in a suit and tie, which was unusual for an Israeli. Israelis take pride in their relaxed dress code even at the highest levels of government. Ori introduced the woman by her first name, Devora, and told us that she was a professor in the Biotechnology and Food Engineering Department. The young man—introduced simply as Yaakov by Ori—was the government liaison officer to the president of the university.

After a few preliminary remarks by the director—he asked that we call him Ori—he told Tikva to make her presentation. She did an excellent job of putting our project in perspective and making a plea that Ori and his staff take our proposal seriously and do whatever was in their power to make it happen, not just to save Arab lives but, hopefully, to bring a lasting peace to the Middle East. After Tikva's presentation we took a coffee break because it was only around 9 a.m. Conversation was cordial and nonsubstantive for a while, and then Ori got down to business.

He had an agenda printed out, and the first item of business—after opening remarks and Tikva's presentation—was a teleconference with Yancey and Bobby back in Lansing. "I put Professor Stetson's presentation first because it is already past two in the morning there and we shouldn't keep him up any longer than necessary, do you agree?" he asked me.

"Yes, certainly," I said.

In short order we had Yancey and Bobby projected on the screen, and their voices came out of the speaker on the table. Skype had come a long way over the last couple of years, and their images, now in hi-res, were very clear and not nearly as jerky as they used to be. Yancey was smiling, and we could see our images in the corner of the screen so we were aware of what he and Bobby were looking at. I introduced Yancey Stetson first and then Bobby by his real name, Barindra Padawal, and then I introduced the others at the table to them.

Yancey gave a concise and very specific description of his enzyme solution suspended in a liquid protein: how it worked, how it was fabricated, and its overall effectiveness. Yancey then had Bobby carefully and succinctly lay out one possible distribution plan that he recently developed using MSU's relatively high-speed computer.

"Of course, this is just one plan; there are plenty of other possible plans, but they take a long time to generate, considering we have anywhere from one to two thousand centers," Bobby explained.

Yancey and Bobby had been presenting and answering questions from Ori and his team for over two hours. Devora had the most questions from a farmer's perspective, and you could see Yancey was excited that he had found a kindred spirit in the group. After asking Yancey if he would share his recipe and asking Bobby to e-mail his distribution plan to her—which they naturally agreed to—the conversation was about to end when Ori said, "Barindra, are you originally from Goa, and is your father's name Yadu?"

"Yes, I am...I mean, yes, I'm from Goa and my dad is Yadu. Do you know him?" Bobby asked.

"Yes, I do...your family and mine have been business partners for three generations—did you know that?"

Bobby immediately started talking in his old-fashioned Yiddish, bringing smiles and outright laughter to Ori and his staff. Ori was most at ease speaking the ancient Polish Yiddish with Bobby. He had learned the language with its unique Polish idiosyncrasies from his grandparents.

"Barindra, I talked to your father shortly after you were born to congratulate him. I know he's very proud of you. Listen, if your father is still interested in producing Professor Stetson's enzyme, then I think we may be interested too. I know your father's capabilities as a chemist, so I'm certain it will work. Say hello to him for me, and tell him I hope to see him again real soon," Ori said as he ended the conversation with Yancey and Bobby.

We broke for lunch after talking for over two hours with our MSU team, but before lunch I said to Ori, "I think that conversation with Bobby—Barindra—was the definition of *it's a small world* carried out to the nth degree." We all smiled as we walked over to the faculty dining room. During lunch I asked Ori about his family's life on the kibbutz.

Ori told us that his grandparents emigrated from Poland to Palestine in the mid-1920s during the Third Aliyah, the return of Jews to the Holy Land. Ori's grandfather, Isaac Nowinski, was a teenager at the time, but in spite of his youth, he joined the Haganah, a Jewish defense organization, to help defend the Zionists against the many Arab onslaughts that tried to expel the Jewish settlers from the land. The young Zionists wanted to settle in Palestine under the League of Nations Mandate. Isaac came over as part of a Zionist youth group called the Hashomer Hatzair and planned to live on a kibbutz with other like-minded Zionists for the rest of his life.

The kibbutz that Hashomer Hatzair created was called Ein Shemer, and when Isaac was just eighteen, he was one of the first settlers to join. The kibbutz was less than fifteen miles south of Haifa near Hadera. It was on that kibbutz that Isaac met Ori's grandmother, and where they were married and raised three sons during some very bleak times in the history of the country.

Ori's father, Schmuel Ben-Isaac Nowinski, was born there eighty-one years ago and still lived on the kibbutz with Ori's mother. Ori's father and his uncles shortened their last name to Ben-Isaac—dropping Nowinski—to rid themselves of any reminders of the rampant anti-Semitism that was raging in Europe when their parents left Poland. The family remained on the kibbutz, raising a variety of crops, notably fruits from their orchards, which they exported to other parts of the world, while importing rice and spices, mostly from the Goan region of India, and sold them on the open market. It was in Goa that they met and set up a trade partnership with Bobby's family. It was also Ori's grandfather who taught Bobby's great-grandfather Yiddish, and that's why Bobby's accent was so familiar to Ori.

Ori told us, "By the time I was born in 1960, Ein Shemer had prospered, and many of the younger generation wanted to be more than farmers and marketers. When I was seven years old, my father was sent to fight in the Six-Day War with Egypt and its Arab allies. At that time there was grave concern that Israel might be defeated and the country would no longer exist. Israel had just become a country twelve years earlier, and now it looked like it may be gone. There would be no mandate to preserve its existence if they lost; but even if we did win, the mood was that it would cost many lives, which would disrupt the country's progress into the foreseeable future. As it turned out, we were not defeated, and we went on to become a jewel of democracy and scientific progress in the Middle East. I wanted to be a scientist to help bring about that type of country—someone committed to a better and more democratic world through science."

"And you did, Ori," Dad said, "and if we have any say in this matter whatsoever then your country will always live—*Am Ysrael Chai.*" Dad said the Hebrew saying, *the people of Israel live!*

"Amen," Tikva said.

After that Ori told us about his leaving the kibbutz for Cal Tech and meeting his wife. "But, you know, I must admit there are still times when I miss living on the kibbutz—we were one big family, and living so close to the land is a marvelous thing for a child growing up."

"My family is also from a farming kibbutz," Devora said, "and I, too, miss working the land. It was fun talking with your colleague, Yancey. I could tell instantly he was an American farmer before he was a professor. I could also tell that he, too, misses working the land."

After lunch we went back to the conference room, and I made my presentation on the slugs and how I figured out the process for remutating them back to their original species.

"I find it fascinating that you're willing to go to all this trouble to change them back to a simple garden pest that will still have to be controlled anyway. Why don't you simply eradicate them or render them neutral?" Ori asked.

I then explained that all that had been carefully thought out. We came to the conclusion that it would be impossible to treat this sub-species any other way without causing irreparable harm to the soil. "Actually, our approach is the best of all approaches from a farming and ecological perspective," I said, "and I think Yancey's presentation covered that for the most part. But if you like, I can get him to further clarify why we have settled on this process…"

"No, that's not necessary," Devora said. "I fully understand your approach and agree with you. These slugs are the strangest I've ever seen, with properties that have never existed before in nature. I think you're absolutely right in remutating them back while we still can."

"But the problem of physically spreading the enzyme over the infected lands still needs resolving. I'm guessing that's your part of the problem, Pieter, am I right?" Ori asked.

Dad made his presentation about using traditional liquid fertilizer machinery attached to a GM specially-designed truck. "But I must tell you, after seeing the distribution plan that George has been working with, I don't think that a truck delivery system alone will meet our needs. It would take way too many trucks to get the job done in any kind of timely manner to be effective. Some trucks can be used in certain areas, but airplanes would be far more efficient in other places."

After Dad's presentation it was getting late, and Ori said, "I think we've done a lot for one day. We'll continue tomorrow and either come up with an action plan or…"

Yaakov joined the conversation for the first time and said, "Before we even think of an action plan, Ori, I think that some elements of this plan have to be discussed with officials other than the Technion, especially people from the IDF." Yaakov was referring to the Israeli Defense Force—the military.

"Yes, of course they do, Yakie," Tikva said, then switching back to Hebrew she said, "Let's make sure we even have a viable plan before bringing *anyone else* into the conversation. You can update the president, of course, but I think we should wait a little longer to bring in any other government agency." Tikva immediately translated for us, but she wanted to make certain that Yaakov knew she was an Israeli first.

Tikva knew that conservative elements in the government would in no way endorse a plan such as this—helping Israel's enemies survive. She wanted to wait until we had a solid and workable action plan, then she would use her own personal efforts in order to get the plan implemented. She certainly had a lot of courage to think that she could take on the IDF, but she was determined to give it a try. Tikva wanted to prevent a government veto before we had a well-thought-out and developed plan. Ori joined in, saying in English, "As I said, let's continue with just this group tomorrow before we get too carried away. Is that all right with everyone?"

Dad and I decided to meet at Tikva's house later and to debrief Charlie and Mom on how the meeting went. I also wanted to call Yancey and Bobby in the evening to let them know how things went and thank them for putting on such a great show.

Early that evening I Skyped MSU on Tikva's computer. "Hey, Yancey and Bobby, did you guys get any sleep last night?" I asked.

"Not much. Tell me how the presentation went?" Yancey asked.

"I think it went very well. Of course if it wasn't for Bobby's expertise in Yiddish, I think we would be on our way home now," I joked, watching Bobby smile on the monitor. "In any case we're meeting again tomorrow to talk about an action plan. We're far from home yet. We have to sell the idea to the IDF, and that's going to be tough..."

Tikva jumped in after hearing only my side of the conversation and said, "But I'm going to cover that end of it so don't worry, Yancey," she yelled out.

"Well, then it's a done deal," Yancey said.

We talked a little more, filling them in on our presentations. I ended the conversation with, "Hey, and Merry Christmas to you guys in case I don't get back to you on Thursday."

"Sounds like your team is happy with our progress," Tikva said to Dad and I. "What's on our agenda for tomorrow's action plan that we're supposed to be developing?"

"I'm not sure, but Ori said something about an action plan before Yaakov jumped in about meeting with the IDF, so maybe we should try to side-step the action plan bit. What do you think, Dad?"

"I won't be there tomorrow; your mother and I will be heading down to the city center tomorrow. She wants to show me some things, and I want to familiarize myself with the bus terminal before we have to be there on Friday for our tour. I don't think you'll need me tomorrow," Dad said, "but if you want my advice, I'd downplay the action plan talk. Couch your dialogue in terms of *continuing efforts* and see what tasks need to be assigned to everyone. Then establish a timeline for completing the tasks and meeting times—that would be virtual meetings, of course—for updates. Keep Yaakov involved as much as possible but continue to make it clear that you're still not in any position to discuss the project with other government agencies."

"I see, carry out the action plan, but don't call it a plan—is that what you're saying Pieter?" Tikva asked.

"In a sense, yes, I'm just trying to be sensitive to Yaakov's position without getting him in trouble. If you talk about a 'plan,' then he has to tell his superiors, but if you're still developing a general concept, he's not obligated to get them involved yet," Dad said.

Tikva looked at me and said, "Wise words, George; we'll do it that way, okay?"

I nodded in agreement, and then Charlie said, "I'll be visiting my family's friend in the Architecture and Town Planning Department—maybe I can meet you guys for lunch or something. I'll call you around noon on your cell."

"Then it sounds like everyone's busy tomorrow, so we're all set," I said.

We sat down for a typical Israeli light meal: salads, sides, and excellent Arab bread dipped in olive oil. The kids did most of the eating since we were all still full from the lunches we had, but with some wine that Charlie and Mom picked up in town, and some fresh flowers on the table that they also picked up—even though it wasn't *Shabbos*—I was in good spirits. *Maybe we can do this thing after all,* I thought as I drank my glass of Carmel Appellation Sauvignon Blanc. I didn't know that Israel had such amazing wines.

Yaakov Uhlman was a strange character with a dark personality. He was in his late thirties or early forties. He was short, about five-foot-five, and although he was always impeccably dressed, wearing a jacket and tie, he looked out of place for an Israeli university administrator. He was not good looking and had a dour expression on his face most of the time, which more or less amplified his homeliness. But there was something about his manner that led me to believe that he exercised more authority than one would expect from someone who was *just* a liaison officer from the president's office. I think Dad knew that and that's why he wanted to make certain Yaakov was not marginalized. Yaakov, like many petty bureaucrats, appeared to want to exercise his limited—but potentially obstructive—powers to the maximum.

On Wednesday Tikva and I met once again with Ori, Devora, and Yaakov to further discuss the project. We worked out what additional tasks we would be responsible for, like coming up with the optimal enzyme delivery procedure. Ori and Devora would look into other Israeli institutions for support and financing, and Yaakov would continue to watch our progress until such time that an "action plan" was necessary for us to proceed further.

We also agreed on holding bi-monthly meetings via Skype to update everyone with our progress, and we set the end of March next year as a tentative go/no-go date. In other words we gave ourselves three months to come to a final agreement as to whether the project lived or died.

We were just finishing up when my cell phone buzzed. It was a text message from Charlie telling us where to meet her for lunch. She'd be there waiting for us unless I texted her otherwise.

"Good-bye and my best wishes for success," Devora said. "I think we have a major project here, not just for Israel but for the whole world. Don't loose faith no matter what happens."

Yaakov, surprisingly, nodded in agreement and didn't push us about meeting with the IDF or any other federal agency. I think he saw what was happening and knew that frequently it was the quiet diplomacy that got the action done, and I think he really wanted this project to succeed.

Charlie was waiting for us in the large student cafeteria on campus. She was at a table with an older gentleman who looked to be of mixed Asian and Anglo heritage.

"Tikva, George, I'd like you to meet Professor Reginald Shao from the faculty of Architecture and Town Planning. Reggie is an old friend of the family from Birmingham who moved to Israel—was it 2006, Reggie?"

"That's right, Charleen," Professor Shao said in a clipped British accent. He looked to be in his mid-to late-fifties.

"Reggie spent a lot of time at our place talking politics and planning with my father, and I would love to participate. I knew he had relocated here and was delighted that I would be able to meet up with him again." Pausing and then looking at Reggie, Charlie said, "You never wrote me, you know—I was hurt," Charlie said, feigning disappointment.

Reggie smiled and said, "I heard from your father that after your stint at Birmingham you went to the University of Michigan for your graduate work. I should have written to you then because that's where I received my planning PhD. I fully intended to contact you, Charlene, but..."

"I know...one can get awfully wrapped up in one's work. No matter now," Charlie said. She then told Reggie to tell us about his work and how excited she was that it tied so nicely into what we were doing.

Reggie was always interested in the role of planning as it related to emerging populations from ethnic groups not indigenous to the area. He became disappointed with the UK's efforts to absorb immigrants from the former British colonies, especially those having darker skins.

"As you can see, I'm of mixed race myself—English mother and Chinese father," Reggie told us. "I often felt the pain of not being recognized as British. People would frequently ask me where I was from. And even though I would tell them that I'm from England, they would still persist with, 'Yes, but before that, where did you come from?' like my family were aliens from another planet."

His publications on working with and assisting Pakistanis and Indians who immigrated to England grabbed the attention of the planners at the Technion. He published articles about helping them become an economic force in their own right and how they should receive the same benefits and other perks that native-born Brits receive.

Reggie was hired by the Technion to participate in its Center for Urban and Regional Studies, where his knowledge of the economic aspects of migration planning made him the best candidate to work with the Arab and African populations currently living in Israel. Reggie went on to explain, "I couldn't help but get excited when Charleen told me what you were all about here. We were all well aware of the major crop damage that was caused by a nonnative species of a garden pest in Syria and Iran. The issue is very keen with me since many of the people in the populations I work with came from agricultural communities in their own countries. They frequently find it difficult to adapt to an urban workforce, and I've been trying to get them involved in some of the farming kibbutzim that they might fit into. But, if you know anything about Israeli kibbutzim, you know that's a difficult thing to tackle. Most farming kibbutzim are very old now, and it's like asking them to adopt new family members who are not ethnically the same as the Eastern European families who founded the kibbutz."

"But how does your work tie into ours?" I asked.

"I think I might have an idea as to how we could solve your problem of getting Israel to participate in neutralizing the slugs," Reggie said.

"Really? How?" I asked.

It turned out that Reggie worked closely with the Ministry of Agriculture and Rural Development along with some United Nations agencies that were friendly towards Israel's Minister of Foreign Affairs, the MFA. The MFA had an agency called MASHAV, Israel's Agency for International Development Cooperation, and that's who he had developed plans for. He explained that in order to get anything done in Israel, you needed a plan that detailed the economic, social, and political benefits to Israel for any program that required federal funding or support, and that was his specialty when it came to foreign workers' programs.

After listening to Reggie, I asked, "I'm still not seeing how that helps us get the slugs neutralized in Syria and Iran. I doubt if you have any joint programs with those countries or, for that matter, any country in the coalition. How could you come up with a plan that includes cooperation from the coalition?"

"Don't be such a skeptic, George," Charlie said, "hear him out."

Reggie went on to explain that they had a number of low-key "cultural exchange programs" in coalition countries in the hopes that those people who were aided would not want to wage war against Israel.

"I didn't know that Israel did humanitarian work in coalition countries. You certainly wouldn't know that if you listened to the coalition's rhetoric against Israel," I said.

"Things in the Middle East aren't always as they seem," Tikva said, joining the conversation for the first time.

"In any case I'm offering my services to develop a plan for you that would get government approval for you to carry out your project."

"Wow! You have no idea how relieved that makes us. Sorry to have been such a doubting idiot before—I didn't quite see that coming, but, yes, yes...by all means, make us a plan. What do we have to do?"

I looked over at Tikva and saw her eyes filled with eagerness and a smile on her face as she said, "I guess that's my role in this affair, Reggie. Let me know what I need to do—help write proposals, make calls, contact people, anything to expedite the plan. My services are at your disposal."

"I'll definitely be taking you up on your offer, Tikva." Reggie then looked serious as he took hold of both of Tikva's hands and said, "Everyone at the Technion knows about the loss of Avi Gittleman, and we are all committed to see to it that his loss was not in vain."

Reggie then looked at me and said, "I'm also being self-serving in this—let me tell you why. I have a population of North Africans that I've trained to do modern farming. I'm hoping that they can be employed to train the Syrian and Iranians to actually carry out the distribution of your enzyme. I think these North Africans—even though they are Israelis now—will have a better chance of acceptance in the coalition countries than Israeli Sabras. Also, I have a number of grad students who will use this opportunity for their master's project on regional planning. So you see, everyone wins here," he said, smiling at us.

There were hugs and warm wishes all around as we left the cafeteria.

Our last of couple of days in Israel were unhurried and well spent. Dad was especially pleased with the news of Reggie's involvement and the MFA. He said that was probably all we needed to keep Yaakov off our backs—at least for now. The folks loved their tour of Bethlehem, and as we left Israel we were all more determined than ever to go forward with our project and save the world.

chapter 13

IT WAS AT our weekly meeting on Wednesday, March 16, just a couple of weeks away from our deadline, when I realized things were on schedule to have everything done or in place for the treatment plan. Since things had been going exceptionally well, I had that nervous feeling that everything would probably collapse—but not today. We had set early April for our team trip back to Israel to initiate the implementation plan and finally get the project up and running.

Noreen and Charlie were once again attending our meetings, which added to our feeling of certain success. "Let's take stock of where we are right now," Yancey said to start off the meeting.

Noreen was the first to respond. "I think that we're still at three minutes to midnight, but I must admit that for some reason anti-Israeli rhetoric from any coalition state has definitely decreased. I'm not sure why. I think something must be going on that we're not getting from any publicly available source."

"What do you think it might be, Noreen?" Charlie asked.

Charlie, at almost six months pregnant, had quite a pronounced tummy. She was so small to begin with that once she started to show, her pregnancy became quite obvious. She decided to attend the meetings again so that she'd be the one who would update Tikva either by phone, e-mail, or Skype.

"I'm not sure. There are so many possibilities, but they would all be only speculation on my part," Noreen answered her. "My gut feel is that somewhere behind the scenes diplomacy must be going on, but who's doing it and with whom is anybody's guess. I think the highest probability consortium is the United States and Syria. Syria needs wheat and other grains, and I'm guessing the United States is offering them relief for their backing-off on the saber rattling. But as I said, that's pure speculation. I have absolutely no corroboration as to what's really happening."

"I think you're right on that one, Noreen," Yancey said. "Charlie, maybe you can run it by Tikva and see what she's hearing. I know she's been in touch with Yaakov, and if anyone in that group at the Technion knows what's happening politically he should."

Charlie updated us with news from Israel, which was the best news of all. It seems that Israel—or at least the Technion group—was well into the project. "Reggie and Yaakov are working very close with the MFA to develop the economic plan. Ori is on board technically with Devora, and the two of them were put in the position of guaranteeing the technical success of the project, but they didn't mind—"

"Yeah, I know. I've been on the computer with her—Devora—many times these last three months," Yancey said. "She's very sharp and really knows about farming techniques in the Middle East. I think I'm learning more from her than she's learning from me."

"And that's a good thing, isn't it, Yance?" Charlie said with a smile. "In any case, they are on point. You know, as Tikva fills me in on the project details, I realize that I never fully understood the magnitude of this venture. It will take an army of people to carry it out. What with planes, trucks, training sessions, and hundreds of farmers from three unfriendly countries, covering millions of hectares of land—I must admit that I'm overwhelmed at times."

Yancey explained, "People always underestimate the size of farmlands by just looking at maps. But once they've walked a few hundred acres or a couple of square miles, they get impressed with just how much land a section of farm acreage consumes. Yet on the map, it's just a dot. And in the lands we'll be working on, there are a whole lot of dots."

Noreen smiled when she heard that her husband was still very much interested in the everyday elements of farming in the Middle East. She recalled how excited he was when he first learned that he was going to Lebanon, and she detected that excitement once again.

"You are right about that, Yancey," Bobby said. "But I think I've finally got the optimal distribution program worked out—or I should say distribution *programs*."

Alan Wackfield at IBM had once again given us time on one of their Blue Gene computers. With an elegant brute force algorithm that Bobby developed looking at the myriads of possible solutions to the TSP, he came up with the most efficient and least costly that centered around 1,250 locations. He also had a number of backup plans just in case terrain, politics, or other unknown local factors came into play during the treatment process.

Bobby briefed us on the plan, telling us that he based it on the use of three major organizing centers: Al-Hasakah, Syria: Hamadan, Iran; and Mosul, Iraq, with Mosul being the main center for the whole operation.

"Why those cities?" I asked.

Bobbie went on to explain that Reggie pointed out that Al-Hasakah and Hamadan would be the most accepting of an international program with a large number of foreigners present. With Syria on the west and Iran to the east of Iraq, he suggested that we needed to use some place in Iraq as our main base and felt that Mosul would be the best location for that.

"We also decided to do some prophylactic treatments on that northern section of Iraq that borders on Syria and Iran just in case the infestation had spread," Bobby said in conclusion.

IBM was so impressed with Bobby's ability to take full technical advantage of one of their Blue Gene supercomputers that they offered him a full-time high-level position when he completed his PhD, but he told them that he planned to return to India when he was through.

Bobby added, "Oh, I almost forgot to tell you that Ori has been working with my father on producing the enzyme, and I think they have the price way down—I think it's much less than a hundred million, closer to fifty million, but Tikva should have that data. Also, after our trip next month, I'll be going on to Goa to see my family and to touch base with my father on the project—if we get approval, that is."

We broke for lunch after Bobby's update, and since there was just my report on my dad's progress with the GM trucks and liquid fertilizer spreaders, we decided to do that after lunch. Noreen and Charlie wouldn't need to be there for that; Yancey and I would fill them in later about Dad's progress.

Later the three of us returned to finish up our meeting, which would probably be our last before heading off to Israel. In Israel we planned on putting the finishing touches on our tasks and working with Reggie on finalizing his overall plan that he would have to present to the MFA for funding.

Dad had been able to drum up seventy-four trucks and fertilizer spreaders in Europe and the Middle East that could be brought in to do the ground treatment, putting the total at over thirty-five per country with a couple of spares for our use in Iraq. Bobby pointed out that would be more than sufficient to complete at least six lifecycles of the slugs, considering that small crop-dusting planes would be doing the larger open tracts of land. If some trucks broke down, it may take a little longer to finish, but he thought that seventy-four trucks were more than sufficient.

"How did your dad pull that off?" Yancey asked. "I remember last year he was having some difficulty getting GM's support for the project."

"Boris helped," I said. "It seems Boris promised GM a sole-source follow-on project for the military's CROSSHAIRS program—essentially, a military Humvee—that would more than make up for the loan of the trucks and other equipment. When Dad presented the offer to GM, they couldn't refuse."

"Nice work, and a thank you to Boris," Yancey said. "So, is everyone packed and ready to go?" he asked.

We wouldn't be leaving for a couple of weeks yet, but it was Yancey's way of saying that we should make certain that all our ducks were in a row before we left. Bobby was nodding his head with his charming smile on his face. He was psyched about going to Israel and then on to Goa to work with his dad on the design of the enzyme plant. If all went well in Israel, we felt that we would be able to start spreading the enzyme by early fall.

***

That evening Charlie and I felt relaxed for the first time in over a year. We knew that we had at least a year or more of hard work, and probably two more years after that, to fully realize the benefits of all our efforts, but soon it would no longer be totally in our hands.

"How about a drink?" Charlie asked me.

From the ultrasounds we were fairly certain that our baby would be a girl, and we already knew her name would be Marike.

"I'd love one. Fix yourself some juice too, and we'll have a toast." When Charlie brought us our drinks, I said, "To Marike. May our daughter live in peace for her whole life."

I was smiling on that mild day before St. Patrick's Day. There was a promise of spring in the air. It felt good to be in mid-Michigan where one really appreciated the coming of spring as the snow melted away and the fields began to look ready for plowing and planting.

"What are you thinking about?" Charlie asked, as we sat on the couch looking out the window over our brown lawn—soon to be vibrant green— and the houses on our street. I was sipping my Scotch and Charlie was enjoying her mango fruit juice.

"I'm thinking that once we bring the soil back to life, all will be well in the world. That somehow the soil's death from the slugs is some kind of metaphor for the way the world is—unable to blossom and grow in the current political climate of hate, distrust, and radicalism. I'm thinking that if we can bring the soil back to life to be productive again, then maybe we can make the world fertile for peace again. I don't know, I'm probably full of shit, but that's what I'm thinking."

"I'm thinking you're suffering from delusions of grandeur. Don't take yourself so damn seriously. None of us are really that important in the whole scheme of things. Yes, I'm feeling good that we seem to be accomplishing something impossible, but I have no false hopes that it will create world peace and all that other good stuff that you're alluding to. Let's just take what comes and be happy with small successes and hope it all goes well from here on. Can you do that, George?"

I pulled her close to me and we snuggled till well past sunset. I knew she was right, but then again, I'd always been the dreamer.

We met on Monday, April 11 to fully debrief Noreen and Charlie on our trip to Israel the previous week. Bobby was in Goa visiting his family and waiting for word from us on what to do. We had gotten back yesterday, and we were too tired and discouraged to talk about all the details and the unexpected outcome we had experienced. Noreen and Charlie were obviously very interested in how the meetings went and wanted to know right away. We told them that the project was on hold because of politics and that we would fill them in today.

Yancey and I proceeded to tell them what happened—how from the very first day we sensed things were not going to go well. I started. "The first meeting had way too many people there to begin with, and it made us uncomfortable right off the bat. We sensed that conflict was already in the air between Reggie and Yaakov, which surprised us since they seemed to have been working so well together lately. We—that's me, Yancey, and Bobby—were in a large conference room with Ori's team—Devora and Yaakov—along with Reggie and two of his doctoral students. There were five other people we had never met before; one was from the president's office and one from the Minister of Foreign Affairs, and the other three were from some other government agencies, but I couldn't tell you what those agencies were."

Yancey added, "The dialogue kept changing between Hebrew and English, which was hard for me and George—that's one reason we didn't know who the other three men were. I suspect, though, they were all somehow related to the military. Also, throughout the meeting people seemed to come and go; and some new people, who were never introduced to us, arrived at different times and then left."

"Was Tikva there?" Charlie asked.

"No, not the first day. We were led to believe that the first day would be all updating and that Tikva wouldn't be needed until the second day's working session, so she stayed home," I said.

I went on to explain how political it had all gotten and that we were totally marginalized, sitting there for the most part while the Israelis loudly discussed the project. "It seemed that Reggie's draft plan was given to these other agencies' people by Yaakov before anybody had a chance to even discuss it. Ori was in the awkward position of having to play peace-maker in his own house, so to speak."

Yancey stepped in. "I can't quite explain the dynamics, but it seems that Israelis are like one big family, only they argue a lot more than most families. It may look like they're going to come to blows at times, but you soon realize that they argue like sisters and brothers and the blows don't come no matter how angry they are."

"What was the argument all about?" Charlie asked.

I told her that it appeared that the person from the Foreign Affairs Ministry and Reggie had been working on the whole project, developing the necessary plan detailing the various benefits, and were ready to start the process of getting formal ministry approval. However, Yaakov and the other person from the president's office felt that the project was well enough along to bring in the IDF. Yaakov told us that any project involving work in "hostile areas" by Israeli citizens needed military approval and that was why they were there.

"So was the IDF just pissed that they had not been brought in earlier?" Charlie asked.

"I wish it was that simple, but it wasn't," Yancey said.

I said, "From what we could gather from the conversation—with help from Devora, I might add—it appeared the military were entirely against the project and would in no way approve it."

"So is that it...is it over?" Noreen asked, shocked. "All that work, all that hope, and now what? Are we asked to sit around and watch people starve and go to war for ideologies and outmoded beliefs..."

"Let's take a break," Yancey said, "and we'll come back and finish our report. I know it seems hopeless right now, but we don't think it is, and we're going to keep at it. Noreen, Charlie, don't you two get discouraged yet; we haven't given up the fight. Are you still with us on this?"

Both answered in the affirmative but with noticeable resignation in their voices.

We took a short break for lunch and, during a lull in the conversation, Charlie asked, "How were Tikva and the kids? Did you give them the gifts from the folks?"

"Yeah...they're fine, considering everything." I took a bite of my sandwich and then said, "But you know, Tikva had noticed that the tension between Israel and the coalition seems to have diminished lately. I asked her why she thought that was, and she felt it was related to some issues of anxiety in the coalition over food and other resources. She said the coalition had enough trouble and probably didn't want to take on Israel...at least for now."

"What do you think, Noreen?" Yancey asked.

"I'm not sure. They are having trouble keeping everyone in the coalition in line because of the economic issues; but if anything, it's under these kinds of conditions that make for the best rallying cries. You know, blame it all on an outside enemy."

We sat quietly for a while, thinking about Noreen's remarks and commenting on how complicated it was to do anything in that part of the world no matter how good our intentions were. "You know what they say about good intentions and the road to hell," Yancey said in his typical Midwestern affect.

After a while I said, "I'm wondering now, Noreen, if your earlier premise about something going on that we don't know about is coming into play here. It did seem a bit strange to me that all this military interest seemed to come out of nowhere. I'm not sure what went down at the Technion since the people from the other agencies rarely spoke English. From the little that I did understand, and from what Devora told us, it seemed to me that they were trying to tell us—that is, the whole team including the Technion—to stay out of this for now. That it was none our business and essentially we all should just back off. What do you think, Yancey, did you get that feeling?"

Yancey thought for a minute and then said, "Now that you mention it, the next two days of meetings between us and Ori did seem to be less than enthusiastic. Reggie was still upset by the whole episode on Tuesday, but he was still committed to completing his plan. Ori, on the other hand, seemed to be a bit preoccupied, which isn't like him; and Tikva, as we said before, was disheartened but still willing to keep on working. Looking back now I think that you may be right. I think our team was told, in some way, that we needed to hold off for some reason that was much more important than starting our project right now. And by 'we,' I agree with you, George, it's not just our little group here in East Lansing; it's Ori, Reggie, their teams—all of us."

"So what do we do now?" Charlie asked.

"Find out what that reason is and take care of it," I said.

Yancey looked at me; he was a little surprised but smiling and said, "Okay, cowboy, what's your plan?"

"Boris," I said. "He didn't get those trucks for Dad for nothing. He knows if anything is going on out there that's 'bigger than us' and he should tell us what it is. Let's go talk to Boris."

On the plane to DC on Thursday, Yancey said, "I think the best approach might be the straightforward one: tell Boris the project is in trouble and ask for his advice on how to get it back on track."

"You don't think we should tell him that we know he put the slugs out there and now it's time to call in the cavalry?"

Yancey smiled at my battlefield image. "If I thought for one minute that Boris would be straight up on that one I would, but...no, I think we thank him for helping us get the trucks, then fill him in on everything, and then ask for his advice. I think he's the type of person who likes to be in the godfather role, so let's just kiss his ring and see what happens."

That night Yancey and I further hardened our approach for our meeting the next day. We knew that Boris was probably well aware of what was going on, since DARPA worked very closely with State and State usually knew what Israel was doing in a broad strategic sense. If we were right in assuming—but never actually validating—that Boris' people modified the slugs into a weapon and put them out there in the first place, then they would be the ones to want to control them—not us or a bunch of peaceniks from the Technion.

I said to Yancey, "I guess you're right about letting Boris think we need him, but what do we tell him? He'll wonder why we came to him with our problem. Why didn't we go to State or DOD and ask for their support?"

"That's easy," Yancey said. "Remember it was Boris who convened the conference on the slugs, not the other agencies, so it would only be natural that we asked him. Also, State was there at the conference, so they could always be brought in by Boris on this one too. No, I don't think it will be any problem convincing him that he was our logical choice. But, best of all, we know him and he thinks we like him."

"You mean we don't?" I said sarcastically.

Yancey just smiled as we finished our meeting and left the hotel dining room. "See you early in the morning—let's meet at seven for breakfast," Yancey said, and we went to our rooms.

I called Charlie to see how she was doing, watched a little TV, and then tried to get some sleep, but as usual my busy mind kept me from falling soundly asleep. I kept thinking about our meeting tomorrow, playing out all kinds of scenarios in my head, and they all came to the same ending: Boris doesn't help. When I woke up at six, I was sweaty and exhausted as I slowly got ready for our meeting.

———————

"George, Yancey, so good to see you two again. How are things going with your project?" Boris asked as we came into his office. I wasn't sure what he meant by *your project*—did he know what we were doing in Israel or was it our remutation project that he was referring to? I guess it really didn't matter because after we both sat down, Yancey immediately filled him in on our Israeli mission and updated him as to our current status, which, for all practical purposes, was *dead in the water.*

Boris listened intently and hardly asked any questions; he seemed to know more about our work than even I suspected. "So why have you come to me?" he asked after Yancey finished.

"We'd like your help," I said. "Since you helped Dad get those trucks, we feel that you have some commitment to the success of the project. We're not politicians or diplomats, but we know you know how to deal with those people, so we're asking for your help, or your advice, or whatever it is you feel you can offer us."

"*Those people*—you say that like they are some kind of vermin," Boris said with a noticeable sneer in his voice. "Who the hell do you think is keeping your asses safe? It's not your scientists, or your pansy-assed academics with all your touchy-feely shit. It's *those people*. It's the career diplomats and bureaucrats along with the policy makers—the politicians—and their ability to keep a realistic view on who in the hell you're dealing with out there. They don't play for marbles; they play for lives and freedom. Your father knows that, George, and you should too, Yancey," Boris said, now looking at Yancey.

"Boris, I didn't mean any disrespect—" I started.

"I know, I know, but I get a little tired of people who have never had to make a life-or-death decision in their entire lives looking down their noses at those of us who do have to make those decisions. You get into areas that you have no business being there in the first place, and then expect us to bail your asses out. Do you have any idea at all what you've gotten yourselves into?"

"We would like to think—" I started to say when Yancey cut me off.

"I'm sure we don't, Boris, just as I'm certain that *you* do know, and that's why we're here. We, or rather the whole project, need your help, and we're hoping that you can salvage the program. If you want us out in order for you to do that, then so be it. If you want us to stay involved, then that's fine with us. We just want to help end the infestation and get the land back to being arable again...that's all we want."

"That's a modest request," Boris said, a little more relaxed than he was a moment ago. Sitting back in his chair, he said calmly, "However, the United States government wants a lot more. The government not only wants what you do, but they also want to establish a peaceful coexistence between Israel and all its neighbors. The government is more than willing to offer assistance to people in the coalition for humanitarian reasons, but without safeguards for Israel—and other democratic regimes in the region—it would be foolish to aid and abet Israel's enemies." Then he asked us, "Can you do that—defend Israel? Are you in any position to make those kinds of commitments? I don't think so—that's why we need *those people.*"

"You've made your point, Boris, and again, I apologize for speaking so callously. So...are we in or out?" I asked.

"Oh, you're in, of course, but under new rules. Can I depend on you for complete cooperation, or are you only interested in being some kind of maverick peacemakers who want to take on the whole world?"

"Why don't you tell us what you have in mind so we can better answer your question?" Yancey said.

"Fair enough, but how about a break. We've been at this for a while and I need some nourishment," Boris said in a most hospitable manner.

We agreed, and as if on cue a late morning snack was brought in to Boris' office. We all wanted to freshen up a little anyway and looked forward to the break. It had been a rough session for me, and in the visitors' washroom Yancey assured me that I didn't blow the meeting. In fact, he said, it was because of what I unthinkingly said that we finally understood what it was all about and how much Boris was really involved, and that was good. And the fact that Boris seemed to anticipate what would happen but still wanted us involved was a good sign for the project.

We were both smiling as we sat down for our snack with Boris. Maybe the project wasn't going to die after all.

.Boris filled us in on what he and his colleagues in the State Department had been doing since the infestation destroyed the food crops. Arrangements had already been made to deliver United States surplus grain supplies to the Middle East—paid for, I might add, by United States taxpayers through farm subsidy programs. In return, the rhetoric had to stop—which, for the most part, it had. There were still rants coming from some extremist groups that were not part of any coalition agency, but promises were made to at least disavow those groups. Those arrangements were well in progress when, much to Boris' surprise, through his own Israeli contacts—probably the Mossad—he found out about our work in Israel. If we had continued at the pace we were going, then the whole deal might have fallen through. He and his colleagues felt that it was a little too early to be helping the Syrians and Iranians get rid of their slug menace. There was no doubt that they would eventually control the slugs, thanks to the information we supplied them at the conference last summer, but not just yet. That's why the Israelis stopped—or as Boris put it, *temporarily halted the project.*

"Have you heard of the Office of Technology Transition?" Boris asked us. We shook our heads, and he continued. "They're responsible for making policies about any technology that can eventually be used in weapon design and production. They don't look kindly on technology that has the potential for weapon usage being offered to any other country—friend or foe. Sadly, as you can see, your technology—slug remutation—has that potential. You might make a case that it's similar to antimissile defense systems, which is governed by international treaties."

"Are you saying that we broke the law?" I asked incredulously.

"No, no...not you. Your work was strictly for promoting agricultural pedagogy and farming practices. You aren't in any way responsible for illicit weapon—or antiweapon—development." Boris paused and took a drink of water before continuing. "But, if someone in India knowingly produces your formula with the idea of using it to aid an enemy of one of our allies, then they may be in violation of a number of international agreements."

It hit Yancey and me like a ton of bricks: he was saying that Bobby and his father might be in trouble.

"So how does that come into our 'complete cooperation' you asked for earlier?" Yancey asked with his arms folded on his chest and a noticeably distrustful look on his face.

"Don't get so paranoid—we're not going to strong-arm the Padawal family. All I'm saying is that you can't do it in India on your own. First of all, neither you nor the Israelis can come up with the money it will take to make Yadu's plant and produce your enzyme. However, I can."

"You're willing to fund the enzyme plant? Why?" I asked.

"Because it will be a lot cheaper to build the plant there than anywhere else in the world, including here in the United States, and less of a political hassle for us. But it would have to be for agricultural purposes only, and once the slugs were controlled, the plant would have to continue on as an agricultural chemical processing plant as proof that it was not built for a single purpose. That's what I mean by cooperation. If you agree to that I'll give you a name of a company in India that's willing to finance the operation for a reasonable return on their investment. The only other agreement I would ask of you is that you don't start your neutralizing program until Yaakov Uhlman tells you when. Can you abide by those conditions?"

I looked at Yancey, who was looking at me, before he said, "How much of this *agreement* can we share with our colleagues in Israel?" "Ori Ben-Isaac has been made fully aware of the protocols necessary to achieve his goal. I'm certain that the administration at the Technion has briefed his staff and others involved on what they must do to achieve their goals as well. I know that Professor Reginald Shao is very excited about having his plan adopted and getting on with the training implementation elements for his group of émigrés. Yes, you may share our discussion and your responsibilities as I've outlined them here, but it should be made clear that you are in no way representing or speaking for any US government agency," Boris said, acting more like our boss than our colleague.

"Deal," I said, looking at Yancey for approval while extending my hand to Boris.

At noon on Monday, we met to discuss our DARPA meeting with Noreen and Charlie, although I'm certain that Yancey had already told Noreen all about it, just like I had already told Charlie.

"You were right, Noreen. There was some behind-the-scenes negotiating going on between the US and Syria as well as with Iran. And it still seems to be going on," I said.

Noreen thought for a minute and then said, "But from what Yancey told me over the weekend, it seems that there are a number of agencies involved here. The fact that Boris had some company's name in India ready to finance Bobby's father's plant tells me that the CIA must be active in this whole thing as well. My guess is that they—the CIA—planted the DARPA-engineered slugs in the coalition states. And now the State Department wants to use the opportunity to influence Middle East policy in relation to Israel. It's the same old business-as-usual…"

Yes, Noreen, but so what?" Yancey said somewhat impatiently. "If we're able to get our program accomplished, who cares what federal agencies were involved in the whole damn thing? We're just trying to end it. You're making it sound like we're in bed with the devil."

"Aren't we?" I said. "If not the devil, then at least Dr. Strangelove."

"Does that bother you, George?" Yancey asked me with the same impatience he displayed to Noreen.

"I keep hearing my brother-in-law, Gerry, warning me about the evils of government intervention in science and using our discoveries for weapons. I used to think he was paranoid, and frankly, I wasn't really that concerned. But now…"

"If Gerry was only here to guide us, I'd feel better about the whole thing too," Charlie said, "but he's not, so we have to decide for ourselves." Charlie took a deep breath and then said, "I had a long talk with Tikva over the weekend, and she knew that something was up. Ori told her not to get discouraged, that the project was just being delayed for a bit in order to put Israel in a better political position for carrying out the effort. She was not sure what that meant, but it didn't surprise her that the US was involved."

"Was she supportive of Boris' plan?" Yancey asked.

"Yes. She's a realist, and when it comes to politics in Israel, she told me that everyone has an opinion—or two—and wants to be involved in the decision making process, and that's why your meeting there a couple of weeks ago seemed so chaotic. But she's willing to wait if it means there's a better chance for ultimate success," Charlie answered.

"Let's face it, there's a zero chance for success from our vantage point if we don't do as Boris asked," Yancey said. Then he asked with more patience and a little resignation in his voice, "What did she think about Yaakov's role in all this?"

Charlie explained that, according to Tikva, Yaakov was always the one who apparently would have the final say, since that's what his role was. She told Charlie that he really worked for the government, not the Technion. Ori's staff and Reggie knew of his power, and maybe that was why they were mostly upset with him when the project was put on hold. Actually, there wasn't much anyone could do other than support Reggie's plan until Bobby's dad started to produce the enzyme product, which would be in place by summer's end. Finally, we all agreed to put Bobby in touch with the company that Boris told us about and then fine tune all our plans while we waited for Yadu's product to be manufactured.

"I think it's all we can do," Noreen said. "I'm not thrilled about accepting DARPA's ultimatum that it's their way or the highway—especially since Boris blackmailed you into accepting CIA money for the enzyme plant—but what choice do we have? I think that we have to go along with them for now, but if another more morally justifiable option presents itself, we should go for it. We should spend our time doing more than just fine-tuning the plan; we should continue to search for other options. At least, that's what I think."

Charlie was the first to second Noreen's proposal, and Yancey and I had no quarrel with her either. *Will the anxiety ever end?* I thought as Yancey closed the meeting and all of us went on to do our individual normal academic duties.

chapter 14

MARIKE GERALDINE CHEN-BRACHMANN was born on Saturday, June 11, 2016, at 3:06 a.m. She was a beautiful and healthy baby, nineteen inches tall and just over seven pounds, with pitch-black hair and laughing almond eyes. Charlie had been in labor for over twelve hours, and when it was finally over, I cried my eyes out. My parents were at the hospital throughout the entire ordeal, and shortly after she was born, Dad called Charlie's parents in England, on that bright Sunday morning over there, to tell them the good news. Happiness reigned on two continents.

Ma and Ba Chen were planning on coming into East Lansing a week later to stay with us for a month or so and help with the baby. I was—in some sense—looking forward to that, remembering their stay with us in DC almost five years ago and wanting to get to know them better. We planned on having the baptism and Chinese naming ceremony at the same time while the Chens were in town.

Noreen was also there with us right from the beginning, and I can't say enough about her solid Midwestern ethic: washing diapers until the service started (no throwaways for us), making two or three casserole dinners at a time, bringing the girls over to help clean the house, and so much more. There was little doubt that Noreen and the girls were thrilled with Marike and couldn't wait till she was awake so they could hold her and play with her—what a great family! Yancey gave me a bottle of good Scotch—Lagavulin—which I shared with him the second night we were home.

I must admit that for the first time in my life, I finally felt like an adult. I guess that's what being a father is all about, but I also must admit that I wasn't always sure how I was supposed to act around my baby. I wasn't the *kootchy-kootchy* type, but I did love to hold her and kiss her soft little cheeks. On the other hand, I wasn't thrilled with changing her poopie diapers or walking around and rocking her while she was crying. But I knew I loved her and her mom more than life itself, and that's all I cared about then. *I am a pansy-assed academic after all*, I thought, while smiling to myself.

The baptism was held on Sunday, July 10, one month after Marike—or Ricky, as fourteen-year-old Maxine Stetson called her—was born. We asked the Stetsons to be Marike's godparents, and Noreen held the baby while Yancey stood beside her throughout the baptismal service. When the priest said, "It is your task as sponsors to confess with the whole church the faith in our God, Father, Son, and Holy Spirit, in whose name this child is to be baptized..." and some other things about their duties as godparents, finishing with, "This, then, you intend gladly and willingly to do?"

They both whispered an audible, "Yes, we do." Mom and Dad were understandably teary through most of the church service, thinking of Mackie, but they were now beginning to relax and enjoy themselves and couldn't wait until it was all over and the Chens were back in England so that they would be the only grandparents in the area to spoil our daughter.

The traditional Chinese naming ceremony, which is supposed to take place a month after the child is born, followed in my parents' home right after the church service. The Chens hosted the naming service and had everything brought in for the guests, including dozens of hard-boiled eggs dyed red, along with the traditional plates of ginger and dishes upon dishes of Chinese food. Friends from Ann Arbor, East Lansing, and Warren, along with family members were all there. It was a grand celebration with a lot of banners covered in Chinese characters for good luck scattered throughout the house.

We didn't leave Warren until well after ten with a carload of food—including lots of hard-boiled eggs—to take back with us. Charlie and the baby slept all the way back to Okemos. The ride home was pleasant and quiet. Ma rode in the back with Charlie and Marike and I could see her dozing off through the rear-view mirror. Ba was up in front with me. We talked little on the way home, but about ten minutes away from the house he said, "You make us very happy, George...very happy; thank you."

I just smiled and looked briefly in his eyes, which were wet with tears, and nodded my head. They would be leaving on Tuesday, and I was a little scared because then it would just be me and Charlie to take care of Marike. *Can we do it all by ourselves?* I wondered.

It was midnight by the time Charlie, Ma, and Marike were in bed, but Ba and I were too stimulated from all the partying to sleep, so we stayed up a little later, and for the first time we had a substantive talk about my work.

"You know, George, I still keep in touch with Professor Shao—Reggie—and he has told me all about your work in Israel. You know I'm an urban designer, but Reggie's interest has always been in the larger urban planning context. His publications about integrating immigrant rural populations into the urban core—especially populations having different racial characteristics—are seminal. He sees a future where the urban-rural distinctions will be removed; what with modern communication technology and advanced scientific farming methods, these populations will fit seamlessly into urban environments more than ever. Do you agree, George?" Ba asked me.

"I never really thought about it that much before, but I would think that's the next big hurdle to overcome in gaining more tolerance for dissimilar members of a society. I know that Reggie's work, especially his plan, is the cornerstone of our remutation project and that it will be a big step forward for Israel in trying to establish peace with its neighbors. I just hope it all goes smoothly...that's all I can wish for," I said. I was getting tired now, and all this talk about work was making me even more tired.

"He tells me that one of his colleagues, a Mr. Yaakov Uhlman, is making things most difficult for him. Uhlman was at first working very close with Reggie, but he now seems to be distancing himself from the project, and it has caused concern for Reggie. Reggie thinks that Mr. Uhlman is somehow holding the project up. Do you know anything about this? Can you...uh, correct the situation?"

I was taken aback by how he even knew about Yaakov and that he was asking me (I presume) to get Yaakov off of Reggie's back. I simply told him that as far as I knew it was all about local Israeli politics, and it would iron itself out soon. I then told him that I was getting very tired and wanted to go to sleep. He agreed, saying he was getting tired too. But I could tell that he was not at all satisfied with my answer, and we would have this discussion again—soon.

I laid awake, thinking about Boris telling us we had to wait for Yaakov's approval before starting the distribution program, and I began to suspect that things might not be going as well as I'd thought. The baby had taken up most of my energy the last couple of months, and I hadn't really thought about the project. Before I knew it, Marike was up and crying for her 4 a.m. feeding, and Charlie was stirring, getting ready to answer her demands. For some reason I couldn't fall asleep when Charlie was feeding Marike, so it looked like I wouldn't be getting much sleep that night after all.

We spent the next morning helping Charlie's folks pack to go home. They had a 7:30 p.m. flight out of Detroit Metro and wanted to be at the airport by five. We offered to drive them, but they wouldn't hear of it. They hired an airport shuttle to pick them up at the house at three, just to be on the safe side, and they were all packed and ready to go by noon. I wondered what it was about older people always wanting to get to where they're going early. I hoped I didn't get like that—they never seemed to relax.

Shortly before the shuttle was scheduled to arrive, Ba sat down with me again to talk about the project. "You say that the trouble with Mr. Uhlman is just local politics, but from what Reggie tells me I don't think so. I think the problem is much deeper and Mr. Uhlman is just, uh...pawn, a person reporting to someone much higher. It's your project, right? Then you must find out who that person is that Uhlman takes his orders from and get it resolved, or your project will go nowhere."

"I've been out of touch for a couple of months now," I told Ba, "but I promise I'll get on it and see what's really going on. If, as you say, Uhlman is just doing what he's told by someone else, then I'll try to find out who that is. And if we have any influence with that person—or agency—then I promise to try and resolve the issue, whatever it is. We've put too much time and effort into the program to see it end like this. That's the best I can do, Ba, okay?"

"Okay, George, okay. When I talk with Reggie again I'll tell him you're looking into it and will get back to him when you find out anything, is that all right?"

"That's fine, Ba."

The shuttle showed up a little before three and had to pick up one other person on the way to Metro, but the driver assured them they would be there by five. So with lots of hugs and kisses for me, Charlie, and Marike, the Chens left for their trip home. Marike had just been fed and changed and was falling asleep in Charlie's arms, so we put her down and sat down with a deep sigh of relief—mixed in with a little anxiety. We were alone now and felt a little like we were babysitters looking forward to when the parents would come and pick up their kid. We were afraid to make noise for fear of waking Marike and having to do everything on our own when the phone rang.

"Hi, it's me, Noreen. Are you two getting settled in now that Charlie's parents have gone home?"

"Actually, we're just sitting here holding our breath and hoping Marike won't wake up for a while; but yes, we're all pretty much settled in. What's happening with you guys?" I asked.

"Not much—I made a chicken casserole, and as always I made too much. Would you like some for dinner?"

"You know, that would be just great. Neither of us feels like cooking right now and..."

"Say no more, Yancey and I will be there shortly to help get you through that first day of being on your own. We fully understand how it is," she said.

I told Charlie what Noreen said, and she smiled with relief. She immediately started straightening up the place, getting the house ready for their arrival. I was glad that Yancey was coming too. I wanted to tell him what Ba told me, and I needed his advice on what we had to do to get it fixed. If Ba was right, then we needed to act quickly, and right now I couldn't think straight enough to deal with something that major. I was trying to concentrate on the issue and see if my brain could focus on all the players in Israel,

India, and here in the United States and determine who we should be contacting when Marike awoke and wanted to eat.

———————

The Stetsons arrived shortly, and immediately Charlie and I relaxed. Noreen took charge and got the casserole in the oven and started helping Charlie with the baby. I couldn't get over how much joy Noreen took in Marike; she was all smiles when the baby was up, and she relished every little nuance. "Look, look...she's smiling—no, it's not just gas, it's a real smile," Noreen said while holding her and touching her at the side of her mouth as Charlie attended to Marike's diaper in the toilet.

After we ate Yancey and I went into the front room to talk and have a little after-dinner drink.

"You said that your father-in-law thinks our project is headed for the scrap heap. Did he tell you any more than what Reggie told him?" Yancey asked.

"I think that was enough. I haven't talked with Tikva or Bobby, have you?"

Yancey looked a bit concerned. "Yeah, I have, and I must admit that things have slowed down to a crawl. Bobby tells me they're having difficulty with the financing, and he doesn't know why, and Tikva is always being told that Ori and Devora are busy and they don't need to meet with her. She's definitely concerned that something's going on, but she can't find out what it is. She also said that Yaakov won't even answer her phone messages, and that really bothers her."

"Have you talked to Reggie? From what Ba told me, it's Reggie that's having the worst of it with Yaakov. Has he told you that too?" I asked Yancey.

"No, I haven't touched base with Reggie, but I will now and try to find out what's happening. He has the largest job to do once we have the enzyme ready, so his inability to get anything done worries me as much as Bobby's dad not being able to get financing. I don't know what to tell you, George, but I am worried. Will you be coming in to the office any time this week? If you are maybe we can talk to Reggie together."

"I'll make it my business to come in, uh, how about Thursday?" I asked.

"I'll e-mail Reggie tonight and set it up. In the meantime see if you can think of anything else that we should be doing about the situation, okay?" Yancey said.

I said that I would, but right then there was absolutely nothing that came into my head that I could do. I felt so helpless and a little nervous, too, when the Stetsons went home.

I would usually talk with Charlie about things like this, but she'd been so involved with the baby that I hated to bother her; however, when we finally went to bed around ten—while it was still light out—I told her what Ba had told me and what Yancey said.

"Have you talked to Dad?" she asked.

"Huh? No, why—do you think I should?

"I think he's wiser about these things than we are. I think he pegged Yaakov from the beginning, and he certainly might have a better idea as to what's going on than we do. Give him a call—it can't hurt. Besides, you should call anyway to thank them for arranging the baptism and letting my parents host the naming ceremony at their house. Be a good son, George... and now let me sleep. I'll be up soon enough."

I was relieved after talking with Charlie. She made it all sound so simple. Maybe now I'd be able to sleep for the first time in what seemed like months. I'd always listened to Dad's advice—*he's level-headed and intelligent and he makes good decisions*, I was thinking as I dozed off into a sound sleep before I got woken up by the demands of our daughter.

———

I called my parents to thank them for everything they did on Sunday. "How's our little Mary today?" My mother asked. She decided to call Marike Mary, just like she did for my sister, but I wasn't going to call her Mackie. Charlie and I liked Marike pronounced the European way with a slight roll on the "r" and the "i" pronounced like a long "e" so that her name sounded more like "Mah-dreek." I told Mom all about her activities, even though there really was not much to tell: she ate, she slept, she pooped...oh, and yes, she smiled—things that for some reason moms loved to hear.

After we chatted I asked her to put Dad on. I had recently recalled that Dad had been in the ROTC when he was in college, and when he graduated in 1984, he went into the service as a second lieutenant to serve his two-year tour of duty. He was honorably discharged as a captain in 1986, the year he and Mom got married. He never talked much about his military career, and all I really knew was that he was stationed, for most of his tour, at the Defense Logistics Agency (DLA) in Alexandria, Virginia, less than ten miles away from Arlington, where DARPA is located. It seemed that part of DLA's mission was to support our foreign allies in procuring various supplies to keep their military mission's defense ready. That was the extent of my knowledge about Dad's military career, until today.

Once he was on the phone, Dad filled me in on the history of our Israeli policy during the years he was stationed in DC. As it happened, 1985 was a very rough year in Israel's financial history, with rampant inflation and a severe government-imposed austerity program. By June Prime Minister Shimon Peres' monetary policies hadn't kicked in enough to control prices and keep the Israeli Defense Force fully prepared for war after Israel pulled out of Lebanon. President Reagan made it clear to all federal agencies to help the Israeli government whenever possible. America was still reeling over the 1983 attack on the Marine barracks in Lebanon, killing over two hundred soldiers. Reagan ordered the Marines entirely out of the country in 1984, so when the Israelis left in 1985, Reagan wanted to be sure that the Israelis were in a position to fight a war if they needed to.

Dad told me that it was early in the summer of 1985 when he met a young Israeli procurement officer at the DLA who was looking to get as much as he could to supply the IDF with sorely needed military materiel. "You say his name was Yossi Gittleman? Was he related to Avi?" I asked.

"He's Avi's older brother. They were about seven years apart and weren't very close. Avi wanted to be a scientist and Yossi was strictly a military man. The three of us became quite close then—"

"The three of you? You knew Avi back then?" I asked.

"No, no. The third person was Boris, Dr. Boris Bethelheim at DARPA. We all worked together to get Israel as much equipment—both military and just plain old ordinary supplies—as was legally possible. Boris helped more than me on the weapon side, but I did all I could to get Yossi the other supplies. Yossi stayed for over five months in Washington, and we put him up in Bachelor Officer Quarters in Alexandria where I was billeted. We were about the same age—of course Boris was older—but Yossi and I spent a lot of time together. He was like a brother-in-arms to me, and we kept in touch for many years after that."

Dad went on to tell me that when he found out that Gerry and Marike would be working in Avi's lab, he contacted Yossi for the first time in over twenty years. It was during that contact that he learned that Yossi was a senior officer in Mossad—or so Yossi implied. Mossad was the Israeli Intelligence service and was involved deeply in covert operations, including conducting assassinations of suspected terrorists.

"I never told you any this before," Dad said, "because I wasn't certain how you might take it, knowing how antiwar you were."

"Oh, Dad, I wish you had told me this before," I said with a touch of exasperation in my voice. "I would have understood so much more—like you referring to Tikva as your Israeli family not, as I originally thought, because she was Avi's wife—and you should know that I've never been ashamed or upset about your military work in or out of GM."

Dad then continued to explain his renewed relationship with Yossi. I think he was relieved that I never judged his military work as something to be ashamed of. In any event, it seemed that Yossi was not as easygoing as he was thirty years ago, or even twenty years ago. He never married, and the Mossad hardened him so much that he was no longer fun to talk to. In fact, it took him a long time to divulge the fact that he was working in a "covert Israeli agency," but he suggested that he was just a pencil pusher and not an operative. Dad said when he called to tell Yossi that Marike and Gerry were coming to Israel, Yossi didn't appear to be all that excited about them working at the Technion, but Dad found out later there was a good reason for that. He said that they talked for about half an hour on the phone, but that was the extent of their reunion.

"I think that Yaakov Uhlman might be working for Mossad, or at least as a Mossad informant. It's only a gut feeling, but I think I'm right on this one. I think that's why he's been so distant and not forthcoming with what's happening with your project," Dad said. "As you can guess, Mossad works in extreme secrecy, and their intelligence and operations are very difficult to discern with only limited knowledge, but I just have this feeling."

"So what can we do?" I asked.

"Right now, nothing. I think, if anything, it's time that Yossi and I talked again. If you talk to Tikva, don't tell her what I've told you about

Yossi. It wouldn't surprise me if she didn't even know that Yossi is Mossad. As I said, he was never close to Avi, and Avi might not have known either. I'll talk to him and get back to you when I find out anything. I think you should continue working as if this is a routine delay and things will pick up again. Keep a good attitude. I'll talk to you again soon, George. Take care and give my love to Charlie, and kiss our little angel for me."

———

Nine o'clock Thursday morning I was in our lab at MSU with Yancey. I had already filled him in on my conversation with Dad, and Yancey said that it put a whole new meaning on what was happening. I wasn't sure why, but Yancey said he'd explain it after our talk with Reggie. He also said we should take Dad's advice and tell Reggie that it was just a routine delay and we shouldn't panic—at least not yet. When we called Reggie, it was three in the afternoon in Haifa. Reggie told us the same thing he had told Ba about thinking that someone was holding up the project and blamed Yaakov for not telling us who it was.

"You may be right, Reggie," Yancey said, "but we have no concrete reason to believe that's the case, at least not now. Neither Ori nor Tikva has indicated in any way that something is really amiss and that it's nothing more than a typical Israeli bureaucratic slow-down. Don't you get that feeling too?"

"No, I don't—not this time. I think it's more than that. Look, Yancey, try to pry into it a little more. I think you'll have better luck at it than I can. They think I'm some kind of paranoid half-breed and I get the runaround a lot over here."

"Okay, my friend," Yancey said with a chuckle. "George and I will poke around some more, but don't stop working on getting everything in place for the distribution program. The project will happen—I can't say for sure when, but it will happen."

We weren't certain that Reggie was all that convinced that we could find anything out. Israel had a very open society with almost all facets of government programs open for debate, discussion, and dissecting to the nth degree—that is, all except security. When it came to Israel's internal security, only a few nongovernmental organizations could question their practices.

Israelis, for the most part, trusted their government almost blindly to keep them safe. And if, as Reggie suspected but didn't verbalize, Yaakov was privy to any security aspect of the project, then Yaakov wasn't about to tell anyone about it. Why he thought that Yaakov, or anyone else for that matter, would tell us was beyond me, but I think he attributed more power to us than we actually had, or could ever have, as outsiders.

"So what do you think, Yancey?"

"I'm not sure, but after what you told me about Yossi Gittleman, I'm beginning to think that Reggie is right, that someone is trying to put a halt to the project. Let's grab some coffee or something and I'll explain my thoughts, but it will have to wait for further confirmation until we can act on it. As it stands now, I'm not sure how long that will be. I should also say that if your dad's right, we may never be able to do the project with full Israeli cooperation."

My heart skipped when Yancey made that last remark because without full Israeli cooperation, the project as we knew it would be dead—just like the soil in Syria and Iran.

It was now Thursday, July 14—Bastille Day—and over coffee in our lab on campus I asked Yancey to explain what he thought was going on. He told me that Yaakov was the key. "From what your dad said, Yaakov is not the messenger between the Technion and the IDF, as I originally thought, but he's the messenger from Mossad, which makes it that much more difficult to get any substantive information about our project's status. Mossad doesn't have to tell a thing to anybody as to how or why it responds to a threat. Whether the threat is real or imaginary or just remotely possible, Mossad simply reacts and they often react with deadly consequences."

"But I don't understand. What possible threat could our remutation program pose to Israel?" I asked.

"That's the tough part; we'll probably never know. All we do know—rather I should say *can assume* for now—is that the remutation project is suspected of posing some kind of threat to Israel, and Mossad has been put on alert. Consequently, Yaakov, who probably knows even less than we do, is waiting for their go-ahead. As I see it, we have only a couple of options: first, we could wait for your dad to talk to Yossi Gittleman and see if that gets the problem resolved; and second, we contact Boris again to see if we can get Yaakov out of the loop. I don't have much hope for that last option."

"And if neither of those options works, what do we do—give up?" I asked.

"I haven't thought that far ahead yet, so let's just stick to those two options, unless you have some others to add."

In the evening I told Charlie all about the latest problem with Yaakov and explained Yancey's theory about why we were put on hold.

"Seems strange to me," she said, "but if Reggie is also concerned about Yaakov holding up the program—and then there's my dad's comments about someone more powerful being involved—it does make sense that it's Mossad. But for the life of me, I can't imagine why. Unless, of course, they perceive our whole program as some kind of terrorist plot against them—but how would that work?"

I thought about what Charlie was saying for a bit, and then it hit me. "Reggie's training program using immigrants with different ethnicity to train the Syrian and Iranian farmers. Could that be a coalition plot to do just the opposite—to possibly get the immigrants out of the country where they can be trained in terrorist techniques so that when they return to Israel they would be an established internal terrorist threat capable of doing all kinds of damage? In fact, that may be the reason the coalition countries aren't putting up a huge argument against the project. They see this as an opportunity to create an internal disruptive force in Israel itself. I can almost picture the whole thing organized around the three cities Reggie selected for our operation centers. They could just as easily be perfect locations for conducting clandestine terrorist training at the same time we're carrying out our control program."

"Whoa there, George, I think your overactive imagination is at work again. I just can't imagine they would go to all that trouble just to train a few bad apples to try and hurt Israel..."

"Not a few—a few *hundred*," I said. "That's almost like having a mini-insurgency force in a country the size of Israel. And then who knows how many others they may have recruited that won't even be going on the mission..."

"Stop right there. You know absolutely nothing about military operations, and your paranoia is certainly a bit overactive right now. I think you should talk this over again with Dad, who is at least militarily trained, before you get all riled up over some comic book adventure story. Enough!"

Charlie was at best agitated over my arguments. She turned away from me for a while, but then picked up the conversation again. She looked at me, only now she spoke more softly and with noticeable concern in her voice. "All this terrorist talk about secret agents and Mossad conspiracies against *your* program is enough to make me worry about your state of mind. Have a drink and come to bed. Marike will be up again soon enough, and she should be your only concern now," Charlie said. But her tone wasn't dismissive; it was more that if I was right, then maybe I was onto something that was way over my head.

The next day I couldn't wait to run my theory by Yancey to see what he thought. "George, I suspect that there's an infinite number of scenarios we can create as to why Mossad has put us on hold, and yours is just one of those," he said. "I think it best we wait till you talk with your father, and in the meantime let's just assume that the project will happen sooner or later as he said. My personal feeling is that whatever it is that's holding us up won't be nearly as dramatic as you perceive it to be." Yancey was not very impressed by my analysis and said in a matter-of-fact kind of way, "Have a good weekend, George." He then rethought how he had responded to me and added, "The weather is supposed to be nice. Maybe you'll come over to our place for a barbecue on Sunday."

I wasn't feeling much better after that conversation. I felt like a ten-year-old kid who had just been told to mind his own business after seeing his neighbor steal some tomatoes from another neighbor's backyard. But these weren't tomatoes I saw being taken, these were lives.

The next day, which was Saturday, I called Dad and told him about our conversation with Reggie and Yancey's feeling that Mossad was behind the delay. I then told him my thoughts about the Mossad, worrying that a terrorist cell might be trained to operate in Israel using our program as a guise.

"I don't know what's causing the holdup of the farm program, but you present a plausible argument," Dad said, relieving me of the thought that I was going bonkers. "I've tried getting in touch with Yossi again, but he hasn't got back to me yet. It may be a while before he does, but I know he will eventually. On Monday I'll call Boris just to let him know what's going on. He has a lot invested in your program also, so it will be interesting to hear his perspective—that is, if he'll give it to me," Dad said.

Even though we were talking on the phone, I could sense by Dad's tone of voice that something else had caused him to be concerned. "Look, George, this may be more complicated than either you or I can imagine, so don't be disappointed if the project is...uh, transferred to another agency and our role somewhat reduced," Dad said somberly. "You and your friends have done a marvelous job getting it to where it is now. I think you should feel satisfied that no matter who finishes the project, it was you that made it possible to be resolved in the first place, okay?"

Chills ran down my back. I knew that he was in protect mode. He'd already lost his daughter to an Arab terrorist in Israel, and he wasn't going to loose his son. I think he was saying that he'd be setting a course to get us out of the project because it might not be safe for me anymore. And I knew there would be no way to stop him if I was right.

I told Charlie what was going on and how I felt about my conversation with Dad. She listened very carefully this time and said, "George, if Dad really feels that way then maybe we should let him do what's best for us. He's been around and knows these people personally. Let's wait to see what happens and not try to push it until Dad gets back to you. Can you accept that?"

Do I have a choice? I thought.

———————

At Yancey's barbecue on Sunday, I sat with Yancey for some time, strategizing our next moves. It was a beautiful, dry, hot Sunday in July, and the weather was not conducive for working. I think we both had other things on our minds—the coming semester and what we'd be teaching, writing up a paper for the next agricultural society meeting—so the thought of just waiting to see what happened sounded easy enough to accept.

"Then we'll have to leave it at that. Keep an ear open as to what's going on and simply wait for your father to get back to us," Yancey concluded.

I nodded and caught Charlie looking at us out of the corner of my eye. She seemed to understand what we had concluded and looked at peace, sitting there on a blanket in Yancey and Noreen's beautiful green backyard. I took another sip of my beer and thought how cool and refreshing it was. If only our lives would always be this peaceful and worry-free, I would ask for nothing more. But I knew they wouldn't be.

chapter 15

IT WAS JUST after Labor Day, and we were well over two months behind on the project. Classes had already started at MSU and still no word from Yossi. I stopped bugging Dad about it and left it at that. Dad said he would get back to me as soon as he heard from him, and so I continued to wait. His conversation with Boris over six weeks earlier had given him little new information about the current holdup. Boris was not impressed with my interpretation. He simply told Dad that if what I believed about the terrorist training program was actually true, he, Boris, would have known about it because he'd been privy to international terrorist issues ever since Osama bin Laden was killed by Navy SEALs in 2011. It would appear that DARPA developed the SEALs' arsenal and worked closely with the National Security Agency (NSA) on evaluating terrorist threats. This all seemed credible—that is, if you could believe Boris, but I didn't say that to Dad.

Things in the Middle East had quieted down considerably, and Noreen found out that food supplies were being supplemented by some outside intervention. We knew it was our surplus food program that was responsible for that intervention, but the fact that the grain supplies were from the United States was not universally known for political reasons. United States aid programs seldom get the coverage they deserved from Middle East countries for fear of local backlash. The slug infestation had not progressed much farther than the fields we had targeted for treatment, but the land was in worse condition now and would require significantly more work to bring it back to life. Bobby would be staying in India, working on an independent study program under Yancey's tutelage, developing the computerized processing for his dad's plant. It appeared that some money had started trickling in to build the physical plant but not enough to furnish it with the equipment and raw materials needed to make the enzyme product.

In Israel Reggie had finished his plan and had it accepted by the foreign affairs officer he was working with. He was well into training the trainers he would be sending over to start the treatment phase. He was still worried that he would not be able to do it before the hard winter set in, which would greatly hamper the project. But nobody was stopping him and he even made trips to the three cities to look over potential training, staging, and housing sites.

He had no difficulty getting visas using his British passport, even though he did not hide the fact that he was on the faculty of the Technion. Yaakov had not stopped him but had made it clear that no Israeli workers would be allowed to leave yet; he still gave no reason why they couldn't leave other than the Technion's president had not authorized it yet. Tikva was aware of all this, and, although she felt frustrated by the delay, she had lived in Israel long enough to know that bureaucratic decisions sometimes took exceedingly long and irrational routes before finally being implemented. As long as some progress was occurring, she didn't feel like she could push it any faster.

We held our first meeting of the school year on Thursday, September 10. It seemed that Thursdays would be better for all of us as a time to meet. Charlie was on maternity leave for the first semester, and she arranged to have someone come in on Thursdays to take care of Marike while she got away to shop, do some work here at the college, and just get out of the house for a few hours by herself. Marike was down to one feeding at night—between two and four in the morning—so we weren't as tired as we were when we first brought her home. A fixed routine was starting to form in our lives once again, and that was comforting.

"I still think it's only three minutes to midnight," Noreen said at our meeting, "even though it appears that things are very peaceful over there. In fact, it may even be a little less than that. I think the temporary relief that the surplus grain created is just that: temporary. There have been absolutely no substantive talks or actions on any coalition country's part that would lead me to believe that peace with Israel is on anyone's agenda. I also think that the loss of their grain crops and no hope for having a reasonable harvest next year will again create the unrest that led to the recent crisis. In other words, I'm not a happy camper."

"If that's the case, then even if we are in time to start the treatment this year, it still may be too late to ward off a serious crisis. It all seems so damn futile—why are we working our asses off if it's all for naught?" Charlie said.

"I can understand why you may feel that way, Charlie," Yancey said, "but it has been my experience that if you keep at it and don't lose your enthusiasm, only good things can happen. Let's not give up hope just yet; we're not licked on this one, right, George?"

Yancey was looking to me for support, but I just nodded and didn't add anything. In a way I must admit that I was feeling exactly like Charlie. I just wanted to go back to doing my own research and stay out of these so-called applied research programs. I was looking forward to having Dad get us out of this project—maybe I could get a couple of papers out of it and that would be fine with me. On the other hand, I had invested so much emotionally into the effort that I didn't want to give up without a fight. To say I was conflicted would be putting it mildly.

The worst part of it all—from an academic viewpoint—was that nobody else in academia was the least bit interested in my work. Acidic slugs did not turn other researchers on, and my remutation efforts did not seem to excite anyone beyond a mild curiosity. No federal agencies were looking to fund my efforts and no nongovernmental organizations were knocking on my door asking me to join them for any joint research projects, including IBM. It seemed that it was only Yancey, our wives, Bobby, and me who believed that we were actually saving the world. After all this research, heartache, and work maybe it was just one big waste of time after all. And, maybe—just maybe—I was really trying to make the murders of Mackie and Gerry not be in vain.

Yancey sensed my feelings and said, "Okay then, we wait for George's dad to get back to us, and be prepared to get back at it again if he brings us good news. Remember, there's always Boris. He's our ace in the hole, and we all know how much he needs this treatment program to be successful or he's probably out the window. We're not doing much on the project right now, so we should still be able to do our other work. George and I are preparing a joint paper for the ag society meeting and that's enough for now. Everyone, let's take a deep breath and promise that we will support each other no matter what the outcome is, okay?"

Yancey's pep talk worked—well, somewhat. Whether I wanted to or not, I guess I was still committed to seeing this through. I just wished that

I felt more enthused about it and honestly still believed that we could make a difference in this fucked up world.

A couple of weeks later I found out from Dad that he, Yossi, and Boris all met in DC for a secret meeting on the project. But it wasn't until months later that I learned all the facts from him. Boris and his contacts set up the meeting at an Israeli safe house in DC. From what Dad told me, it was a real cloak-and-dagger kind of event. Blindfolds and unmarked vehicles at different times and at different places were used to get Dad and Boris to the meeting. It was at that safe house that the three brothers-in-arms of over thirty years ago were at last reunited. Only now they were all much worldlier, and their old collaboration for outfitting the IDF with secondhand clothes and equipment was certainly not the issue. The current issue was the survival of Israel and the Middle East as we knew it.

Dad told me that Yossi started out by telling him, "Pete, you know that that entire emotionless diatribe I said over the phone last year was just an act. I was thrilled to hear about your daughter coming to the Technion, but I couldn't let anyone who might be tapping our phone know that just in case they wanted to take out their hatred for me on them. I know you think that Avi and I weren't close, and that sadly was partially true. But I loved my brother and was very proud of what he was doing. My work, on the other hand, was so dangerous I knew that if I, in any way, appeared to be too close to Avi, I would be putting his life in danger—and that went for your family too."

The room was in a low-cost housing section of the city and was simply one room, a kitchenette, and a bathroom. The furniture was shabby and in disarray, and the place seemed dark with only two windows exposed to an enclosed courtyard. Yossi stopped talking while looking around the room and reflecting on what he just said. Then he continued, "But, as it turned out, I put him in danger anyway. The attack on his lab was actually an attack on me. I've made many enemies in the terrorist ranks, and because they couldn't get to me they took it out on him. When your daughter and son-in-law were collateral damage to that attack, you have no idea how sick it made me. And it only got worse when I found out that Marike was pregnant. And now your son and daughter-in-law are also involved, as is Tikva and you...and you too, Boris—enough!" he said, looking directly at Boris. "I want you all out of it now. Just give it up and go on about your business. I need no one else's blood on my hands. Israel will handle the problem herself."

"You're worried about me?" Boris said, incredulous. "I'm probably on every terrorist hit list in the world right now. One more listing is not going to make that much difference. In any event, what makes you think we need you to pull this off?"

"Stop it, Boris," Yossi said. "You know we can we do it ourselves without Pete's trucks or your Indian processing plant. As for the university kids—your son and his colleagues, Pete—they were superfluous right after Boris' so-called conference on remutation when they told you, Boris, how to control the slugs. We got all we needed from them at that time from our own contacts. My advice is to simply tell them to back off—it's out of their hands now and we'll take it from here. In any case, we're in no rush to neutralize the slugs just yet, thanks to your Arab food program, Boris. We'll put more pressure on the coalition for other concessions..."

Yossi and Dad had been sitting on the couch with Boris sitting in his chair in front of them when suddenly Dad stood up and said to Yossi, "Yes, of course you will, like you have been doing for decades now without any real promise of peace. Yes, do that—ask for more concessions, and when they're not forthcoming simply kill off more land from farming. That should do it." His sarcasm was palatable.

Yossi stood up now and started to slowly pace in the small room. He then responded to Dad. "Pete, I never knew that you became an Arab sympathizer in your old age. Do you honestly believe for one minute that the Muslim terrorists really want a peaceful coexistence with Israel? You should know, as Boris does, that at their first chance they'll take over Israel and kill us all. If we don't keep them weak and disorganized, it will be the end for Israel. Is this what you want? To let them get organized and strong and of one voice? If that takes place then the second holocaust in less than a hundred years will happen. And this time it will be me, Ori Ben-Isaac, Devora Kaytz, Tikva, and even Reggie and his team because they work for us. I don't think you want that to happen."

"Of course I don't. But unlike you, I think there is another alternative. The world is getting much smaller, and the desire for the total destruction of

Israel is not on the agenda for most young Muslims. Food, jobs, education, and freedom are more important to them, and if you don't help them get it, they will destroy you and their own leaders as they did just six years ago. I think it's time Israel took a chance on rational decision making and made the Arab lands fertile again, if only for humanitarian reasons."

"What do you think, Boris?" Yossi asked, still pacing, "Are we irrational or realistic?"

"Both," Boris said. "I agree that the coalition leaders are still very anti-Israel and would welcome the complete takeover of your country. But I also think that it's time to step out there and solve their food issue. I think you're right that you don't need us anymore and you should do it yourself. But that could also be risky. We still have a better chance of getting you into Syria and Iran than you do on your own. But if you think you can do it, then be my guest."

Yossi stopped pacing and was quiet for a while, and then he bent over and gave Boris a big hug. He then walked over to Dad and hugged him too, and then said, "That you are still willing to let your son stay involved after losing Marike is beyond brave." He then said to both of them, "I'll keep you informed as to what's happening. Boris, I'll let you know through the usual channels and you can update Pete, okay?"

And with that the meeting ended, and the three parted the same way they came: in secret.

When Dad got back from DC on Sunday, September 20, he simply informed me at that time that he had made contact with Yossi and that the Israeli government was now taking over the project. Boris was also informed of this, and so it would not do us any good to try and pressure Boris to stay involved, even if the GM trucks Dad got were no longer needed. If they wanted any more advice from us, they would contact us.

And that was it. I couldn't get out of my mind how much Dad kept saying, "We are no longer needed."

At our meeting on the twenty-fourth, we sat around not offering anything in the way of alternatives. I, naturally, told Charlie right away and then called Yancey to fill him in on Dad's conversation as well. So our regularly scheduled Thursday meeting was a bit anticlimatic. "I suggest we temporarily suspend our efforts on the project until we are called to participate in the treatment. As George says, it would appear that 'we are no longer needed.' Does everyone agree with that?" Yancey asked.

"I'll still keep my eye on the political situation and let you all know if anything happens that might need our immediate response," Noreen said. "At this point all I can do is pray that the situation doesn't get any worse and that Israel acts in time to prevent more damage. I don't think we'll ever know who put the slugs out there, but that no longer matters. I think you two—George and Yancey—need to make certain that it doesn't happen elsewhere in the world, and you should come up with a rapid response plan if it does..."

"And just who do you think will fund that?" I asked. I loved Noreen totally, but there were times when her unrealistic sense of our capability to control things just grated on me, and this was one of those times. The four of us—well, at least three of us—had been sitting there dejected over the idea that we no longer had any control over our project, and I think the frustration that came with that knowledge got to me.

Yancey detected the strain in my voice and, trying to ease the situation, said calmly, "George is right. There's not a whole lot of national or international worry about the slugs right now, so getting funding to develop some kind of a response plan is almost out of the question."

Yancey looked over to Noreen, whom he could see was hurt by my harsh response to her suggestion, and said, "But you are right, Noreen, that our work is not done. You know that for quite a while now Charlie, George, and I had planned on presenting papers and publishing articles about the slugs—obviously, leaving out all the political intrigue. That will take time of course, but at least we'll let everyone know that a danger to the world's farmlands exists and that we have developed a mitigation process. That may at least start to generate some worldwide interest. I think that's all we can do for now."

With that last statement, our little research group was formally dissolved. Yancey talked with Bobby over the weekend and brought him up to date, assuring him that his dissertation research was still viable. In the meantime, Charlie and I talked with Tikva and got her sense of what happened at the Technion. We also told her our decision about formally ending the project here in the States, which she said she regretted but understood our problem. Charlie also touched base with Reggie, and afterward she let Ba know the status of Reggie's treatment program.

And that was it. I can't say I felt good about it, but I was relieved to finally have permission, as it were, to do other things. Competent people from the Israeli government had taken over the project, and maybe that was the best way to leave it. Yancey put it in perspective when he pointed out that we'd be writing and publishing about the threat and offering relief if it should happen, and that was a good thing. After all, we were a pretty small, powerless, and insignificant little group, and it was arrogant of us to think that world peace actually rested on our shoulders. We should let world peace fall into the hands of others. However, as it turned out, that wasn't such a good idea after all.

New Year's Eve of 2016 had come and gone, and it was now Thursday, January 5, 2017. Yancey and I were both wondering what was happening on the remutation project. We hadn't been informed by anyone lately, and Charlie's weekly (or less) talks with Tikva gave us no clue as to what the Israelis were doing to get the project going. We had been in touch with Bobby, who told us his dad's plant was producing product and shipping it to Israel, but that's all he knew. It seems the early partnership they had had with Boris' company dissolved for some reason, but Bobby's dad found some other local investors to pick up the plant and make it go. Bobby learned that the majority of the funds actually came from some Israeli companies involved in international investing. But he strongly suspected they were front organizations for the Israeli government.

Yancey and I still met informally on Thursdays to keep abreast of what was happening with the Middle East food situation. MSU let us keep the research space until such time that another faculty member with funding needed the room. It seemed a bit lonely with just the two of us sitting at the table, but it was good for us to be able to talk about the current slug infestation while we prepared our upcoming talks and papers. Yancey said, "I've been thinking, George, that if the remutation project is underway, I don't recall any effort being considered to restore the soil, am I right?"

"I think so," I said. "I think we decided to wait on that one until the project got started. We knew that it would be a year or so before restoration could start, and I think we decided to wait on developing that aspect of the project. What are you getting at?"

"I don't know—I guess I'm getting antsy over the project's status, and I was thinking that we should get involved again, and coming up with a soil rehab project might be one way for doing that. What do you think?"

"I think that's more in your area than mine, but if you want to get involved some way, then do it. I'll support you in any way I can. Are you thinking about any particular process or just exploring some options?"

"It's more like a little of both. When I was in Lebanon, over two years ago, one of my colleagues was into vermiculture—you know, worm farming—for composting and fertilizing in a totally organic manner. He's now working in Qatar at their solid waste management center; it's the largest in the Middle East. I was thinking that maybe I'd touch base with him and find out what his thoughts are on restoring the farm lands in Syria and Iran. I don't know...it can't hurt, right?"

"Sounds like a reasonable thing to do. I don't think we need Israel's or Boris' permission to investigate that angle. Why don't you give him a call and at least see if he knows anything about what's going on in the coalition about the lost farm acreage, and if so, what are their plans on restoring the soil. Want me to do anything?" I offered, not really knowing what I could do.

"Yeah, why don't you run this by your dad but in a more proactive fashion. I mean, don't lie, but if you could make it sound more like we're maybe planning on starting some kind of soil rehab project with Lebanon and Qatar—which I actually might—I think we may get a rise out of Boris. That might shake loose some idea as to what the hell is happening over there. Could you do that?"

I smiled at Yancey and said, "Did I ever tell you that behind that solid Midwestern affect of yours there's a very devious man?"

I told him that I would touch base with Dad on the weekend and see what I could find out as well as plant the seeds of us getting active again. In spite of all my misgivings about working on the Israeli project once more, I had to admit that I was excited about the prospect. It would be interesting to get Charlie's read on what Yancey was proposing, knowing that she was glad to be out of the business.

I found out later that night what Charlie thought, and I was quite surprised.

Marike, at almost six months old now, was beginning to sleep through the night, and life got a lot easier. She was also a lot more fun to be around too—smiling, laughing, and doing what most six-month-old babies do, but she was our six-month-old baby and that's what made it so great. Charlie had been shopping most of the day, and when I got home the sitter was gone and Charlie was putting away the groceries. Marike was still sleeping, and while Charlie took care of the groceries, I told her about Yancey's plan for trying to find out what was going on with the project.

"That's brilliant," Charlie said. "I've been dying to know myself. Whenever I would ask Tikva, she would get a little upset for having been left out of the loop by Ori, so I stopped asking her. I figured that if something exciting or new was happening, she'd tell me. You know, George, I miss being involved. As frustrating as the project was at the end, the feeling of impotency—not be able to do anything of importance—was getting me down. But now I want to be involved again. So what's your plan?"

I really didn't have any plan, as such, but more of an idea as to what I would say to Dad to get the desired results.

"He'll see right through you, George," Charlie told me. "I think you should be straight out with him. Sure, tell him Yance's plan to contact his old colleague and possibly put together a soil treatment program, but you don't have to embellish it. Tell him we want to be involved again and see what he says. I think you might be surprised at his response."

Charlie was certainly right about that last part—I was indeed surprised by what Dad said on Sunday when I called. He filled me in further on all the details of his conversation with Yossi and Boris a few months back. He told me that Yossi was worried about our safety, and he said that frankly he was worried too. He suggested that we leave it alone—let the Israelis handle it and wait for them to ask us to get involved yet again. He also cautioned me and Yancey about preparing a soil reclamation program without letting Israel know. That might change the entire dynamic in a way that could destroy Israel's chances for success.

I wasn't sure how that worked, but I got his drift and noticed, for the first time, how concerned he was with our safety. He even felt that Ba was in danger because of his close association with Reggie. It was then that I realized that my father had let his love for me, Charlie, and the baby color his judgment. I let him continue on with his cautionary tale and listened respectfully before thanking him for his advice and ending the call.

"Well, that's not what I expected," Charlie said when I told her about the conversation with Dad. "I thought he'd be glad that we were being so constructive and planning on the future once the slugs were under control. So what are you going to do, George?"

"I guess all I can do: run it by Yancey on Monday and see what he thinks. Do you have any ideas?"

"Not really. But I think I'll call Reggie. I won't mention anything about Yance's plan but just feel him out about what's going on and what he sees in the way of progress. You know, I'll keep it general and try to get as much information as possible to help us make some good decisions about all this."

Charlie stopped playing with Marike and was putting her in her crib for a nap when she said, "I can see Dad's point about our safety after learning that Marike and Gerry were..." Charlie never could say *killed* or *murdered* without getting overcome with sadness. She continued, "And they didn't even know about Yossi. Here we are working with that guy, so maybe Dad is not as paranoid as you think."

Professor Kassim Faysal was a Maronite Catholic originally from Lebanon who was currently on leave from the American University in Beirut and working in Qatar. He was setting up a vermiculture effort for composting organic waste using Egyptian worms that would thrive in Middle Eastern countries. Yancey found him on the Internet, and after a couple of e-mails he called him.

"Kassim, how are you? So good talking with you," Yancey said.

"Yes, yes...it is me—Yancey, my friend, how are you? Still working with those rogue slugs we found a couple of years ago? I've read your papers published with Brachmann—they were brilliant; changing them back to becoming harmless again... what a coup. Have you had much success?" Kassim asked.

Yancey explained the work that he and I did when we developed the slug remutation process, but he didn't tell Kassim about the soil treatment program we helped develop with the Israelis. Nor did he mention anything about the enzyme plant in India. *"Anyway, that's where we're at right now, but I was wondering if you know anything about the slug infestation problem we discovered over there. Do you know if it still exists, or who may be treating it? I was also curious if your vermiculture project could be used to restore the land again. That is, could the worms raise the pH in such a way as to make the land fertile—and even more important, could your worms live in such an initially low pH environment?" Yancey asked.*

"That is funny that you should ask, Yancey. I've recently met some Iranian scientists—agronomists, I think—who are currently taking care of the problem. They claim that they learned how to neutralize, or remutate, the slugs based on your published articles, and they too have come to me and asked if I could restore the land. Did you know about them?" Kassim asked.

"No, as a matter of fact, no...I, uh...I had no idea that anyone else was using our work here at MSU to treat the infestation. Uh...that's great, I guess, uh...if you should talk with them again, I'd love to make contact. You know, uh...yes, please have them contact me," Yancey said. He was completely flabbergasted by the knowledge that another treatment program was in progress and apparently far enough along to be looking into land restoration.

"That may be difficult, Yancey. I think scientific exchanges between your country and Iran are what your government calls restricted." Kassim was quiet for minute and then said, "But I'll tell you what I can do. You know we farmers are not political, and I'm certain that they might be very interested in talking with you. Maybe I can arrange something on neutral ground—like Qatar—where you could informally meet with them. Would that work for you, or are you uncomfortable with that?" Kassim asked.

Yancey told me that he agreed to meet with them, informally, and on the pretext of visiting with Kassim to study his vermiculture program. He then arranged for travel to Qatar, receiving university travel support for the short trip. Yancey got the funds by promising to publish a follow-up article from his earlier work in Lebanon taking into account the use of vermiculture to restore the land. After all, it was perfectly reasonable that if one cleared up a catastrophic infestation that left agricultural land unusable, one would want to explore the various improvement programs that might be around. The composting plant in Qatar was probably the largest in the world and could possibly offer the mitigation they were seeking. If other visitors were at the plant from other countries, well, that might be a nice way to exchange ideas—informally, of course.

———————

On Monday, January 9, Yancey and I filled each other in on our conversations with Dad and Kassim. "How in hell did Iranian academics get involved with the program, and where are they producing the enzyme-protein soup? I can't believe that they are that far along by just having read our papers in the open literature. They would have to be pretty far along technically to pull that off, and I don't think they are," I told Yancey.

"We should find out soon. I'm leaving in less than a month—Saturday, February 4 to be exact—and I'll be back the following week. Why don't we plan on one more meeting...say, Thursday the second?" Yancey said, looking at his iPad. "We'll go through one more update on everything and flesh out what it is I have to find out and how I play it, okay?"

On Thursday, February 2, Charlie, me, Yancey, and Noreen met at the lab to game-plan Yancey's trip. Charlie had recently been able to talk with Reggie on the status of the remutation program and wanted to fill us in on that conversation as well.

"He said that they're all set up and have actually started the training program, especially in Hamadan, Iran. They have product stored in Mosul, and as soon as they feel the weather is warm enough—probably in a few more weeks—they'll start spreading the enzyme solution. They have planes, trucks, and all sorts of equipment ready to go. He then told me that in Al-Hasakah the process has been slowed down by the Syrians, and he's not sure why. But in any case, he was quite up-beat and felt certain that the treatment portion would be completed by late spring or early summer at the latest," Charlie said.

It was like old times with the four of us sitting around the table, planning our strategies for saving the world. Too bad Bobbie wasn't here—he would have enjoyed working on this new element of actually restoring the land. But that wasn't what we were really doing; we were trying to get involved in the program again by finding out what everyone else was doing.

"That's it!" Yancey said. "I'll bet anything that these Iranian scientists are from Hamadan and they're already anticipating soil rehab. Wow! This trip should prove very interesting. So how do you think I should play it?" We all got excited at the prospect of being in the thick of things again and paid no attention to the inherent dangers Yancey might be facing on this trip.

"I don't think you should be telling them that you've been working with the Israelis," Noreen said. "Even if they were to admit—which I doubt they will—that it's the Israelis who are funding their project. I think you should play it just as you set it up: you want to learn about soil rehab using large-scale worm composting methods as the natural follow-on to remutation. I think you can be as curious as possible about how they carried their remutation program out, since it was yours and George's work that solved the hard part of the problem in the first place. That shouldn't cause them to be suspicious of your motives."

Finally, I began to think about Dad's warning and raised that issue. "But what about Dad's advice telling us to stay out of it for fear that we might be endangering our lives and hurting Israel's chances for success?" I asked. "Now that we feel fairly certain that it is our program under Reggie's plan that's being conducted, shouldn't we be backing off from it now?"

There was silence while everyone thought about my question, and then Yancey said, "I think we have an obligation to satisfactorily prove that it is our project—if it's not ours, then whose is it? And if it is an Arab-based project, are we obligated to inform Ori? And finally, from a purely academic point of view, aren't we obligated to learn as much as we can about the results obtained by applying *our* theoretical research to practical problems?"

It all sounded very reasonable when put that way, but something was still nagging me and, as it turned out, Charlie as well. We looked at each other for a second and then Charlie said, "Yes, to all your questions...but the one that scares me is the second one about informing Ori if it isn't ours. I think that could be the most dangerous situation if it was true. Because if it was true and it is an Arab project, then it would be hard to predict Israel's—and Boris'—response to that. I think that's where Dad's warning comes in to play. If you notify Ori about your findings, Yance, then it shouldn't be hard for the Arabs to trace it back to you and then to us. And we could be targets if Boris and Israel don't think that they're getting enough concessions from the coalition for cleaning up the infestation and they react belligerently. It would be just the excuse that the terrorists would want in order to justify doing some harmful act either in Israel or even here at MSU…"

"I think that's a stretch," Noreen said. "But I do agree with Charlie that if Yancey does find out, with a high level of certainty, that it's not our project, then we should think very carefully about what our next steps should be. Why don't we just leave it that way until you get back, Yancey? We'll worry about who needs to know what's happening and what they need to know once we have all the facts."

We ended the meeting with lots of hugs and good wishes for a safe trip to Yancey. To say we were worried would be putting it mildly—not so much for Yancey's safe travel but for what he might find out on his trip. All we could do was sit and wait for his return. We didn't expect to hear anything of importance either via phone or Internet from him while he was in Qatar for fear of his messages being intercepted, so our wait would be tense.

PART IV
OUTCOME
Winter 2017

chapter 16

WE HADN'T HEARD very much from Yancey since he left the previous Saturday—just a couple of e-mails with nothing very informative in them.

Then on Wednesday afternoon, February 8, I got a phone call. "George, it's your mother. You have to come home as soon as possible. Your father has had a heart attack, and they rushed him to Beaumont Hospital. I'm here with him now, and he's asking for you..."

"My God!" I said. "When did this happen? Is he...is he...will he be..."

"Yes, he's alive and he will survive, but he's scheduled to undergo surgery soon, and he wants to talk to you first..."

"I'm on my way—that's Beaumont on Thirteen-Mile Road, right?"

"Don't speed. The roads may be slippery. Whenever you get here will be fine. The doctors say he's out of danger now, so drive careful. I'll be here. I love you, and thank you for coming. Oh, and make sure Charlie and the baby will be all right if you're gone for a while..."

"They'll be fine, Mom. I'll see you soon." Mom was so matter-of-fact it scared me even more. I could tell she was scared out of her mind by the way she showed almost no emotion, but knowing her, she just didn't want to make me worry any more than I needed to. Unfortunately, she didn't accomplish that goal.

Charlie had heard my end of the conversation and was sitting down with her eyes open so wide I could see the fear in them from across the room. I told her what happened, and she helped me get ready for the drive into Royal Oak where the hospital was located. She kept telling me, "Now don't worry about me and Marike, we'll be fine. Just drive carefully and don't speed...and call me as soon as you get to the hospital."

I left hurriedly and forgot to take my gloves. I hoped I wouldn't need them.

It was around four in the afternoon when I reached Beaumont, and I found out that Dad had been there since around one thirty. The EMTs treated him with aspirin and other drugs for his chest pain and put him on oxygen as soon as the ambulance arrived to take him to the hospital. By the time he got to the hospital, they had decided he needed surgery to unblock the artery that caused the attack. They told Mom that Dad was fortunate that treatment was started so soon and that after surgery he should have a good recovery. The doctor was talking to Mom when I came in, and he explained the procedure to me as well.

"He's only fifty-five, Doctor," I said. "And he's always taken such good care of himself. What's going on here?"

"Yes, he certainly looks quite strong, and that's all in his favor. But you know family history, stress, and so many other factors can lead up to a cardiac event; you can't always predict when heart disease will affect someone. Your dad is going to get the best that modern medicine has to offer, and I'm sure—"

"Yes, I know he will, and thanks. You say stress can be a factor—he has a desk job and exercises regularly. What kind of stress...?"

"No, I didn't say that was the case here, I simply pointed out that in some cases stress—mental or physical—can lead to heart disease. But we don't know if that was true for your dad. Look, George, if you want to see him for a few minutes before his surgery, you should do that now, okay?" the doctor said.

I walked into Dad's room and saw him lying in the bed, and for the first time in my life my father looked frail and vulnerable to me. There were all kinds of monitors and IVs hooked up to him. His eyes were closed at first, but he must have heard me coming into the room because he opened his eyes and looked over at me.

"George, glad you made it before my surgery. I'm scheduled to go in between five and six so I'll make this brief," he said in a weak and tired voice.

I came over, took his hand, leaned over, and gently kissed his forehead. I had never kissed my dad's forehead before and was moved to tears when I did it. "How're you feeling?" I asked almost in a whisper.

"I'm fine now—very tired, but I'm feeling fine. They tell me I'll be all right, but I wanted to talk with you before the operation."

"It can wait, Dad. What could be so important that it can't wait for a couple of hours...?"

"George, listen to me now. I want you to stop this work you're doing in Qatar. You never knew this, but it was Iranian terrorists that attacked the Technion, and they are totally unpredictable. Your friend, Yancey, is in serious trouble, and if you can get him out of there then do it as soon as possible. But please, for my sake and your mother's sake—she, by the way, knows nothing of this—get out now before they harm you too. Do other kinds of research and stay away from any projects that might take you into the Middle East. Will you promise me that?" he asked.

I was totally confused, but I didn't want Dad to be any more stressed than he was already, so I said, "Yeah, sure, Dad—I'll get out of it. I was planning on doing that anyway. And yes, I'll contact Yancey and tell him to come home—I promise you. You can count on it, okay? Now relax and get some rest, and I'll talk to you again after the operation. Again, I promise I'll do what you say on this one. I've always taken your advice before, haven't I?"

The attendants came shortly and took Dad off to the OR prep station. Mom and I went into the family waiting room and tried to relax a little while they operated on Dad. Mom looked at me and must have seen something in my face. "George, don't get so upset. Everything will be fine—the doctors said so. You know his grandfather had heart trouble, so he probably inherited it, but today it's not a death sentence. He'll be fine...you'll see." Mom kept rubbing her finger on her cheek below her eye like she was trying to wipe away a tear, afraid that I might see her cry.

I put my arm around her and said, "I know he will, Mom. He's so tough that it will take more than this to keep him down."

What Dad said hit me in two ways: first, how did he know that Yancey was in Qatar already since I hadn't told him? And second, I suspected that his worrying about me probably generated the stress that led up to the attack. *What a selfish asshole I am,* I thought, *putting such a burden on my family.*

When Dad came out of the OR and into the ICU, he was still very much out of it, as one would expect. The doctor said the operation went very well, and they were optimistic about his recovery. However, he said we should just let him sleep now, go home, and come back tomorrow. We should call first because they might even take him out of the ICU in the morning. With the modern computerized equipment and imaging techniques they used, there was no need to crack his ribs and that meant a significantly less painful and much quicker recovery period. We waited for a while anyway and just watched him sleep.

Around eight at night I followed Mom home and decided to stay the night so I could see Dad first thing in the morning. I went to sleep in my old room, which was now a guest room, and thought about the times I spent there while growing up. I could almost hear Mom yelling up to me, "Stop reading those comic books and get to sleep!"

I thought about Mackie's room, which they had refurbished into a nursery for Marike. That was nice for us, but probably very hard for them. They didn't do much to my old room—since Mackie fixed it up for me and Charlie after we were first married—other than remove more of my junk and repaint it. However, in my bed I felt warm and comfortable. I was so totally exhausted that I fell asleep without any trouble for the first time in a long while.

———

Dad was out of the ICU when we went to visit with him on Thursday, but he was still very groggy. I'm not sure he even knew we were there. We were informed that he was recovering rapidly, and they would probably try to get him up and walking that afternoon, which surprised us.

"We're thinking about sending him home on Saturday," the nurse told us. "With no reason to keep him here, he should be starting his outpatient rehab program next week and could be back to work, if he wants to, in around three weeks." She was quite upbeat and seemed to be knowledgeable about his condition. "You can tell just by looking at Pieter that he's in great physical condition, takes care of himself, and I know he will do what's expected of him to get well, so don't worry—I'm certain he'll have an excellent recovery."

Mom was actually smiling when she said, "Georgie, I'll stay here with your father, and if I need you for anything I'll call you, okay? You go home, and we'll stay in touch. Give Charlie and our little angel a big hug and kiss from us. Maybe you can come in with the family next week some time. Thank you so much for being here now." And with that she gave me a big hug and many kisses. She hadn't called me Georgie since I was a little kid, but I didn't mind.

When I got back to Okemos, I told Charlie what the nurse had told us about Dad's recovery, and you could sense the relief in her voice when she said with a deep sigh, "Thank God!" She told me that she had informed everyone that needed to know at MSU about Dad and had been in contact with Noreen. They still hadn't heard from Yancey, but assumed he'd be home sometime on Saturday or Sunday. He had an open ticket, so he hadn't scheduled a flight back yet because he was uncertain how long he'd be staying in Qatar. But he tentatively set Saturday the eleventh as the day he would be leaving. I didn't tell Charlie what Dad had told me about getting Yancey home—she was worried enough without having to put up with that burden as well.

I immediately composed the following e-mail to Yancey:

Dad had a heart attack and I need you here to help out with my teaching schedule. If at all possible come home ASAP.

I knew that Yancey would read between the lines since he and I never taught the same courses and we never sat in on each other's classes. If nothing else, I was hoping that I would get a response from him as to when he'd be here, but he never answered my message. I knew something was wrong, and with Dad's warning I was terror stricken.

I didn't tell anyone—Charlie, Noreen, other faculty members—about my concern and tried to analyze on my own what I needed to do. I waited two more days, which seemed like a lifetime, and when Yancey didn't come home on Saturday, panic set in.

First of all I contacted Bobby in India and updated him briefly about Yancey's trip to Qatar and my father and asked how things were with him and his family. I really just wanted to know if Bobby and his family were all right. I kept the conversation very brief and avoided any talk about Israel or Reggie by saying I just wanted to update him and there was no need for him to waste his time filling me in about the project since I was fully aware of what was happening—even though that obviously wasn't the case. I felt guilty not warning Bobby, but I just felt I couldn't do that over the phone. I desperately wanted to call Israel and talk with Ori and Reggie, but I had promised Dad I wouldn't. I had no idea what to do.

Late on Sunday I called Noreen from the house. I knew that she was beginning to worry about Yancey. She said, "It's not like Yancey to leave me in the dark as to his whereabouts. I know it's hard to communicate from over there, but I know he could call or e-mail me, and he hasn't. He doesn't answer his phone either, but that doesn't surprise me. He left his charger here, but I should think he'd have access to one there. Look, George, do me a favor and try to reach him too. Let me know if you do reach him and see if you can find out when he's coming home, okay?"

I assured Noreen that he was fine and that knowing Yancey he was probably out in the field and unreachable. I felt a lump in my throat and a pain in the pit of my stomach for saying that. I'm glad I was telling her this over the phone; surely if she could see my face, she'd know that I was lying.

It was Sunday evening and I was totally at my wits' end about what to do. What could I do without raising all kinds of red flags that could do us more harm than good? And then the phone rang.

I grabbed it instantly and heard, "Hello, George, it's me, Dad. How are you?"

"Dad! Great to hear your voice. I knew you got home yesterday but I didn't want to bother you. I was planning on calling you..."

"I know, I know. Listen, George, have you been in contact with your friend, Professor Stetson? I hope he had a successful trip and is home now."

I nonchalantly said, "I'm under the impression that he's out in the field, so we haven't been able to reach him. I'm sure he's having a good time, he'll be home in a day or two."

A slight pause, then Dad said, "Yes, yes...fieldwork—it's hard to stay in touch when you're in the field. I understand. Anyway, I'm feeling good and will have some home rehab for a few days before going back to their rehab unit at Beaumont. I just called to say hello. Mother tells me you might come in with the family this week. I'd love that. Well, take care, I'll call again soon. Oh, by the way, are you in your office tomorrow? I was thinking just in case Professor Stetson tries to reach you there..."

"Yes, yes…I'll be in tomorrow, and uh…I'll keep you posted. Love you, Dad. Take care and thanks for calling."

I'm positive he was telling me to be in my office tomorrow. I had only one class and that was in the morning, so I would make it my business to be in my office the rest of the day. *What does he know?* I wondered.

———————

I was in my office all afternoon, and I didn't receive any unexpected calls on my office phone or my cell. It was past four, and I usually went home early on Mondays, but I hung around a little longer, waiting for the call that Dad implied would come. I was packing my things in my briefcase when a man dressed in gray slacks, a short gray jacket, white shirt, and black leather bowtie walked into my office. He had a logo on his cap that I didn't recognize—I just assumed that he was wearing a messenger's uniform. He claimed that he had a package for me and asked for some picture ID. When I showed him my MSU ID and driver's license, he handed me a large cardboard envelope marked PERSONAL, and without saying another word he left.

I closed the office door, and, after a brief hesitation, I nervously opened the envelope. For a split second I was a little afraid that it might not be safe, but I knew Dad would have told me if he expected me to get something dangerous. All that was inside was a brief note telling me to call a telephone number with an area code I didn't recognize. I was also instructed to use a land line, not a cell, and that I was to call the number at three tomorrow afternoon. The note was not signed, but there were two initials on the bottom, BB. I assumed immediately that stood for Boris Bethelheim. I looked over the envelope for any other markings or signs of where it came from—there weren't any.

When I got home, I didn't say much to Charlie. She was busy with the baby and making dinner, but later in the evening after Marike was put to bed and we were in the living room, I had to tell her what was going on.

"I'm scared, George. I'm really scared. What have we gotten ourselves into? What in hell is going on?" she said.

"I honestly don't know, hon, but I'm scared too."

"Should we call Noreen and tell her?" Charlie asked.

"No, no. She's worried enough as it is. Let's wait until I talk to Boris before we call anybody, okay?" I said.

Then Charlie, on the verge of tears, said, "Right now I just feel like running away—but I don't know where we'd run to."

"Oh, honey, honey," I said as I put my arms around her. "I'd think if it was a life-or-death situation, I'd have been told to call right away...or maybe we would have been taken away by now to some safe place or something. Let's not panic and just follow it through until we find out, okay? I guess I'm troubled too by all this cloak-and-dagger shit, but after what Dad told me about his meeting with Yossi and Boris last year, we shouldn't be too surprised. It will be okay..."

"I hope you're right about this, George. But I'm thinking all kinds of irrational thoughts now. I'm worried—I'm worried about Marike and you and Yancey. I want to call someone—Tikva, Reggie..."

"That's because you feel that if they're calm and safe then so are we. But that may not be the case, and in fact right now they may be in more danger than we are and may not even know about it. That's why we have to remain cool and wait until Boris fills me in. Can you do that?"

Charlie assured me she could and urged me to come home early tomorrow to make the call from our house. She would see to it that no one was here and I would have complete privacy. Her knowledge of communications told her that I would probably be calling on a scrambled line and also that my end would be monitored to make certain that no one else was listening in.

That night seemed to last forever.

———

I was home by two thirty on Tuesday, which meant that I had to hang around and do nothing while waiting to call. I checked e-mail and my watch over and over to make certain that I didn't miss the appointed time. At around five minutes to three, I picked up my phone. My hand was shaking as I dialed the number given to me. I heard nothing and then some clicking sounds and then Boris saying, "Hello, George. Look, before we start talking just say, 'Hello, Boris,' or any other short greeting, okay?"

I did as instructed and waited briefly while, I presume, some kind of voice recognition system was analyzing my voice print. Then Boris started talking again.

"George, what I'm about to tell you is in the strictest of confidence—can I trust you to keep it that way no matter how difficult it may be?"

"If it helps me to understand what in the hell is going on concerning Yancey, then, yes, by all means, I'll keep your confidence."

Boris didn't acknowledge my agreement but simply started talking. "In about an hour, Noreen Stetson will have visitors from the United States State Department. They will be informing her that her husband is being held by the Iranians on a trumped-up foreign espionage charge..."

"Oh, no, Boris—not Yancey, he's the sweetest, most dedicated guy in the world. Why did they pick him?" I cried.

Boris ignored me and continued. "They'll also tell her not to believe anything she reads in the media—that they're on it and they will have Yancey safe at home just as soon as they possibly can. Shortly after that the media will be bombarding her with all kinds of questions and telling her all kinds of bullshit, but she shouldn't listen to it. State will keep her updated at all times on every issue, and she should trust them, not the press," Boris finished.

I did all I could to keep from screaming, *It's your fucking fault*, but just said, "It will kill Noreen to think that Yancey is in trouble. What's really going on? How can I help?"

"Take your father's advice and stay out of it. I promise to fill you in on everything once it's all settled—and it will be settled to our satisfaction without Yancey getting hurt. Look, trust me on this—I'm telling you it's all power politics, and we can handle it. You should be there to support Noreen and tell her to listen to the woman from State. She's a career bureaucrat that really knows her stuff. Don't call Noreen now—wait till she calls you and Charlie, which my guess would be around four thirty."

"We can do that—support Noreen. But, Boris, I'm depending on you to get Yancey out of there unharmed. Will you do that?" I asked, trying to sound commanding, but I'm certain he wasn't impressed.

"You can count on it, George. By the way, if you talk to your father, send him my best and tell him I wish him a speedy recovery. I'll talk to you again soon, and don't try to call me at this number again. After we're done here the number will no longer exist." That last comment about Dad was

Boris' way of telling me that Dad knew what was going on and supported Boris' efforts.

I filled Charlie in on my talk with Boris, and she was noticeably upset, as expected. "What the fuck does he mean by 'power politics'? If it's what I think it is, then Yancey could be dead already and nobody would know it. George, what are we going to do?"

"Exactly what Boris said we should do. We're amateurs in this, and we've already gotten into enough trouble by not listening to the pros. Now try and hold yourself together, we're going to have to be strong when Noreen calls. We're all going to get through this somehow, and we can't do it if we start to panic and act chaotically. Will you be okay?" I asked, wiping tears from my own eyes.

Marike woke up, and Charlie went to take care of her, but before she left the room she was nodding her head, even though she was crying.

Noreen called on schedule, and before the media onslaught, she brought the girls over to our place and planned on them staying for a while. The State Department representative came along with her and the girls to brief me on how to behave when the media showed up here. She also filled me in on what was happening, and it was exactly as Boris said. I, of course, acted like I hadn't heard it before.

It didn't take long before the TV cameras arrived. We had already darkened most of the house on the inside and closed all the blinds, leaving all the outside lights on. I introduced myself as the family spokesperson but any official information would have to come from the State Department or MSU, and any questions concerning the event itself had to be directed to them.

"Yes, Mrs. Stetson and the girls will be staying with us for the duration," I answered one reporter.

"Is it true that Professor Stetson had been working with Israel on a special project inside Iran?" another asked.

"As I said earlier, any questions concerning the official State Department press release will have to be addressed to them."

And so it went. I kept my cool and requested that Noreen and the children be left alone to cope with this tragic misunderstanding in the privacy of their own home and their church. Yancey's arrest in Iran was breaking news on the six o'clock local news and national news at seven, with delayed coverage of my press conference at eleven. We knew our house and the Stetson house would be under twenty-four-hour surveillance by the media, so we had to be extra careful not to be blindsided by them when going out.

The media was saying that Iran was accusing Yancey of developing biological weapons for the Israeli government that were used in Iran to destroy their crops. Iran claimed Yancey was trying to find out how the Israeli weapon program was proceeding by traveling from Doha, Qatar, to the Island of Kish in Iran, where he was apprehended. They claimed that he had confessed to his involvement, and the Iranian government was considering its options: to either try him for espionage or simply sentence him directly based on his confession. Either way, they alleged he had committed a capital offense against the Iranian people and would have to pay for it.

The State Department had no comment other than to say that the charges were entirely false. The Israelis agreed with State and claimed the whole incident was based on lies and that neither Professor Yancey Stetson— a highly respected internationally known agronomist—nor anybody else in the world had ever tried to destroy Iranian crops with biological or other weapons.

To say we were all scared out of our wits would be putting it mildly. A capital offense meant they could execute him if they found him guilty of the charges, and the Iranian court system had one of the world's worst reputations for human rights violations. Things did not look good. But we kept our cool and did as we were told by the State Department, keeping a low profile and trusting in State to do its job and bring Yancey home safely.

As weeks passed and the media circus around Yancey's arrest quieted down, we began to relax a little. We had assurance from the International Red Cross through its affiliation with the Muslim Red Crescent Society that Yancey was alive and well. They even sent us pictures of him in which he looked a little gaunt but straight as a bean pole and apparently unharmed. We weren't told where he was being held or if he would go on trial. We were simply told that negotiations were continuing. Who was negotiating was also not specified, but our State Department contact said that they were doing the negotiations and that we would just have to be patient for the time being.

After all the initial hoopla was over, we fell into some kind of a routine around work, school, children, and being with each other that kept us sane and supportive, but not very happy. Every day we hoped that this would be the day Yancey was released, but as each day passed and less and less was heard, our hopes were fading. Charlie and I noticed that Noreen was losing weight, and it didn't look good on her. She was a little chunky to begin with, and the weight loss made her face seem thin and frail. Her hair was noticeably becoming gray, and we were worried about her mental state.

"Today's my day off," Charlie said to her one Thursday, "and you and I are going to the hair dresser to get spiffed up for Yancey's homecoming." That helped to lift her spirits a little bit, but her quick smile and shining eyes seemed lost now, and she looked to be staring into space most of the time. We did our best to keep her focused on Yancey's return. The State Department representative was always upbeat when she called us, telling us that negotiations were going as well as could be expected, and they were still very confident of Yancey's release. When we pressed her as to what the negotiations were all about, she never really told us.

"The negotiations have to do with sensitive international relations that take time to iron out; but believe me, Yancey is safe and he will be brought home," is all she ever told us, so we stopped asking her about the negotiations.

Time dragged on as winter ended and spring moved forward. The last three months had seemed like a million lifetimes.

But finally it happened. On Friday, May 12, we got word from State that Yancey would be arriving back in the States tomorrow, and he would be kept at the new military hospital in DC for a few days to check out his health before letting him come home. If we wanted to, we could visit with him there until his release. Noreen called to tell us the news and was almost in a state of hysteria. At first I couldn't tell if she was telling us whether Yancey was dead or alive, but it finally came through that Yancey was coming home. Charlie and I packed up Marike and went over to the Stetsons' to celebrate with them. It was all tears and laughter and dancing...and simply great relief. I was so pleased for them—and us—that I cried with them. After a while we made our plans to bring Yancey home. We decided that Noreen and I would go and Charlie and the girls would stay home. Fifteen-year-old Maxine Stetson—or Max as she liked to be called—would help Charlie out with Marike and twelve-year-old Beth until we got back with Yancey in tow. We decided that it would be best for the girls to stay here since we would be home in a couple of days anyway, and we had no idea how seeing Yancey would impact them without fully knowing Yancey's mental and physical condition.

"I can't thank you and Charlie enough for all you've done for me and the girls. I don't think we could have made it without your support," Noreen said to me after I made the flight and hotel arrangements. "I know that Yancey and I will never, ever forget what you've done for us."

Charlie and I both hugged her with the kids looking on; we were all smiling for the first time in a long time. The tears were still coming—including Marike's, who was tired and hungry. She had just started to walk and was tugging at her mother's skirt, not understanding what was happening. We all had to laugh while Max picked her up and comforted her. Yancey was coming home and that's all that really mattered now—not the safety of the world, nor the Middle East food shortage, nor a possible war, nor anything else...Yancey was coming home.

chapter 17

WHEN WE WALKED into Yancey's room Saturday morning we noticed almost immediately that he was in great physical shape—a little lighter, but other than that he seemed okay. He was sitting in a chair and wearing Army fatigues, and he certainly didn't look like he need to be in a hospital. He jumped up as soon as he saw us coming in. Noreen and Yancey embraced almost immediately. They hugged each other for a long time, and both were crying softly. I was thinking that maybe we should have brought the girls, but seeing how much Yancey and Noreen would need some private time, I was glad that we had decided to leave them at home. I left the room so that they could get comfortable with each other and returned when I heard Yancey call me.

"George! Get your ass in here and let me see you," he shouted.

It was now my turn to hug him and tell him how much I missed him. "At least I hope that you learned enough about vermiculture to have made that fucking trip worth all the aggravation," I said, trying to put a light spin on his *adventure*.

Noreen had brought clean clothes and toiletries and told him that, according to the doctor, he could leave the hospital that afternoon and spend Saturday night and Sunday with her in the hotel. He had to go back to the hospital on Monday while they finished up his physical and went over his lab tests, but if all went well—as they suspected it would—he could go home Tuesday. After we all got through the very happy and emotional greetings, we started to talk.

"Actually, I got in last night," Yancey told Noreen and me, "and you'll never guess who was here to debrief me…"

"Boris," I said.

"Yeah. Now how did you know that?" Yancey asked.

"Oh, just a hunch—I'll fill you in later," I told him.

He told us that for the most part he was not ill treated—that is, no torture or sleep deprivation, or endless hours of questioning. He was kept in a small cell with no other prisoners and the isolation got to him, but he filled his mind with work, and they did give him writing materials—though he wasn't permitted to send any letters out—and that was about it. He kept a makeshift calendar and knew exactly when he was released and how many days he was there in prison. What bothered him the most was that he did not know what he was really in prison for and what they wanted from him.

"I felt that I was a pawn in some bigger political issue that I was in no way involved with. All they told me was that I had been arrested for being in the country illegally and spying. But whenever I tried to tell them that I was hijacked out of Qatar and brought to Iran, they just ignored me. It was then that I realized that the truth didn't matter, that it was all some big game that I had absolutely no control over. And that's when I was frightened the most, when I realized that I had nothing to say about the situation and was no longer in charge of my own life."

I didn't tell Yancey about my dad's warning that he should get out of Qatar and about Boris' phone call, since it was too early after his release to get him excited over things that I could tell him later. I did tell him that Dad had a mild heart attack and that he was back to work and well on the mend.

I left Yancey and Noreen alone Saturday night and most of Sunday while they stayed in their room. They had a lot of catching up to do. We did go out for a great dinner in Georgetown on Sunday night, and it was so nice seeing Noreen smile again. Yancey was still a little somber and seemed to fade out occasionally, but that was to be expected after three months of solitary confinement in an Iranian prison. His affect was not unlike prisoners of war (or so I've been told) and their early reactions after being released. They had already called Charlie and talked to the girls a number of times. Charlie promised to have a great home-cooked Chinese dinner waiting for them to celebrate Yancey's homecoming. That is, if the media didn't get in the way.

At our dinner on Sunday, Yancey talked about his arrival in DC. "It was strange," he said, "that it was just Boris and a guy from State who debriefed me on Friday afternoon and evening. Their questions were pedestrian at best—how was I treated, what questions did they ask me, did I know where I was, and the like. They didn't seem at all to care that I had been hijacked in Doha and flown to Kish where I was arrested while still groggy from a knock-out drink they gave me."

I told him that all that could wait for now, that he should just relax and enjoy his freedom. "Come home and get back in the swing of academia for a while. It's the end of the semester, and I'm sure you want to get caught up on your courses and students. After you've settled in for a while, we can try to find out what really happened over there, okay?" I said.

"Sounds reasonable to me," Yancey said. "I actually don't give a damn about the whole Middle East situation right now. I'm all for getting back to the grind of teaching and research. The Iranians let me keep my notes on some future research I want to do, and that's where I'll start. George, let me tell you some of my thoughts..."

"Not now, Yancey," I said, smiling. "I think now you should be enjoying your family and friends unencumbered, as it were, by other issues."

"Okay, George—you're right about that. There are more important things that I should be thinking about right now. Um...let's get back to the hotel," he said, yawning and smiling at Noreen, "I'm getting tired."

There was no media clamor when we got back to Okemos, and it would appear that nobody really cared what happened to Professor Yancey Stetson. We only knew of one small article in Sunday's *New York Times* saying simply that he was released. The article briefly reviewed the circumstances of his arrest by Iran over three months ago, and then went on to say that the Iranian government released him for humanitarian reasons. And that was it. There was no comment from the State Department, and the international community didn't even mention the issue according to Noreen, who tried to research the incident on the Internet.

We went right to my house because the kids were there and so was Noreen's car. To say that Yancey's girls and Charlie were glad to see him would be an immense understatement. Screams, hugs, kisses—everything you can imagine from a family reunited after three months of terror was played out in the few minutes after our arrival.

After dinner we sat around talking for a while about the lack of media interest. Yancey said, "I could care less, and, in fact, I'm glad there's been no great hoopla. At least not until I have a much better idea of what it was all about." Yancey stopped there and then, looking very thoughtful, said, "Oh, I know that our work in Israel probably led up to it, but there are many researchers from many other countries that have worked with Israeli scientists on a whole host of issues other than farming—including military ones—and they weren't harassed like I was. No, this was for a lot more than our work with Ori and the Technion. But for now I'm taking George's advice and sticking to local issues."

"That's good advice, and I think we should all follow it and let things just cool down before we try to do any deep analysis," Charlie said.

"I fully agree," Noreen said, "but I think that, knowing Yancey like I do, he'll not let it rest until he knows what's happened. Am I right, Professor Stetson?" she said with that knowing, loving look on her face.

Yancey looked at her tenderly and said, "You know me too well, Noreen. Look, let's give it a month or so, and then, say...after Marike's one-year birthday party in June, we'll do our own debriefing to see what this might have been about. Bobby will be back by then, and he should be included. And let's all agree not to communicate with anyone just yet—Boris, Tikva, Reggie, or anyone else we've worked with. We can do all that after some reasonable planning, okay?"

We all agreed that taking a month's break would probably be the wisest thing we could do now. Let everything get back to normal and then plan our next moves—if there were any next moves—before drawing any conclusions about Yancey's abduction. We were all still feeling very vulnerable, and even though it wasn't expressed by anyone, you could feel our angst in the room.

When the Stetsons left for home, I hugged Charlie and Marike as we started to clean up after the dinner party. Later I called Dad to tell him that we were back from DC and that Yancey was in good physical condition. He said he was glad to hear that. He asked if we'd be coming into Warren for Marike's birthday party next month, but I told him we would be having it here in Okemos, and we wanted them to be here too. Her birthday was on a Sunday, and if the weather was nice we'd hold it in the backyard. After talking with Dad, Charlie talked to Mom about the party she was planning for Marike, and that was it.

I heard from Israel the next day—Tikva called when she learned from Ori about Yancey's release. How Ori found out I could only speculate, but I explained that Yancey needed a rest from the slug program and that we would call in another month for a full update, but we needed to let it rest for now. Tikva understood completely and simply wanted to wish Yancey and his family well from the entire Israeli team.

It seemed so strange that for the first time in what seemed like forever we were not worried about Yancey being in Iran. I wondered if that's how families with sons and daughters in the military overseas felt: constantly worrying about their loved ones' safety. I suddenly had great empathy for their situation and fervently hoped that I would never have to feel that way about any family member.

As for my family and me, it finally looked like things were looking up and that everything was going to work out after all. Whether that would be true in other parts of the world or not didn't seem to matter to me now because I no longer had, or wanted, any say over world events. I slept well that night for the first time in a very long time.

———

Marike's birthday party was held on June 11, which was a beautiful, sunny day, and lots of friends, family, and neighbors were there to celebrate with us. Dad and Mom were there and couldn't get over how well their *little angel* was walking all by herself. She was also babbling a few words, which pleased them to no end. The Stetsons were there, of course, and so was Bobby, who had recently returned from India. It was truly a fun-filled occasion. Max followed Marike around like a *little mother* while Beth in turn followed her sister, trying to learn how to take care of a child in preparation for her future role as the babysitter.

Off in a corner of the yard, I saw Dad talking with Yancey. They both looked very serious, and I couldn't help but wonder what it was all about. When the party wound down around six in the evening, it was just us and Mom and Dad left to clean up and put things away. When that was all done and Marike was acting like a very tired and irritable young child, which is what we'd expected after all the attention she was getting, Charlie put her down for a short nap. Mom went with her, and I was finally alone with Dad.

"What was all that serious talk you and Yancey were having earlier?" I asked him.

"Nothing, nothing...I was just filling him in on some information that I wasn't sure he was aware of about his abduction."

"And how, might I ask, would you have heard about this *information?*" I asked with noticeable irritation in my voice. "And why wasn't I informed about something as important as that since it might have concerned me and our project?"

"I told you, George, in the hospital to *get Yancey out of Qatar,*" Dad answered with some irritation in his voice as well.

I shook my head and said, "Yes, but you never told me why I should warn Yancey, and I wasn't about to ask you anything then. Remember, you were about to have heart surgery! I just assumed that Boris or somebody else gave you some kind of heads-up about Yancey's situation...but if there's more to it than that don't you think I should have known too?"

"Of course I do, and that's exactly what I was telling Yancey. I told him that I thought we needed to get together to talk about what's been going on, so I asked him to arrange a time for all of us to meet," Dad said.

I felt stupid for getting so short-tempered with him—after all, he'd been involved from the beginning and had been nothing but supportive of the whole project. He's the only one who fully knew of the true danger and tried to keep us out of harm's way all along.

"Sounds good, Dad," I said in a much more conciliatory tone. "Did you say when and where you wanted to meet?"

"I left that up to Yancey; he'll get back to me when it's all arranged. Look, I think the danger for you and your team has been significantly reduced, but I also think—as I've said before—that it's time for you to, uh... ease off, so to speak. The project is being carried out and your involvement is no longer needed—"

"Yes, you've told me that, but it's sort of like our baby in some way. I know the project has a life of its own now and that we can easily get out without any impact whatsoever on the outcome. But that doesn't stop us from being concerned about it and wanting to be informed of all the details. After all, there's some universal knowledge about environmental science and agronomy that's going on here, and I'm obligated—rather, my university is obligated—to report on it for the entire international academic community. I'll take your advice and stay away from trouble, that's for sure, but I need to stay involved."

"I can understand that completely, George, and I'm very proud of you and the work you've done. Let's leave it at that—that you won't do anything dangerous, but you'll make known the scientific and practical outcomes from your project. Look, here comes your mother. We'll talk about it more at the meeting, okay?" Dad said as he got up to take my mother home.

When the folks left, Marike was asleep and the house was quiet. Charlie and I finally had a few minutes to ourselves. I filled her in on what Dad said about a meeting, and she was looking forward to finally understanding, if we could, what it was all about.

Charlie said, "I think if anyone knows what the hell went on in Qatar—or more importantly, why it went on—it would be Dad.

I went back outside and sat in the yard for a while longer. I wondered if Dad would really tell us everything, or if he even knew everything that happened to Yancey and our project. I knew he would have privileged information from Boris and Yossi. I got the feeling though that a meeting with our group would not necessarily be a place where he could divulge any truly sensitive information. Not because he would be concerned that *he* might be held accountable, but rather for our own safety because there might be some things that were better off not divulged. Things like who actually planted the slugs and why they did it. I was looking forward to the meeting with some trepidation, but also some hope—finally—for closure over Yancey's ordeal.

———

On Thursday the fifteenth, we held our last project meeting to tie up some loose ends and prepare for Dad's meeting on the twenty-ninth. We hadn't finalized a place for that meeting or an agenda, but since it was Dad who called the meeting, we felt he should set the agenda.

"Yancey, you never filled us in on exactly what happened in Qatar, and I could understand that. We know all about the three months in Iran, but how exactly did you get there from Qatar?" Charlie asked. "Do you think you can tell us now?"

Yancey slowly nodded his head. You could see that it still pained him to talk about the incident, but then he told us the whole story. "You know, of course, that I was to meet with Kassim," he said, "and we were going to look over his worm processing plant for a possible soil reclamation program in the affected countries. He was going to have a couple of Iranian agronomists there that I could meet with informally to learn about the remutation project that *they* supposedly carried out."

"That's where I got lost—that they claimed that they carried out the remutation effort and not Reggie. How could that be?" I asked.

"Unfortunately, George, I never found out. I met those guys the day after I arrived, and I could tell you right from the get-go they weren't agronomists. From the way they responded to my questions, I knew they probably weren't even farmers. They talked more like people who dealt in large mechanical projects—engineers or equipment makers—because they kept talking about machinery and manufacturing plants that they had built in Iran. They spoke no English so Kassim had to do all the translation, and I could tell early on that he was nervous. I don't think he knew what was going to happen, but he was definitely afraid of something. They were more interested in finding out why I was interested in soil reclamation since it was their project and they were handling it. I decided not to get too involved with them because I suspected that something else might be at issue—I didn't know what, but I knew something wasn't kosher."

"I wish you had just turned around and found some excuse to come home then," Noreen said.

"No, hon, there was no way I could do that then. I thought about leaving early but not that early. On Tuesday—I guess that was the seventh—we decided to all go out for dinner at a lovely little restaurant in downtown Doha. At some point before dinner was even served I knew something— probably chloral hydrate—was put in my water or juice, and before I could do anything about it I woke up on a small plane headed for Kish." Yancey paused here and then, looking at me, he said, "Kish is a small resort island in Iran less than two hundred miles from Doha across the Persian Gulf. When we landed in Kish, some men—Iranian military types, I guess, dressed in civilian clothes—took me off the plane, and the next thing I knew I'm being arrested for being in the country illegally. Kassim and the two *engineers* were nowhere to be seen, and no one was listening to my complaints about being abducted in Doha. The big problem was that no one would speak English other than to ask me basic information—my name, what country I was from, and the like." I could see that Yancey was getting irritable and wanted to take a break when Bobby broke into the conversation.

"Were you scared?" Bobby asked.

"In some sense, yes, because I was duped into going there. In another sense I felt that once I could talk with someone in charge who spoke English, it would all be cleared up. That was pretty naïve of me though. In any case, you know the rest: I was taken someplace around four hours away in a darkened van, put in prison, and there I remained."

Yancey paused again, but sounding more relaxed he told us, "I've tried to make sense of it, but I'm still not at all clear on what really happened. I'm sort of torn between the incident being a huge mistake or some kind of power play I just happened to stumble into. Either way I hope Pieter can explain it to me."

I asked, "Do you think Kassim was in on it? Maybe it had something to do with Lebanon and the coalition. And those two fake agronomists you met with, do you think that maybe they were some kind of secret agents?"

Yancey looked thoughtful before answering me. "It could be any of those things and a hundred or more other likely reasons. All I can say with any certainty is that it definitely had to do with Israel and our work there. Because that was the one thing they kept harping on when I was interrogated—what did I do in Israel in December of 2015, and was I planning on destroying Iranian food crops. I, of course, admitted fully to being in Israel but totally denied that I was there plotting to sabotage their food resources."

We stopped pressing Yancey for any more information. His voice was getting agitated again, and I could tell from the way he was looking into his lap and nodding his head that he must have been thinking about his capture and arrest, so it was time to end the meeting.

"It will be interesting in two weeks when we meet with Dad," I said, "and possibly clear this all up. In any case, I'm busy planning to attend some meetings this fall and talking about the broader environmental issues of remutation. What's everyone else doing?"

"I'm defending early in the fall," Bobby said. "That is, if Yancey thinks I'm ready."

"I'm sure you'll be ready, Bobby. You're the last doctoral student I would ever have to worry about being ready to defend," Yancey said, smiling at Bobby.

"What about you, Noreen?" Charlie asked. "Any poly sci or econ classes you're thinking about taking?"

"No, not this year," Noreen said somewhat somberly. "I'm thinking about a music appreciation course that might be fun, but I'm laying off politics for a while."

Noreen, only in her mid-thirties, was too young to have gray hair, but the ordeal she went through over Yancey's abduction and incarceration had left her light brown hair streaked with gray.

Yancey squeezed his wife's hand, and we all sat there quietly for a while before Yancey said, "The final meeting of the Farmers Save the World Project is hereby adjourned. See you all in two weeks at Pieter's meeting, if not before—time and place to be announced." We were smiling thinly at Yancey's humor—I guess at one time we did think that we would be saving the world.

***

Yancey had scheduled a small conference room in our college's lab for the meeting on Thursday, June 29. The meeting was supposed to start at 11 a.m.; it was now almost eleven thirty and Dad hadn't shown up yet. I was getting worried and was about to call him on his cell when the door opened and there was Dad wheeling in Boris.

"Sorry we're late—my fault, my fault..." Boris was saying as Dad wheeled him up to the conference table. He asked Dad to seat him at the head of the table, claiming that this way his chair wouldn't be knocking against anybody. But it was obvious that it was a power move to let us know that this was his meeting. He hadn't met Noreen or Bobby yet and immediately zeroed in on them, saying how delighted he was to finally meet them.

"Noreen, I understand that you're quite the Middle East policy expert. I would love to spend some time with you, getting your opinions on our policies," he said. And then looking at Bobby, he said, "And Barindra, I understand that you're quite the man with a super computer. I've been told that you can get them to really perform at the limit of their capabilities. Too bad you're not going to work for IBM when you finish here—you're going back to Goa, right? If not, I could always use a man with your talents."

Bobby tilted his head to one side and smiled at Boris' acknowledgement of his talents. Yancey looked at me as if to say, *That's Boris, letting everyone know who's the boss.* I was wondering who it was that told him about Noreen and Bobby because it certainly wasn't us. But that, too, would be typical of Boris—showing us how much information about us he could get without our even knowing about it.

Dad started the meeting off by saying, "Thanks, Yancey, for setting this meeting up. I know that you were all surprised when Dr. Bethelheim came in with me, but you didn't know that it was his idea to hold this meeting in the first place, so he thought he should attend." Then looking over to Boris, Dad said, "Why don't you tell them what's been happening with the remutation project and how it ended up getting Professor Stetson, uh... detained in Iran."

Detained? I thought. *Come on, Dad, you can do better that that. How about almost killed?*

Boris was surprisingly candid, but I felt that he must not be telling us everything. I just sensed that he couldn't possibly tell the whole story—it was much too complex. He explained that there were two remutation programs going on at the same time—one sponsored by the United States working with the Middle East coalition and one sponsored by Israel working directly with the Iranian and Syrian governments. The Syrian program, sponsored by Israel and managed by Reggie Shao, never even got started since it was believed that Syria was going to use Reggie's program as a way of establishing a terrorist cell in Israel, just as I had suspected much earlier. However, the coalition working with the United States (that probably meant Boris) had already treated both countries and the land was well on its way to being rehabbed for farming again. After Boris filled us in with those details, it began to make sense to us as to why things happened the way they did.

Boris spoke uninterrupted for almost an hour, and then at around twelve thirty there was a knock on the door and in walked a group of caterers with lunch for all of us. "Let's take a break," Boris said, "and after lunch I'll try to answer all your questions."

And that was it. We would break for lunch, leaving tons of questions hanging, and then get back to it. We were sort of at a loss as to how we should react, but nobody complained as we sat around, making small talk while eating a very well-prepared lunch of special pasta dishes for all of us. Again, Boris seemed to know what our favorite pastas were and that's what he had brought in. We had to admit later that if nothing else Boris knew how to keep a group of people charmed into submission.

Once the room was cleaned up, Boris asked if there were any questions. Bobby was the first to talk, "Dr. Bethelheim—"

"Call me Boris and I'll call you Bobby, okay?"

"Thank you...uh, Boris. Anyway, I know we didn't prepare as much enzyme product as we initially planned, and I thought that was because the Syrian program was on hold. But our investors started to have us prepare a number of other high-quality farming products. The sales and profits on these products were sizable, but that's Jewish businessmen for you. My father was a little surprised that we didn't finish up on the remutation effort, but he knew we could always come back to making Yancey's enzyme..."

"I sense your question is where did we get enough product to conduct the program?" Boris asked. "Well, we didn't get it from you—you were only making the enzyme soup for the Israeli program. Here in the US we had a duplicate plant that you didn't know about making product for the coalition. We actually had initiated the remutation process months before you even got started in Iran." Boris then looked at Yancey and said, "Thanks to you, Yancey, and your openness with the Israelis and with us at our conference almost two years ago, we were able to produce your enzyme formula."

Yancey's eyes grew wide because he was surprised by Boris' comment. It told him that Israel had been cooperating with the United States from the beginning. Boris continued, "And I should say thank you from your government—and your government too, Bobby—for your remarkable efforts to come up with a way of solving the food crisis in the coalition countries. If it hadn't been for your work, it's hard to say where we would be today, but a war with Israel would not have been out of the question, right, Noreen?"

Noreen was also caught by surprise when Boris asked her a question, so she simply nodded.

I was still confused as to what went on and asked, "Boris, why were there two projects? And why weren't we asked to participate in the US one? I find it strange that since it was our model that—"

"George, George…there was nothing strange about it. We had all the information we needed, thanks to you and Yancey and your team, to carry it out without you. You jumped into Israel on your own—by the way, that was against our advice. In any case, two projects were always our plan since in reality there are still two governments operating in every one of the coalition countries: the coalition's governing authority and the country's own *elected* government. And more often than not, there are considerable disagreements and power struggles between the two."

"So you we were playing both sides of the aisle, so to speak," Noreen said, more at ease with Boris now, "seeing who was really in power—testing your own influence to make certain that you'd be betting on the winning side."

"Like I said before, Noreen, you know your Middle East policy. Israel has the most to lose in these struggles since it still isn't clear who's running Syria and Iran—the old strongly anti-Israel crowd or the more moderate co-alition forces. I say more moderate, but I'm sure you know that Israel's safety is in no way guaranteed under the coalition either. In any case, as it turned out, the coalition won out on getting the program carried through." Boris paused here while adjusting his chair a little to make himself more comfortable. I imagine long meetings like this one had to be hard on him physically.

"So why did you keep the Israeli program still active once you established your program and were implementing it through the coalition?" Yancey asked.

"Good question," Boris said. "The Israeli government was using the project for determining the strength and character of the opposition forces in those two countries. Ori, Reggie, Tikva—they had no idea what was happening. Even poor Yaakov Uhlman—who thinks he's Mossad—didn't know there were two projects going on. He only knew that the one in Israel was for more than trying to establish good relations with the Iranian government. That's why poor Reggie was confused too. He began to suspect that his plan was not being implemented as fast as he wanted it to be because of ulterior motives on the part of some high-up elements in the Israeli government."

Boris looked over to Charlie and said, "That's why Reggie talked to your dad, Charlie, to get to you and George to see what was going on, but you kept telling him it was just routine Israeli bureaucracy holding things up. He knew that wasn't so, but he also realized that you didn't know either." Charlie stared in wonder at Boris, trying to figure out how he knew all that. Boris continued, "That caused Reggie to push the Syrian project sooner than Israel wanted to. Israel thought that Syria was going to use Reggie's plan to infiltrate terrorists and wanted more time to get the names and locations of the terrorists, but Reggie's impatience forced them to pull out too early to accomplish that."

"Yossi told me that too, Boris," Dad said, "but I'm still not sure that was really the case. It might have been Yossi's own paranoia thinking that Syria wanted to do that, and the fact that Reggie pushed so hard to get his project going in Syria gave Yossi the excuse he wanted to pull the plug."

I was surprised that Dad had been made privy to such high-level Israeli political actions and was now discussing it so publicly. I was also, like everyone else—that is, everyone but Dad and Boris—so overwhelmed with so much information that I needed a break. We still had lots of questions, but they would have to wait. It was getting well into the afternoon by then, and I knew Charlie had to go home to Marike and that Noreen also wanted to get home before long, but I wasn't quite sure how to handle it.

But Dad knew how and simply said, "Look, I know it's getting late and people have other things to do. George, why don't you have Boris and I come over to your place and rest for a while, then maybe everyone else could join us there after dinner—say around eight? Is that all right with you, Charlie?"

After everyone agreed to the arrangement, Boris reminded us that even though our talk today wasn't officially secret, it was sensitive and that we shouldn't be telling anyone what happened in Israel, Iran, and Syria over this last year or so. Nobody objected and the meeting broke up.

Dad went with Boris, who had a private limo outfitted for his wheelchair waiting for him. Dad told me that there was a government airplane at Willow Run airport that had brought Boris and his limo to Lansing and would wait for him to take him back to DC. I guess Dr. Strangelove was a very important person after all.

Both Dad and Boris rested for a while on the patio in the backyard while Charlie put together a dinner for us with whatever we had in the house. I left the two old friends alone and looked after Marike.

The Stetsons and Bobby showed up at eight sharp, and we all sat around the front room for the continuation of Boris' meeting.

"So, where were we?" Boris asked.

"I'm still not clear as to why they kidnapped me," Yancey said.

"Noreen, you can answer that one, can't you?" Boris said.

"Power play by the Iranian government is my guess," Noreen said.

"Absolutely right, Noreen," Boris said. "They knew that their reclamation program was already undermined by the coalition's program and, Yancey, you just happened to be in the right place at the right time. They were going to use you to try and get the coalition to say that the land restoration project was done by the Iranian government and their own internal scientists, not anyone from the West. They also saw the opportunity to put the coalition in bed with Israel even though it was them that made the agreement with Israel for their own project."

Yancey audibly sighed and said, "I knew it had something to do with Israel's involvement. And it turns out that it was the old scorpion and frog story so well-known in Middle Eastern politics," Yancey said.

"What story?" Charlie asked.

Dad told her the story. "The frog was about to cross the Jordan River, and the scorpion asked for a lift on his back. The frog was reluctant and said that he didn't trust the scorpion. The scorpion told the frog that it would be foolish for him to poison the frog in the river because then he, the scorpion, would also drown. So the frog agreed and, halfway across the river, the scorpion stings the frog. And as the frog is dying, he asks the scorpion why he would do something so foolish. The scorpion said simply, 'Because it's the Middle East.'" Charlie smiled after hearing Dad's story, but you could tell it was a painful smile.

Boris then said, "When they found out that Yancey was coming to Qatar, they saw the chance to legitimize the remnants of their old government by showing that the United States and Israel had plotted against them again, and here was living proof in the form of Yancey the American-Israeli spy. It was so amateurish by today's standards that, as it turned out, it totally backfired. I won't bore you with the details on that, but suffice it to say that the

Iranian hotheads—their own internally bred terrorists who carried out the kidnapping—were completely marginalized this time around. That's why Yancey was released without much fanfare."

"But he could have just as easily been killed," Noreen said.

"We had his back, Noreen. And yes, it could have gone bad, but believe me, if that had happened it would have cost them dearly, and they knew that."

"Yes, that's true, Boris, but it is the Middle East," she said.

Noreen's sarcasm was not lost on Boris. I jumped in with, "Can I get anyone anything to drink?"

———

After a short pause for drinks and some small talk, Dad pointed out it was getting late and Boris had to fly back to DC that night. If questions were still hanging, maybe we could deal with them at some future time. "Is there one last question before we end this?" Dad asked.

"Yes," I said. "Who put the slugs out there to destroy the crops?"

"I thought we covered that topic when you and Yancey came to our conference over a year ago. Are you still so certain that it was the US that did it? If so, who do you think placed your slugs out there and how did they do it?" Boris asked testily.

"I have no idea, but I think that it would have been pretty easy to—"

"Pretty easy? On a scale that large? You're a better scientist than that, George. You saw how difficult it was to put together your treatment program in those countries; and the enzyme mixture that you're spreading around was a lot easier to make, transport, keep viable, and distribute than the tons of living slugs that would have been needed to carry out that infestation. You think I did it and you want me to say that, don't you?" Boris pushed.

"Boris, even if you did do it," Noreen said, "we know that you could in no way admit it publicly, so it would be silly of us to ask you that. But we are interested in hearing your thoughts on it. Who could have carried out such a huge undertaking?"

I still wanted to hear Boris finally admit to us that he didn't do it, but I let Noreen's question stand, knowing I was probably out of line. "As I told Yancey and George over a year ago," Boris said, "it could have been so many different organizations, including US agencies, that it's impossible for anyone to know who did it. I should also add that there are many foreign agencies, including some coalition countries, that were capable of pulling that off in order to spread chaos. Many of these terrorist organizations thrive on internal chaos." Boris looked tired; he once again seemed to be adjusting his chair. "Look, as I said before and I'll repeat now, it could have been almost anybody with the capabilities I just pointed out that caused that infestation."

"I think that's enough for now," Dad said. "Like I told you, if other questions are still bothering you, maybe we can address them later. I think we should all thank Boris for holding this extraordinary meeting. I'm going with him to the airport." Looking at his watch, he said. "It's...it's ten o'clock and he's had an arduous trip." Dad was indicating to us that this trip—even in a private plane and bringing his own limo with him—was still very hard on a paraplegic. "We don't travel as well as we used to, right, my friend?" Dad said, looking at Boris.

"Yes, Pete...I think it's time for me to go, but thanks for letting me explain what happened. And on behalf of your government, thanks again for all you've done to help avert a major world crisis."

We all stood around and quietly thanked Boris for coming all the way from DC to explain things to us when we knew he really didn't have to. Dad and the limo driver got Boris into the limo and off they went, leaving us to debrief ourselves on what we learned.

"So that's what power politics are?" Charlie said.

"Yes, it simply means that he who doesn't have power wants it, and he who has it wants more," Noreen said. "It's all about control disguised in ideologies, greed, and ancient distrusts. When will it ever end?"

"Let's go home, honey. It is late and Max is in charge—and that could mean almost anything as she tries to increase her power over us," Yancey said with a grin.

I knew all our questions were not answered nor would they probably ever be, at least in my lifetime. But for the most part, I was satisfied and comfortable that things did seem to finally make some sense—in the political realm at least. It would be a while yet before they made sense to me in terms of justice and equitability in the world, but I expected that it would take more discussions, and I could live with that. I was tired too—it had been a long day, and Charlie and I had lots to talk about over the rest of the summer. But Yancey was home again, Dad was on the mend, and his friend, Boris, was back to work saving the world—I was glad that it was Boris' job and not mine.

chapter 18

It was a beautiful and hot Sunday afternoon, the day before Labor Day, September 3, 2017, and we were over at the Stetsons' house celebrating the end of summer. Classes would be starting on Wednesday, and the routine would be good for me. I was excited but a little sad to have to give up the total freedom of a very nonproductive summer. However, I was looking forward to working on new research topics and teaching new courses with new students. In the past three months, none of us ever talked about our mission into the Middle East; but Dad, from time to time, would update us on Tikva and the kids. Charlie also called her on occasion, but that was the extent of it. I never asked Noreen for a clock update—she was no longer interested in global policy issues, or at least that's what she said. In fact, I think none of the others were very interested anymore. Or if they were they were doing a good job of keeping it a secret.

"Here, George," Yancey said as he handed me a cold beer. "You ready to go back to the grind next week?"

Noreen and Charlie came out on the Stetsons' large wooden deck with slats on all sides to keep little kids—like Marike—safely inside and joined us. Max and Beth were on the grass playing with Marike. We looked so peacefully summer that we could have been a French modernist painting with an American motif. Noreen and Charlie had tall lemonades spiked with gin, and Yancey and I were drinking beer—what a soft pastel picture of real Americana.

"What a glorious day," Charlie said.

"Enjoy it, this is Michigan and winter could start in a week," Noreen said.

"That's all right with me," Yancey said. "I love the peace that winter brings, and you'll enjoy your music class even better in the winter climate I bet." Yancey was thinking how the serenity of a winter snowfall was always more conducive to listening to classical music than the heat and activities of summer allowed—at least that's what he said.

We sat quietly for a while, but somehow I just couldn't resist the moment—the peace and relaxation seemed just right to bring it up again without everyone getting emotionally overworked.

"Do you think that this year we might get back into the remutation program again? I suspect that there might be other parts of the world that could use our knowledge..."

"Count me out, George," Noreen said.

"Me too," Charlie said. "My chair wants me to work on my new research agenda," she said, looking at Yancey. "I told you about that, Yance— think you might be interested in working in the department's bio-chemical energy program with me?"

"Not this year, Charlie. I'm committed to developing new enzymes for farming and will be spending some time in India with Bobby's father. That should be fun, and, who knows, we might even get rich from it," Yancey said with a smile toward Noreen.

I couldn't help but think how little we talked with each other about our other work at the college. The slug issue just dominated our day-to-day schedules so fully that we really didn't know what each other was interested in anymore. Then Yancey looked at me and asked, "What about you, George? I thought that you were going to continue your efforts on different remutation programs for other species. I think you've found a treasure trove of research applications that could keep you busy for years. Have you changed your mind?"

"No, no...I still plan on continuing my research agenda, but I thought..."

"You thought that you could still save the world, right?" Yancey said.

"No, Yancey, not really. I think I realize now that saving the world is not a one-person—or even a five-person—job like I might have thought a couple of years ago. I think when the whole Middle East food situation gets resolved, if it ever does, then all our efforts will simply be a footnote at most. But..."

"But you still can't let it go, can you?" Noreen asked.

"Like I told Dad a while back, it's sort of like my baby, and I would at least like to know what happened. Is there anything publishable we can get out of the whole episode, or is this it?"

"I think only time will tell if that's true—that we in any way averted a major catastrophe like Boris said," Noreen explained. "I think he played us all. If you noticed, he never once said definitively that he was not responsible for distributing those slugs. He kept telling us how so many others could have done it, but he never said that he wasn't the one who did it. I let him off the hook on that one, and he never flinched."

"Yeah, you're right," I said. "But no matter who put the slugs out there, I wonder if it was us who solved the problem. Or could Boris have ultimately solved it himself with his crew?"

"It doesn't matter, George," Yancey said. "It's like so many other scientific and engineering breakthroughs that have happened in the past. Most never lived up to their promise, and the truly successful technical innovations were usually developed for something entirely different from what they actually became famous for. I think it's time we put this one behind us and let the test of time decide what our role, if any, was in all of it. I think you should keep on with your work and treat this experience as simply one more step on your professional ladder." Yancey then got up to look after the charcoal fire in his grill that was now glowing brightly.

Noreen got up as well, saying she had things to do in the kitchen, and Charlie went out on the lawn with the girls and Marike. All of a sudden I felt very alone. I got the feeling that they weren't interested in the project any more and that maybe I was just being like a stubborn, immature adolescent talking about *my baby* when in fact I might have an entirely alternative motive—like instant fame and recognition for a brilliant piece of work.

It was times like these that I missed Mackie the most. She was my advisor; she would know what I should do—but most important, she would keep me honest. *God, how I miss her.* I suddenly felt very melancholy, sitting alone and crying into my beer. *What a schmuck you are, George,* I thought, *grow up! You just turned thirty years old this spring—act your age.*

Thanks, Mackie—I really miss you, sis.

Three years later, in the fall of 2020, Charlie and I had submitted all our materials for our tenure revues and were anxiously awaiting the outcomes. We heard nothing, of course, until April of 2021 when we were notified that we were both promoted to associate professors and granted tenure effective as of the fall.

We celebrated our hard-earned promotions with my parents in Warren on Sunday, April 11. Yancey was also promoted to full professor that year, so in terms of our professional goals, things were moving along nicely. Mom, Charlie, and Marike had gone for a walk, and Dad and I were home alone. It was quiet and we were watching a Tigers' early season game without much interest.

"It would seem that all your hard work and your latest research efforts have paid off nicely for you, George. I'm very proud of both you and Charlie for getting tenure," Dad said. "Not everyone gets tenure today. You really have to earn it, and you two certainly did that—you earned it."

"Yeah, we worked hard, tenure's nice, but we're both very relieved to have that part of our careers behind us. It's nice to have a feeling of permanence in the place where you work. It's also nice from a financial point of view too, and, in fact, we're thinking of buying a house maybe next spring. We'll see what happens when we get back, but it is nice to feel that we belong in the academy," I said.

We were quiet for a while, and then I told Dad, "But...in spite of all the recognition for my work, I really wish I knew what became of our Middle East project. It was the only life-altering project that I ever worked on, and it would have been nice to have seen the final results."

"Why, to prove that your theory works? You know it does, and the beauty of grand models like yours is that they're often smarter than their discoverers. You know Maxwell's model—his six equations that describe all electromagnetic phenomena—was discovered years before Einstein came along with his relativity theories. Yet, when they applied Einstein's relativistic transformations to Maxwell's equations, they actually didn't change. It was as if Maxwell knew he was taking into account relativity theory when he developed the model. But, of course, he couldn't have. Maybe that type of hidden genius is in your model too."

"Yeah, Yancey told me something like that before about discoveries proving to be more valuable in areas the discoverer never even dreamt of..."

"And I feel that will happen with your work," Dad said. And then with a concerned—or was it a troubled?—expression on his face, he said, "Forget about the Middle East project. If it would make you feel any better, then I can safely tell you that what you did was very successful, so why don't you leave it at that?"

"Huh? How do you know that? What do you know about the program that I was never informed of?"

"All right, all right...enough time has passed that I think it's safe to tell you what actually happened. Hopefully, though, this should end it. If I tell you everything I know, will you promise to end it now—to let the project be and just go on with your life? Will you promise me that?"

"God, Dad! How can I promise you that unless I know what it is that actually happened, and how that will impact on me, my work, my colleagues? Tell me, and give me the benefit of the doubt that I will do as you promise only if I can live with what you say. Is that fair enough?"

Dad turned off the TV and slowly got up and went into the living room. He returned with two glasses of Scotch and a little water. Handing me one glass, he sat down and said, "All right, George, here are the missing parts that you've been wanting to know about all these years."

"You know Boris retired at the age of sixty-eight, almost three years ago. Before he retired, I met with him in DC—just a friendly visit to touch base with an aging and respected colleague. It was the year after Boris' unusual meeting with you and the Stetsons—unusual because Boris rarely traveled out of DC. We were talking in his office about all that he had worked on, all the programs we were involved with, when he asked me, 'Pete, was I a bad guy? I know I had little tolerance for our enemies and said some pretty nasty things about them, but was I a bad guy?'

"I told him, 'No, Boris, you may have been a little off the wall at times, but, no, you are not a bad guy. In fact, you helped the world either get rid of or neutralize many bad guys in your career, but you were not one of them.' Then Boris said, 'What if I told you that I was in part responsible for the slug infestation in Syria and Iran? What if I admitted to you that I had conceived of the program? Would that make me one of the bad guys?'"

."We knew it all along! We knew it was Boris—" I said.

"Just wait, George…wait until I'm finished," Dad said. "I told Boris that it all depended on how and why the plan was carried out—and even then I told Boris that I could not judge his actions. But he persisted and told me after he learned about the slugs' unique properties, he proposed the infestation plan to his director, and she seemed to approve. Boris explained how he thought that it would be a way to get the coalition countries to fall in line with our Middle East policy, and she apparently agreed with that. But the CIA would have no part of it. They said it constituted using biological weapons, and they didn't want to chance it even with Boris' eloquent arguments that the slugs couldn't possibly be considered as a weapon."

Dad said he asked Boris who he did get to do it, and Boris told Dad that he contacted no other United States government agency and decided to kill the program. Then Yossi showed up one day and was looking for a way to get the coalition to stop their saber rattling towards Israel, so Boris dropped the slugs on him and Yossi bought the project.

"Boris said that Yossi implemented the infestation?" I said incredulously.

Dad said that it was probably not entirely Yossi. Boris just supplied him with the seed slugs and Yossi left. How or when they were planted and who actually did the planting Boris said he didn't know. But once the slugs did their job, then it was time for our State Department to get involved at the request of the Israeli Ministry of Foreign Affairs, who claimed they had no idea who caused the infestation either.

"Unbelievable," I said.

"You have no idea how unbelievable the situation became," Dad told me.

Dad continued the story, telling me that Boris told him the real trouble started when Yossi discovered that we had no control program in place, and the slugs were doing their job at a much faster rate than expected. Yossi was infuriated with Boris, calling him irresponsible and accused him of misleading Yossi, and now the world was on the brink of a major war and there was no way of preventing it.

I jumped in, saying, "And that's when we got called in by Boris, right?"

"Well, not just yet," Dad said.

"It seemed that Yossi somehow got the slugs out into the fields in 2013, and by 2014 they were rampant. That's when all the US negotiations were started, but without a control program in place, it was all hollow talk and the coalition knew that. Yossi was initiating his own program but also without much success, and then later in 2014..."

Dad paused at this point in the story, and I could see he was getting emotional. I waited until he felt composed enough to carry on.

"You know, George...in 2014...that's when the Iranian terrorists attacked the Technion. We lost our Mary, and Yossi lost his brother, Avi."

Dad slowly went to the front room again and poured himself another Scotch. When he returned he took a long sip and continued with Boris' saga. Boris told Dad that after the attack at the Technion Boris would not rest until the initial goal of preventing an Israeli invasion was completed to his satisfaction. He pledged that the project had to succeed so that Avi and the others would not have died in vain. Yossi was certain that the Iranian terrorists knew that he—Yossi—was involved, and he wanted nothing to do with the project anymore.

"So, Yossi got out of it?" I asked.

"Don't rush me, George—hear me out. You wanted to know everything, so now you can just listen."

I sat back and sipped my Scotch impatiently while Dad continued.

"Anyway, we and your other teammates all of a sudden got involved with Ori and Tikva at the Technion, and when Yossi found out about it, he wanted us out. You know all about that—I told you about my meeting with Boris and Yossi. But it was too late then, and now the Technion was part of the Israeli plan, mostly by accident. The two-project plan was already taking shape, and there was nothing Yossi could do to stop it, but he did have the influence to control it. Once it was demonstrated that your remutation discovery and Yancey's enzyme product would work, Boris was able to initiate his policy negotiations between the coalition and the State Department. The coalition knew the remutation program was successful, so they began to bargain. Boris and Yossi were working together again, and they were hoping we would stay out of it so as not to complicate matters any more, when all of a sudden Yancey takes off to Qatar."

Dad got misty eyed again. I never realized how emotionally involved he was, but when I thought about it—after the loss of Mackie—how could he not be emotionally involved? Dad continued, "Yancey didn't know that Kassim was sent there by the Lebanese coalition members to develop the land rehab program when he, Yancey, contacted him. And Kassim didn't realize the sensitive nature of the program himself when he invited Yancey to Qatar."

"Oh, shit!" I said. "That must have really sent everyone flying."

"Yes, it did, and my heart attack at that time didn't help either. Boris had just told me that Yancey was a target and would probably be taken for bargaining purposes, but I got sick and warned you too late."

"Oh, boy, Dad, I can't imagine how you must have felt..."

"How I felt didn't matter, what mattered then was only to get Yancey back safely—and Boris did that. Yes, it was Boris who controlled the negotiations between State and the coalition. Yossi backed off and let the US team do all the work then so as not to jeopardize Yancey's chances any more than they already were. I don't know what the coalition got for Yancey's release, but Boris said he didn't care—he'd have given them Miami if he knew Yancey would be returned safely. I don't have to tell you that the Iranian hotheads who kidnapped Yancey could just as easily have beheaded him on TV to make a statement. In any case, it all worked out in the end."

"Did it, Dad? How do we know?"

"George, I don't know anything more than what I read or hear on the news, and that's not very much. But you should know—and that's what this whole talk has been about—that Boris credits you and your team with definitely preventing a major worldwide tragedy. Boris told me as much when he said that if you and your colleagues hadn't developed the slug control program, there's no telling what would have happened. The coalition, as well as Syria and Iran, were so certain that Israel did it—which was partially true—Boris was certain they would have invaded Israel. And after they invaded we could never have acted quickly enough to prevent a blood-bath, so Israel might well have made good on its threat to use nuclear weapons, and if that happened, well..."

Dad just looked at me, and then said, "So you see, George, you and your team did do something great—you did save the world from another holocaust and nuclear war. Nobody may ever know that, but that's not important—we know it and that's all that really counts."

Mom, Charlie, and Marike returned from their walk and asked if we were getting hungry. Neither one of us said we were.

Back in Okemos that night after putting Marike to bed, I finally had the chance to tell Charlie what Dad told me. She was awed by it all and could only say, "We have to tell Yancey and Noreen...they're entitled to know. When do you want to do that?"

I looked at my watch. It was around nine in the evening so I said, "Let's call them and ask them to come over so we can tell them now. It's Sunday and they should be okay with that."

The Stetsons were at the house by 9:30, and almost before they sat down I began telling them the whole complicated story. Unlike me, they never interrupted while they listened to my retelling of Dad's story.

When I finished, Noreen said, "I suspected that was pretty much the scenario, but I'm surprised it was Yossi's people—or his foreign collaborators—who actually carried out the infestation. I thought for sure that Boris did it and that Yossi was just complacent in the implementation until the two-project plan evolved. However, this explanation works for me too."

"Strange how it all came together," Yancey said. "It seems that so much was based on chance. Our asking the Israelis to get involved when they already were, my looking up Kassim only to find out that he was the one developing the soil restoration program. And strangest of all, Boris letting Yossi go forward before he had a control program in place—that strikes me as the epitome of arrogance. How could he have done that?"

"Because I think he knew we would save his ass," I said. "He knew that we would probably develop a control sooner or later and thought he had more than enough time to initiate the program before he needed to control it. He simply miscalculated the slugs' virility operating in the Middle Eastern climate. And that miscalculation could have led to disaster."

"Yes, George, 'you got that one right,' to quote Boris," Noreen said. "But the real outcome from all of this is that we—the four of us and Bobby—did save the world just as we had started out to do. We could have lost Yancey in the process, but others—like Mackie and Gerry and Avi—who were just as much loved were lost, and we must never lose sight of that. I'm glad it's finally over for us, though, I think we deserve a break." Then with a broad smile on her face, Noreen said, "After all, we did what few others have been able to do in years: face the Middle East issue head on and come away from it with our own heads still on our shoulders."

We met socially with the Stetsons again a few times before all of us headed off on our sabbaticals in other parts of the world. We kept in touch by e-mail and Skype whenever we could and found that our trips were enjoyable and academically invigorating for all of us.

Marike started kindergarten in the fall, but she was enrolled in school in England for the first semester. Charlie and I had both obtained one-semester teaching appointments at the University of Birmingham—Charlie's alma mater—in our respective departments. After someone gets tenure, he or she could apply for a paid sabbatical leave, and that's exactly what we did. It was nice living in England from June till December so that Ma and Ba got to know their granddaughter better than they had been able to do with just short visits to the United States.

Yancey and his family went off to India on his sabbatical leave to continue his relationship and fiscal involvement in Yadu Padawal's—Bobby's father's—organic farm products plant. MSU encouraged faculty entrepreneurship when it enhanced the international prestige of the university, and since MSU got some revenue out of it that worked too—like most research driven universities. They stayed in India from June 2021 to June 2022—the whole year.

Noreen was really psyched about the trip. She was so looking forward to studying Indian carnatic music in Goa. She was introduced to Indian classical music in one of her classes and couldn't wait for the chance to actually study overseas. Noreen was a great singer, and she wanted to learn to sing carnatic music in Hindi, and now she finally had her chance.

In fact, we were treated to a musical performance by Noreen over Skype. She was dressed in a formal sari and sang a carnatic song in Hindi accompanied by Max on the sitar. What a treat that was. Marike sat spellbound through the whole performance and kept asking us if that was Auntie Noreen.

Shortly after spending Christmas with Charlie's parents, we packed up and headed back to Michigan, where winter would be cold and snowy. The world situation had not changed very much—turmoil in the Middle East with the coalition trying to hold on to some countries while trying to gain others that hadn't joined earlier. Israel was still in the middle, but food was no longer an issue, and jobs in the Middle East were on the increase. Hope for stability in that part of the world seemed evident wherever one looked.

We were never again needed to solve any global problems, but if we had been I think that the five of us could have done it one more time. But in the meantime I was thankful that the soil was once again alive and productive.

As Charlie proclaimed with a smile when she read about the healthy food crops being grown in the Middle East, "The soil's not dead—at least not anymore. Thanks be to us."